What people are saying about

Boxed In

N.E.David is a natural story-te )ice
perfectly suited to this direct the
young boxer, Barry Mullins. N .nat
makes a reader want to move ь...шıy to finish the first line, to
finish the first paragraph, to finish the first page and to keep on
going to the end. He's also one of those rare writers who knows
what it really feels like under the skin of so-called 'ordinary'
people, and his ability to tell their stories on their terms is what
makes this book truly unforgettable.
Terry Edge, author and editor

For boxer Barry Mullins, opportunity comes hand-in-hand with
trouble. In Barry, author N.E.David has created a hero for the
age of uncertainty. A book that shines fresh light on our times.
Peter Bartram, author of the *Colin Crampton* series

Boxed In is like all the great title fights - it has drama, suspense
and intrigue and packs a major punch. But it's not just a novel
about boxing - it's about people and the places that mould them.
A fantastic book.
James Oddy, *Boxing Monthly* correspondent

In *Boxed In* N.E.David reintroduces us to Baz, first encountered
in one of Nick's short works, *A Day at the Races*. But in this
case it's a more rounded and nuanced Baz, a boxer cum motor
mechanic, more failed than failure as he faces yet another setback
– a setback that threatens the very essence of who Baz is. Nick's
careful prose charts the course of Baz's rise and fall, filling in the
essential gaps as he lives guilelessly trusting unworthy friends

until he finally figures things out.

Alan Gillott, writer and broadcaster

I really enjoyed *Boxed In*. Even though boxing isn't my thing I got caught up in the individual stories and I liked the different viewpoints and tangled destinies. I could see it as a film with some quirky direction by Danny Boyle!

June Taylor, author of *Keep Your Friends Close*

Boxed In

Boxed In

N.E. David

ROUNDFIRE
BOOKS

Winchester, UK
Washington, USA

First published by Roundfire Books, 2019
Roundfire Books is an imprint of John Hunt Publishing Ltd., No. 3 East St., Alresford,
Hampshire SO24 9EE, UK
office@jhpbooks.com
www.johnhuntpublishing.com
www.roundfire-books.com

For distributor details and how to order please visit the 'Ordering' section on our website.

ISBN: 978 1 78535 886 9
978 1 78535 887 6 (ebook)
Library of Congress Control Number: 2018964268

A CIP catalogue record for this book is available from the British Library.

Design: Stuart Davies

UK: Printed and bound by CPI Group (UK) Ltd, Croydon, CR0 4YY
US: Printed and bound by Thomson-Shore, 7300 West Joy Road, Dexter, MI 48130

We operate a distinctive and ethical publishing philosophy in
all areas of our business, from our global network of authors to
production and worldwide distribution.

Prologue

Ken Cartwright

Hi. My name is Ken Cartwright and I come from Chelmsford. Not the greatest of recommendations I suppose, but there you are. Well you could hardly call Chelmsford "the city that never sleeps". Quite the reverse, in fact. There's a soporific atmosphere that hangs about the place, although at times it's quite beguiling. It is, of course, a county town. There is a county hall. In the summer months we get to see some county cricket played on the county cricket ground. And on hot, lazy, August afternoons when the pitch has completely dried out and the spinners are bowling, life assumes a pace reminiscent of an English country village. All of which goes on beneath the spire of a crumbling cathedral which, if we were to be honest with ourselves, is barely more than a large parish church.

Things happen slowly in Chelmsford. This is a city where the most significant event to have taken place since the end of the Second World War was the closure of a ball bearing factory. That and the construction of a by-pass which diverted the great vehicular artery that carries the nation's lifeblood from London to the coast (namely the A12) around the town and thereby consigned it to oblivion. Its once infamous intersection, the Army and Navy roundabout, still, however, remains and is as busy as ever despite the best attentions of the Council's Highways Department. At least it gives the inhabitants something to complain about. But nothing else excites.

There is a nightlife, naturally. After all, this is Essex and Essex girls (and Essex boys) need somewhere to let off steam. But by comparison to a great metropolis such as Manchester, Liverpool or Leeds, it's really a muted affair. Mondays to Thursdays are generally quiet, the odd hen party breaking the silence, and for the most part late-night diners drift out into empty streets. On Fridays and Saturdays, when pockets are full of a week's wage and there's no work to disrupt the following day, things are a little more lively. But even then, it's invariably all over by midnight. And on Sundays? Well, on Sundays, scarcely a dog barks.

So to all intents and purposes, Chelmsford is, quite comfortingly, a town full of ordinary people doing ordinary jobs and leading ordinary existences. But a few years ago, for a short period of time we had a hero, someone who made us all sit up and take an interest. He was just one such ordinary person who, through a series of random and unintentional events, shot to stardom like a firework rocket, lighting up the sky and illuminating our lives.

His name was Barry Mullins and he was a boxer. This is his story.

Part One

A Game Boy

Barry

I couldn't have been no more than fourteen when it all started. Or maybe fifteen, I ain't too rightly sure. Either way it's all of ten year ago now and a lot of water's passed under my bridge since then. I'll go for fifteen on account of the fact that it was just after my birthday when Dad gave me the Game Boy. That'd make it right.

"Here," he says. "Happy Birthday, son."

And he hands me the present as soon as I come down to breakfast. It weren't no surprise, I knew what it was straight off – I'd been on about it for the best part of six months.

The mistake I made (if it was a mistake and even now I ain't too sure about it) was playing with it in class. Only having waited for it for so long, I couldn't wait to get started on it once I'd got it. I thought that if I turned the sound off and sat right at the back, it'd be alright. It was English and Pop Jenkins was banging on the way he does, besides which, he's as blind as a bat and don't ever look beyond the end of his nose.

Anyways, it ain't him that's the problem, it's Parky, the nosy little git, sitting two rows across and minding everyone else's business as usual. And I know he's clocked it because when I shove it under the desk and have a quick look round to make sure everything's okay, he's sat there looking at me with a smirk on his face like he's just found a big bag of sweets. I smirk back but I'm already thinking it would have been a hell of a sight better if he hadn't found out.

So I'm coming down the drive after school, still playing with it, and he's there waiting for me on the other side of the gate. Only now he's got his mate with him, a big lad from Year Eleven, reckons he's hard. I can hear them whispering to each other.

"Shush, he's coming."

"Is that 'im?"

"Yeah, that's 'im."

"Well he don't look nothing. Has he got it?"

"Yeah, look. He's carrying it now."

So I turn it off and shove it in my back pocket because I reckon there's going to be trouble. And as soon as I get outside the gate, Parky steps out in front.

"Give it over, Mullins," he says, and sticks his hand out.

"Give what over?" I says.

"You know bloody well what," he says.

"No I don't," I says. "You're going to have to tell me."

"That bloody Game Boy, that's what," he says. "Give it over or I'll have to come and take it off you."

Now you can call me stupid if you like but I've decided they ain't having it. I've waited six months for it, I've hardly started on it and I ain't going to give it up that easy. Beside which, Mother says I've got a stubborn streak the length of Chelmsford High Street so I guess it comes kinda natural.

"Oh yeah," I says. "You and whose brother?"

Then the big lad steps out so I can see what I'm up against. He's tall and rangy and I can tell he's carrying a bit of muscle under his jacket. Parky's much the same size as me and he don't bother me none but all the same, it's two against one and I guess I should be worried. But for some strange reason I ain't, and there's even a warm glow building up inside. *Bring it on*, I'm thinking, *I'm going to enjoy this*. I slip my bag off my shoulder and drop it down, then make a pair of fists to show I'm ready. Parky starts gawping about like he's nervous.

"Oh," he says, all surprised. "You ain't going to give it up peaceful then?"

"No," I says, "I ain't. You're going to have to come and get it, just like you said."

Now the big lad breaks in. "Cheeky little bastard, ain't yer."

Parky looks round at him like he's expecting some instruction. The big lad nods and shoves Parky forward. As for me, I'm just stood there waiting for whoever comes first.

So now Parky's caught between a rock and a hard place. He don't really want to come after me because he's just discovered he ain't as brave as he thought he was. On the other hand, he can't stand and do nothing on account of his mate's right behind him and watching every move he makes. So to make it look good, he charges in like some kamikaze pilot, fists flailing, in the hope he's going to land one on me. Only he can't.

And then I'm in the fight. And when I'm in the fight, there ain't nothing but the fight. It's like the fight is all of me and I am all of it. And everything that happens in the fight I see it coming a mile off, like well before it starts. They only have to twitch a muscle or blink an eye and I can tell what's coming next – a jab, a cross, a hook, right or left, I know just what they're going to do. So next thing, I ain't there, I'm gone, I've moved that fraction of an inch that makes the difference between hit and miss. Or I cover up and take it on the arm and ride with it so it don't do no damage. But either way they can't hurt me. And every shot they throw, somewhere there's a gap. So I just pick them off, where I like and when I like. That's all I have to do. It's easy. And that's the fight.

So Parky comes steaming in, throwing punches like there's no tomorrow, and I skip out the way. And it ain't a question of whether I hit him or not, it's a question of where I hit him and when. I decide to let him have a few swings first and get himself out of breath. The more swings he has now the more he'll open up and the easier it'll be. Three wild swipes go whistling by, the fourth's a left cross and as soon as he lets go with it, I can see his shoulder drop. And over the top of his arm there's his face, all tightened up and blowing with the effort so before he can say Jack Robinson my right hand's gone straight out and smacked him one right on the end of his sharp pointy nose. I can tell the shot's a good 'un because there's a crack as the gristle gives way and the next thing you know there's a stream of blood all down the front of his nice white shirt.

And now Parky's stood there, dripping red, and he's gone

into shock. "Look at this mess," he's saying, pulling at the front of his shirt. "My mum'll kill me." Then, as it all sinks in, "He broke my nose. The little bastard broke my fucking nose."

"Yes," I says. "That'll teach you not to poke it in where it ain't wanted, won't it."

And just as I'm thinking he's about to pass out at the sight of his own blood, his legs go to jelly and he collapses in a heap on the pavement and sits there whimpering.

Meanwhile, the big lad's well pissed off and starts working up to something.

"For fuck's sake Parky," he says. "What the hell are you doing? Here, come out of it and let me have a go. I'll sort 'im out."

Only in case he hadn't noticed, Parky ain't exactly in it at the moment, sat on the pavement, bleating his head off.

So now the big lad comes across looking for me. Parky was easy but this is going to be a different proposition. Like I say, he's tall and rangy so I ain't going to be able to stand there and pick him off, I ain't got the reach. I reckon I'm going to have to get inside, give him a couple of smacks and then get out again, quick. Only I mustn't get caught because what he really wants to do is get hold of me and give me a bloody good thump and I can't afford to let that happen. I need some space where I can skip about and my back's up against a wall so I step off the pavement and out into the road.

"Where d'you think you're going?" he says. "You ain't running out on me are yer?"

"No," I says. "I ain't running. I'm just giving us some room, that's all."

And I stand my ground and wait.

He comes in slow and deliberate, like he's meaning to cause some damage. He ain't like Parky, all arms and legs, fists flailing, he ain't going to waste his energy like that. This'll be one big shot at a time, planned and measured, like he don't intend to miss. When he gets up close, I can hear him breathing. It's like listening to Darth Vader after a work-out at the gym.

Then I'm back in the fight. Only this time it's different. With Parky it was like machine-gun bullets raining in on you, rat-tat-tat-tat-tat, and it don't matter if one nicks you, you ain't going down. But these are like cannonballs thundering past, huge and heavy, and if you catch one, you're dead. But I can still see them coming so I skip, skip, skip out the way and let them roar down the road so I know it's going to be alright.

First off, he sends in a big right cross. I duck down and let it go whistling over my head. I could go in now underneath and hit him but I decide to wait and see what else he's got before I commit myself. Next is a straight left so I flick my head out the way and let it go over my shoulder. I'm leaning back a bit so I'm not in a position to counter and if he comes in with a quick right it could be tricky. But he don't. He ain't got no quick right. Fact is, he ain't got no quick nothing. It's all big guns blasting off one by one, slow and steady. Now there's a straight right and I let that sail over my other shoulder. Then he starts getting angry. That's good. I like it when they're angry.

"Why don't you stand still and fight, you little bugger," he says.

Tempting. But I ain't that stupid.

He decides to change tactics. He backs off for a minute and we circle each other while he works out what he's going to do next. His forehead gets all knotted up and somewhere underneath you can tell there's a set of cogs whirring. Then he makes his mind up and takes a step forward.

He starts off with a right feint. And just like Parky, he drops his shoulder but I can tell it ain't the real thing. So now I'm looking for the left, and there it is, a hook, and it ain't a bad one either. Only this time, instead of swaying back, I move forward so his fist's behind me and suddenly I'm inside and looking at his unprotected body. There's no quick right to worry me and

I reckon I've got time to get off three shots. I give him a right and a left in the solar plexus then a big right in the chest, just underneath his heart. The last one, I give it all I've got and turn my body into it so it carries all the power I can find. As soon as it connects everything comes to a dead halt, then he's flying backwards and landing on the seat of his pants, flat out in the middle of the road. I wait ten seconds to see if he's going to get up (which of course he ain't) then I put my fists down. And that's it, it's over, that's the fight.

Parky's still sat whimpering on the pavement. His nose is still bleeding but the drips have slowed up and he's just about coping with a handkerchief that's now the same colour as his shirt front. I move in his direction to pick up my bag and he must think I'm after him because the next thing you know, he scrambles to his feet and goes over to inspect the body of his mate laid out in the road. Me, I'm slinging my bag back over my shoulder and heading off in the direction of home.

"You've killed him," says Parky.

"Don't be stupid," I says. "'Course I ain't killed him. What you talking about?"

"You've killed him," he says. "He ain't breathing. You broke my nose and now you've killed Danny. What the hell am I going to tell my mum?"

"Oh shut up Parky, for Christ's sake," I says. "Here, let me have a look."

I drop the bag off my shoulder again and walk across.

So now there's two of us stood over the body, Parky trying not to drip blood on it and me with my hands on my knees inspecting the damage. Though Parky's right and Danny ain't breathing, leastways not that I can see. I start thinking *He looks peaceful enough.* But I don't like the way this is going.

"Look," says Parky, pointing. "His lips are turning blue. Maybe he hit his head on the road when he went over."

"Nah," I says. "I doubt it. I didn't hear nothing."

But he still ain't breathing, all the same.

Then I remember something from First Aid classes or on TV, I ain't sure which.

"Let's get him turned over," I says. "He won't do no good on his back."

I get my hands underneath and so does Parky and we roll him over onto his front. I pull one knee up, then check his mouth. There's the problem, his tongue's wedged down the back of his throat. I yank it forward and give him a good slap on the back. He gives a cough and starts sucking in air.

"There you are," I says. "That's fixed it. Right as rain now."

Parky don't say nothing but he looks like he's fit to burst into tears. As for me, I reckon it's time I left. I shoulder my bag again and head off down the street. I fish the Game Boy back out of my pocket and pick up where I left off. No point wasting any time. If there's any explaining to do, I'll leave that up to Parky. After all, he's the one as started it.

That ain't the end of it though, not by a long chalk. A week later, Dad and me, we're in the Headmaster's office.

Dr Steed

In most respects it was an easy decision to take. After all, the rules on the subject are pretty clear and just for once, the guidance from the Local Education Authority was unequivocal. And I must say that on this occasion they've been very helpful with it all. They have a vested interest of course, I realise that – they have to be seen to be doing the right thing. But it is the right thing, of that I have no doubt.

My initial concern was whether the incident took place within the school grounds and thereby lay within our jurisdiction or not. One could argue the case on that point. Both Parkinson and McGuire maintain that Mullins assaulted them before they reached the gate, but the ambulance men reported that when they arrived, McGuire was lying in the roadway the other side of it. I came to the conclusion that it wasn't really relevant. To try and maintain that it was nothing to do with the school would simply be attempting to abdicate one's responsibility. Someone has to stand up against this sort of thing – there's been far too much shilly-shallying over such matters and look where it's led us. I see it happening every day. I've lost count of the number of cases of bullying we've had to deal with – not to this extent of course, but serious enough in their own right. The youth of today is so wild and disparate that people don't feel safe in going out of doors at night. Where's it all going to end? Why, only the other day a pensioner was beaten to death in her own home. We can't let it continue. And this is one occasion when we have to put our foot down. We simply must not let such indiscriminate acts of violence become a daily occurrence.

The final decision rests with the governing body, I appreciate that. However, I'm sure they won't have a problem with it once the facts of the case have been put before them. And I know it will be difficult but they shouldn't let the fact that Mrs Parkinson is a member of the Board influence them in any way. I have to say that she's been very good about it. She declared her interest straight away – she was bound to, of course, but it does her credit nevertheless. It must be a terrible trial for her. I met her in the corridor the other day on our way to a committee meeting and I noticed how tired she was looking. She laid her hand on my arm and thanked me for my support.

"Dorothy," I said. "Under the circumstances, it's the very least I can do."

My recommendation will be quite straightforward. He has to go. He's not staying in my school. I've made up my mind on the matter.

Barry

So the big brown door opens and Steed shows us in. Dad lets me go first then follows after like he's being polite. Nobody shakes hands though. It don't seem like the kind of meeting where you shake hands.

"Take a seat, Mr Mullins," says Steed and offers Dad a chair. He don't offer me one but I find a spare and sit down anyway. Then he walks round, sets himself down, plants his elbows on the desk and puts his fingers together like he's making a steeple. But that's okay with me, it's his office and I guess he can do what he likes. *If that's what makes him feel good.*

Now this here's a room I've never been in before so I'm having a good look about. I clock a couple of old pictures hanging on the wall and a glass cabinet full of trophies. It smells a bit musty, like it ain't been cleaned in a while and I can see there's dust piling up on the windowsill. Outside, the rest of the kids are in the playground, running around and shouting. They say you only come in here when you're in trouble, so I guess I must be in trouble.

"I presume you understand why you're here, Mr Mullins?" says Steed, looking at Dad over the top of his glasses. Only it ain't really a question, it's more like a statement of fact. Dad ponders for a minute like it's a trick he's trying to work out.

"Well," he says. "I assume it's on account of your letter."

"Correct," says Steed. "We're extremely assiduous in these matters and we take great pains to ensure that everything is properly documented. The Local Authority is very particular. There are strict procedures to be followed, you know."

He lugs a big file across the desk, flips it open and pulls out a sheet of paper. I can just about read my name, upside down, written at the top of it.

"These are the parents' letters of complaint," he says. "You have read them I take it? I did send you copies."

Dad nods. There's no arguing with that.

Old Man Steed thumbs through the file, stopping here and there to consider. Every so often I catch him looking at me out of the corner of his eye like I'm some piece of dirt spoiling the weave of his herringbone carpet. Finally, he looks up.

"So. Were there any comments you wanted to make?"

"Yes," says Dad and clears his throat. "It was strictly self-defence. Them two lads came after my Barry and no mistake."

"I think not," says Steed, squashing Dad flat. "I don't see how that can possibly be the case. Look at him," and he waves his hand in my direction. "There's not a mark on him. You can't mean to tell me that Parkinson and McGuire attacked your son in the manner you've described and didn't leave some evidence of injury."

"Barry fought them off," says Dad.

"Fought them off? Don't be ridiculous, think what you're saying. There were two of them and McGuire is twice your son's size. No, I can't possibly accept that, it's preposterous," and he shakes his head like there's no way it could happen. "It was clearly a vicious and unprovoked assault."

He looks at us from behind his desk like he's giving us a lecture. Any minute now I think he's going to start wagging a finger. I know I shouldn't laugh but I have to work real hard not to. Then he leans forward and comes over serious.

"You do realise that one of those boys almost died?"

"Yes," says Dad. "And if it hadn't been for Barry here," he goes on, jerking his thumb in my direction, "he might well have done. We've his quick thinking to thank for that."

"Ah..." Old Man Steed hurrumphs and colours up. "Be that as it may, we should count ourselves lucky that both sets of parents have been persuaded not to press charges." Now he recovers and begins straightening his tie. "I think I should be allowed to take some of the credit for that. Mrs Parkinson is a very understanding woman. She realises that the school's

14

reputation is at stake."

It all goes quiet for a minute as the three of us sit and reflect on how reasonable it is of Mrs Parkinson not to drop the school in the shit. Then Old Man Steed starts off again.

"Well," he says, "the Authority will inform you of their decision in due course but I'll be recommending exclusion until further notice. In the meanwhile, I'll make arrangements for Barry to attend the annexe at Park Street. So," he says, looking up at us again. "Are there any further questions?"

Which clearly there ain't because he snaps the file shut, pushes it to one side like he's done with it and sets off making that steeple thing again. We look at each other, Dad and me, shaking our heads.

"Then the School Secretary will be writing to you in the morning."

And that's it, the meeting's over.

I leave my question until we're in the corridor outside. I don't want to ask it while we're in there in case it sounds daft.

"So what's with this annexe at Park Street?" I says.

Dad scratches his head and looks flummoxed.

"I don't rightly know," he says. "I suppose it must be somewhere you go when you've done something wrong."

"But I ain't done nothing wrong," I says.

"No son, that's true, you haven't." And he pats me on the back. As if that's going to make any difference. Which it ain't, but we keep on walking to the car park anyway.

"That ain't fair," I says. "I ain't done nothing wrong and now I've got to go to Park Street. The way I see it, that ain't fair at all."

"No," says Dad. "Maybe it ain't. Maybe there's lots of things in life that ain't fair. But sometimes you've just got to accept it and get on with it. That's the way it is. No point wasting time worrying about it."

We stand by the car while he fishes the keys from his pocket. There's a light breeze blowing, flapping at the legs of his trousers and shaking the workplace dust out. Then he looks at me and puts his hand on my shoulder.

"I'm sorry son," he says. "I really am. But there ain't nothing I can do about it."

There's a tired look in his eyes like he don't have the energy to fight it. Perhaps that's what it does to you, twenty years in a ball bearing factory stood over a grinding machine all day. You grind the metal down but maybe it grinds you down too.

He never was one to buck the system, Dad.

Ken Cartwright

I never did get round to telling you what I do for a living. I run the annexe at Park Street. It isn't what I set out to do when I came into teaching all those years ago – things were different then. But somehow I drifted into it. Because that's what we do, isn't it, drift? Drift from one thing to another, one day to the next without ever thinking about what we're doing or why we're doing it. Unless, of course, you have plans. And therein lies the danger – things can always go wrong. What was it John Lennon said? Life is what happens to you while you're busy making plans?

I suppose I must have had plans. I don't really recall, but I'm sure I did. Probably some high-minded ideals about passing on skills and knowledge to the next generation; about watching young people grow up and helping them develop into useful members of society; about fulfilling their potential and about achievement and satisfaction. So where did all that get me? Park Street, that's where. And how did that happen? All because some misguided Head of Department stopped me in the corridor one day and said *"Ah, Ken, glad I bumped into you, you're just the man I've been looking for. You seem to have a good relationship with your pupils. You know, keeping them under control, bags of rapport, that sort of thing. I've got just the job for you. Come down to my office at four o'clock and we'll talk about it."*

And once he'd explained it to me I remember thinking, *Yes, I could do that. It's a challenge but I could do it. It's something worthwhile, working with young lads who've got themselves into trouble, helping to put them back on the straight and narrow. They need as much guidance as anyone else, if not more. Yes, I could do that.* Another high-minded ideal. But then you have to face up to the reality.

I don't say I'm not any good at it. In fact, I like to think I am. I don't stand any nonsense, that's for certain. The boys know where they are with me, I lay down the rules and I make sure they stick to them. Because that's what they've been lacking – a firm hand. I do what I can with them of course, but what does it all amount to at the end of the day? Does it really do any good? At best, I keep them off the streets and out of trouble for a couple of years before they disappear into that dark unfathomable world they seem to inhabit. At worst, I'm a stepping stone, a halfway house between whatever minor crime or misdemeanour they committed last and whatever dastardly deed they're going to inflict on society next. Sometimes I tell myself I'm all that stands between them and a spell in a young offenders institution.

What can I possibly hope to teach them? The most I can aim for is to instil some sense of respect, both for themselves and for others. But not much more than that. Half of them can't read or write properly and most of them aren't even interested. To be honest, it's a victory if I can just get them to turn up for the day, never mind anything else. And that's the failure, that's where the system's let them down – because nobody's ever bothered to *make* them interested. And by the time they come to me, it's pretty much too late. They've been ignored because they're difficult. *Oh, so and so's no good,* they say. *Don't let's waste our time on him, throw him on the scrapheap, he can't be fixed.* So the scrapheap piles up with broken boys. And that's what I do, I suppose – try and fix broken boys. That's my job.

But I never had any trouble with Barry Mullins. I knew from the moment he walked in that he shouldn't have been there. I can usually tell. There were reasons given on his file, but I never understood them. When we met he stood up straight and looked me in the eye, and that's always a good sign. And I thought then *Yes, I can do something with you, I can help, you're going to be alright.* No, I never had any trouble with him at all.

Barry

Dad's on late shift so he drops me down at Park Street on day one. Only he don't get out the car, just leaves the engine running while he waves me out of the passenger seat. I stand there looking at the gates, wondering what I'm supposed to be doing.

"Ain't you coming in?" I says.

"No," he says. "You don't need me in there. You can look after yourself. You proved that the other day. Just hold your head up, show some respect and don't let them other lads give you any stick. You'll be fine."

I think about it for a minute. But it ain't like I can say no.

"Alright then," I says. And I go in on my own.

I wait in reception while they check me off a register, then I get shown into the boss's office. I've hardly been in an office before and now I'm inside two in a week. But it's nothing like Old Man Steed's. It's a lot smaller for a start and nowhere near as tidy. The corners are piled up with rubbish, there's odd pieces of angle iron and such stacked up against the wall and the bookshelf looks like it's fit to collapse. And I ain't in there more than two minutes before this bloke comes bounding in and slams the door shut behind him. He ain't a snip above five foot six but he's got a chest like a barrel and legs like tree trunks. Thing is, his hair's gone missing at the front and I reckon if you peeled back the skin on his forehead you'd find *DON'T MESS WITH ME* stamped underneath. But I don't have a problem with that. I ain't looking to mess with nobody.

"You must be Barry Mullins," he says.

"Yes, sir," I says. "I suppose I must."

"I beg your pardon?"

I figure he must be deaf so I turn up the volume. "YES SIR," I says. "I SUPPOSE I MUST."

"Well," he says. "I've been called a few things in my time but 'sir' has rarely been one of them." Then he turns suspicious and starts frowning. "Somebody put you up to it, did they? There's no need to shout, by the way."

"No, sir," I says. "Only my Dad says I should show some respect."

"Did he now!" he says, raising an eyebrow. "And am I to understand that you always do what your father tells you?"

"Pretty much," I says, looking down at my shoes. Well, maybe not all of the time but it ain't that far off the truth.

"Well that's good," he says. "But let's compromise a little on the point. Humility is fine but not to excess. When you get out of here the only person you'll ever say 'sir' to is likely to be a magistrate, and I have no intention of making you practise for that. You need to show yourself some respect too. So here's what we'll do. I'll call you Barry, you call me Mr Cartwright and we'll be fine. Is that agreed?"

"Yes, sir," I says. "I mean, Mr Cartwright." And we shake hands on it.

So now he can relax and he parks his broad backside against the desk, folds his arms and crosses his ankles.

"So," he says. "D'you want to tell me why you're here, Barry?"

"I dunno," I says. "I got sent."

To tell the truth, I'm wondering why he's asking seeing as he's got the same file on his desk as Old Man Steed had on his. He catches me looking.

"Oh, I don't pay any attention to that," he says. "That's just what the Authority want me to know. It probably doesn't bear the slightest resemblance to the truth. What I want is to hear you tell your side of the story."

"Ain't no story to tell," I says. "I didn't do nothing." I look at my shoes again.

"Ah," he says. "I might have guessed. *You didn't do nothing.* Of course you didn't, nobody who comes to Park Street ever does. If I had a pound for every time I've stood here and heard a boy say that, I'd be a very rich man. Look," he says, getting back up off the desk. "We've got off to a decent start, don't disappoint me now. If we're going to get along together – which I sincerely hope we are – you'll need to do better than that. So why don't you tell me what you did."

"Alright," I says. "I got into a fight with two other lads. But I still won."

"A fight?" he says. "What sort of a fight? Was it guns, bats or knives? I like to know what I'm dealing with."

"It weren't nothing like that," I says. "Just fists, that's all."

"I see. Just fists… No more than that?"

"No more than that."

"Well, that doesn't sound so bad, I've heard a lot worse. All the same, we can't have that kind of behaviour going on here. I won't stand for it and I'll come down hard on anybody who breaks my rules. Do I make myself clear?"

"Yes, Mr Cartwright."

"So you won't be doing any more fighting?"

"No, Mr Cartwright."

"Do I have your word on that?"

"Yes, Mr Cartwright." And this time I nod, just to make sure he gets it.

"Good. So now let me tell you why *I'm* here. My job is to make sure you don't get into any more trouble – I'm here to help you get back on the straight and narrow. And don't think you don't need any help – just because *You didn't do nothing,* as you maintain. You don't want to finish up in a young offenders institution, do you?"

I ain't too sure what that is but it sounds like the kind of place I want to avoid. I shake my head.

"I should think not," he says. "And by the way, can you read and write?"

"Of course I can," I says.

What do they take me for?

"Well that's a good start," he says. "And don't look at me like

21

that, a lot of the boys that come here can't."

Then he sighs like the whole thing's weighing heavy on him and he turns to look out the window. It's like he ain't talking to me no more, he's talking to someone else and he starts off on some spiel about the Authority and teaching and the system and scrapheaps and how he tries to fix broken boys. Half the time I don't get what he's on about. I let out a yawn and contemplate twiddling my thumbs.

Then he looks back round at me to see if I'm still there. Which I am.

And I didn't even know I was broken.

Ken Cartwright

Once the interview was over, I took Mullins on a tour of the workshops. I say workshops because I tend not to use conventional classrooms. True, we do have one room set out with desks and chairs for formal lessons (the Authority stipulates I must spend a minimum of one day a week teaching them English and Maths) but it's not really satisfactory. Chalk and talk simply doesn't work with these boys, they're just not focused enough for that. Half the time they're trying their utmost to annoy each other, while the other half they spend gazing out of the window wishing they were somewhere else. Their minds are empty and their hands are idle. And we all know what happens under those circumstances.

So I persuaded the Authority to give me some funding and had a couple of rooms converted into workshops (you know, mechanics, woodwork, an electrical section, that sort of thing) in the hopes of giving them something practical to do – put them to work if you like. My idea was that if I could engage their hands, their minds would follow. Well, that was the theory, anyway.

But, as you can imagine, things didn't quite go according to plan and there were a few teething problems. To begin with, some of the tools that we'd provided started disappearing, and rather than abandon the workshops altogether I proposed searching the boys on their way out. But the Authority wouldn't wear it (*There'll be too many complaints*) so we reverted to carrying out an inventory check every morning and every evening and now nobody goes home until everything's accounted for. It's amazing how things that formerly went missing suddenly start turning up in the most unlikely of places.

My next problem was the question of what to do about Matthew Brown. It took me a while to figure that out – but that's when I hit on the idea of the garage...

Barry

We come out of the office and Mr Cartwright takes me through to the workshops. We walk in and it opens out into a couple of rooms. One's full of machinery – a drill, a lathe, a press and a couple of other bits and pieces – while the other's laid out with benches for hand work and such. It's like the technician's lab at school only two or three times the size.

There's a few lads dotted about in overalls, working or stood around chatting. I ain't counting but I reckon there must be a dozen of them altogether. I recognise a couple, faces I've seen about town and such. One by one I get introduced. If I'm lucky there's a grunt or a nod but most of them don't even look. Why should they? They've seen it all before. People come and people go and I'm just another name, another number. They'll be curious though, all the same.

Cartwright's tour takes about an hour. By the end of it he's told me the name of every piece of machinery, what it does, how it works and the contents of just about every cupboard in the place. Seems like there's nothing we ain't looked at. It's like it's all his little pride and joy and he can't wait to show me. Come the finish and he's stood there with this look on his face, like he's expecting me to say something nice about it.

"So," he says. "What do you think?"

"Yeah," I says, nodding slow. "Brilliant."

"And did you see anything you might be interested in?"

"What d'you mean?" I says.

"Well, did you see anything you'd like to have a go at?"

There's a long silence while I consider my options. I'd like to give him something to go on and I don't want to lie if I can help it.

"The fact is, Barry," he says, "when you leave here in a year or so's time, you're going to need to get a job. I know it's a difficult question, but have you ever thought about what you want to do with the rest of your life?"

The rest of my life? How the hell should I know? So maybe he's a magician. Because it's like he's got a pack of cards and he's asking me to pick one. Go on, he's saying, pick a card, any card, and then he'll do a trick with it. And it don't matter which, they're all the same – drill, lathe, press, mechanic, fitter, electrician, it don't matter a toss, just as long as you pick one. Then it'll be alright. Then you can be somebody, do something with your life. It's easy, he's saying. All you've got to do is pick a card.

So happens we're stood next to a bench with some tools on it. I reach round and take one. I reckon it makes no odds which so I just take one because that's what he wants me to do. Turns out it's a ring-spanner.

"I dunno," I says. "What about this?" And I holds it up.

Now he's looking at me, real grateful, like I'm the answer to some kind of prayer he's been making, then he beckons me over.

"Come with me," he says, and we head towards the door.

Now I thought we'd done the lot but it seems like there's at least one room we ain't been in yet. Cartwright's got a key and when we get in the lights are already on. And the reason we ain't seen it yet is because it's separate from the main building and tacked onto the side. There's an up-and-over door at the front and round the edges there's all work benches and tool cupboards full of stuff – cans of oil, boxes of nuts and bolts, wrenches, hammers and the like. In the middle there's space enough for a car – only there ain't no car, just an old engine slung up on a cradle underneath a big pulley wheel with a chain. But the engine's half in bits with the pieces piled up on one of the benches, all shiny metal glinting under the fluorescent strip.

All of a sudden I get this feeling we ain't entirely on our own. Mr Cartwright walks round and sure enough, this kid scrambles up from the floor behind one of the cupboards where he's been sitting and backs up against the wall. No word of a lie but I've never seen a wimpier looking bloke in all my life. Underneath his overalls I shouldn't think he's more than three bits of string tied together – and pretty thin string at that. I just hope he don't want to shake hands because it'd be like squeezing a piece of wet fish. But that ain't likely since he's pressed hard up against the wall and shying away like he's scared stiff. It's like watching a spider running away from the light.

"Matty," says Cartwright. "This is Barry Mullins," and he points in my direction. "He's going to be working with you in here."

It don't take much to see Matty ain't too happy about it.

"Don't worry," says Cartwright. "He's not going to hurt you."

And he looks round at me just to make sure I understand. But he knows that anyway which I guess is the reason he brought me in here in the first place.

"I'm just going to fetch you an overall," he says. "I'll lock the door while I'm gone, just in case."

Just in case of what though, he don't say, but I guess that's something I'll find out soon enough. Cartwright slides out and the door clicks shut.

"So," I says. "What gives, Matty?" I back off to give him some space otherwise he's got nowhere to run. But he still don't want to look in my direction.

"I dunno," he says. Then, "You ain't going to touch me, are you?"

"No," I says. "I ain't coming anywhere near you." The way this is going I figure I'm best off changing the subject. "So what's with the engine? You stripping it down?"

"Sort of," he says. "I ain't really bothered."

Then it goes quiet for a couple of minutes, the way it does when blokes don't have nothing to talk about and they're wishing they was somewhere else. I start poking about with the shiny bits of metal on top of the work bench, wondering what they are. I figure it's no good asking Matty because it's like he said – he ain't really bothered.

"So," I says at last. "What you doing locked up in here then?"

"You'll find out," he says, and he keeps looking the other way. Pretty soon Mr Cartwright comes back with an overall.

"Has Matty shown you what to do?" he says.

"Sort of," I says. He hasn't, but it don't seem to matter much.

"Good," he says. "I'll let the two of you get on with it then."

And suddenly he's gone and the door clicks shut behind him.

Now you don't have to be Albert Einstein to figure out what we're supposed to be up to. This here's a garage and that there's a half-dismantled engine. The idea is you take it to pieces to see how it works and then you put it back together. I pull the overall on and start work. There's a set of them ring-spanners on one of the benches and it takes me the rest of the day to finish stripping the engine down. It ain't exactly rocket science and I get the feeling I ain't the first one to do it neither, all the nuts and bolts coming undone so easy an' all. I take half an hour for lunch (Mother's put a pack-up in my bag) and then I'm back at it. Cartwright pokes his head round the door from time to time to make sure everything's alright, then locks it up again on his way out. Matty don't want nothing to do with it and just sits behind his cupboard, doing bugger all and watching me. I can feel his eyes on the back of my neck the whole time, like they're boring a bloody hole in it.

Anyways, come the finish there's an empty engine casing on the cradle and an even bigger pile of shiny metal bits on the side bench. I don't know what they are or what they do, but they're there. I'm just about done when Matty pipes up at last.

"You know what he's going to make you do now, don't you?" he says.

He talks, then.

"No," I says. "What's that?" I'm a bit snappy seeing as how he's left it all to me, but I'm grateful for a bit of conversation.

"He's going to make you put it all back together," he says. "That's what."

"I kinda guessed that," I says. "A bit pointless taking it all apart otherwise."

We sit around waiting 'til twenty past four when Cartwright shows up for the last time. Matty hauls himself to his feet and they disappear off down the corridor.

"You stay here until I get back," says Cartwright.

I change out of my overalls and get ready to leave. Five minutes later he's back again and he lets me go with the rest. I reckon he must have let Matty go early – on account of him being different an' all. Walking across the car park, I don't half get some funny looks.

I'm home for just after five. Tea's at six so I slump in front of the TV for an hour. Dad's late shift don't finish 'til eight but as soon as he gets in he wants to hear all about it. I tell him all there is to tell – about Cartwright, the workshops, the garage, the lot – everything except the bit about Matty. I reckon I'll keep that to myself 'til I've worked out what's going on. The minute I start on about the engine Dad's eyes light up and before I can say *Don't bother*, he's clambered up into the loft and he comes down with this book, WORKSHOP MANUAL – HILLMAN HUNTER HK3 1965. There's a picture of the car on the front and on the inside, diagrams of it all broken down into bits.

"First car I ever owned," he says. "Light green with a cream stripe, she was. Wire wheels too. A real beauty."

And before you know it we're talking pistons, con rods, crankshafts and gudgeon pins and a shed-load of things I've never heard of before. It's like discovering a whole new world you didn't know was there. Dad gets all fired up, but then it starts getting late and I have to get off to bed.

"Here," he says, and he hands me the book. "Take it. It ain't no use to me no more. I got shot of that car a long while since."

"Thanks Dad," I says, and I take it up to my room.

I don't do much in the way of reading books. Never wanted to. Christ knows why but I start reading this one. And when I do,

I can't put it down. Half past eleven and I'm still reading it when I fall asleep. And that's how I got into motor mechanics. Strange how these things happen, ain't it?

Barry

So next day I'm back at Park Street bright and early, half past eight on the dot. I decide not to take the book in with me. Something tells me it wouldn't be a good idea just yet. Besides, I want to see if I can recognise the parts from that big pile of shiny metal bits without having to look them up. I put the overall on and make a start. Matty's already there, sat in the corner, same as before, not moving. Only now he starts asking questions.

"What you doing?" he says.

"Sorting this lot out," I says. "Fancy giving me a hand?"

But whatever interest he's got, it don't extend as far as doing any work. He just shakes his head and stays put. I go on with the sorting out.

It takes me a couple of hours but I get it all laid out on the work bench the way I want it. I figure this here must be a four-cylinder engine seeing as there's four sets of piston assemblies plus the crankshaft. The top end's a bit more difficult. There's eight valve stems and I have a problem telling inlet from outlet – until I discover they're a slightly different size. After that it's easy. As for the timing gear, sprocket and chain, I haven't a clue but another night with the manual and I should know what I'm doing.

And all the while Cartwright's in and out like a jack-in-the-box, checking up on me. He clocks what I'm doing but he don't say a thing – I figure he's got his hands full on account of them twelve other lads causing him a lot more trouble than we are. Besides, I like being left on my own to get on with it so I ain't complaining.

I try fitting a few pieces together ready for reassembly. I go home at half past four, read the manual and come back the next morning. Same again the next night. Two days and I've built up the best part of the bottom end and it's ready to drop into the casing. Two more days and I've got most of the top end done too.

I'm working that hard I'm close to getting a sweat on. And all the time, Matty sits there behind the cupboard, his eyes glued to the back of my neck, boring away at that same old hole.

Finally, I decide I can't take no more.

"For Christ's sake Matty," I says. "Are you going to spend the rest of your life sat on your backside watching, or are you going to come over here and give me a hand? I ain't going to bite yer."

This time it must sink in because bit by bit he pushes himself up the wall and comes across to the bench where I'm working. But the closer he gets, the more the hairs on the back of my neck stand up until when he's stood right next to me, I can feel them prickling.

"Here," I says. "Hold this for me." And I offer him a spanner.

He reaches out to take it with his hand all thin and white and limp and that's when I realise he ain't the kind of bloke to be doing motor mechanics anyway. Truth is, he'd probably be happier sewing curtains. And it ain't a case of me touching him, it's a case of maybe him touching me. But that ain't going to happen, not in a million years, not if I've got anything to do with it. My compass points north and always has done. And maybe I shouldn't, but there's a lump in my throat and all of a sudden I don't feel too comfortable.

It's taken a while but the penny's finally dropped. Matty's different. So what? That don't bother me none. Just as long as he keeps his hands to himself. And the reason Mr Cartwright's got him locked up in here ain't to stop him getting out – it's to stop the rest of them getting in. And to stop what they might do to him, one way or the other.

So Matty's different. So what?

So now I'm his bloody minder.

I start wondering how long it'll be before somebody kicks off at me. It takes about a fortnight. It's a Wednesday so we're all in the classroom for our day of Maths and English. It works like this. Everyone troops in and sits down, me included, but Matty's left out. Then Cartwright goes and fetches him and puts him up the front well away from the rest. And he don't leave him on his own for a second. When we've finished he takes him back out, then let's us go. At first I just get a few more funny looks, but second time round, while Cartwright and Matty are out, one of the lads comes over. Spike, they call him. He's tall, wears a crewcut, must be sixteen and he's got a bad case of acne.

"I want a word with you," he says.

"Word away," I says. "I'm listening."

"I don't know what you and that little poof do in there, up each other's arse all day, but I want you to give him a message. Tell nancy-boy that if I ever get hold of him, I'll tie his legs round his fucking neck."

"That's nice," I says. "Why don't you tell him yourself?"

"You know bloody well why not. Cartwright's got 'im locked up all safe and sound and I can't get in there."

So Spike's all raring to go – but then my stubborn streak kicks in.

"And even if you did," I says, "you'd have to get past me first."

"Oh yeah," he says, sneering. "And who the fuck are you?"

"The name's Mullins," I says. "Barry Mullins."

"Barry Mullins? That rings a bell. You're the little twot that turned Danny McGuire over. In that case I've got business with you. Danny McGuire's a friend of mine."

"That's good," I says. "I'm glad to know you've got one."

His eyes narrow down to a slit as the shaft sinks in and he pulls back his fist.

"Not here," I says. "Not now. If you want to make something of it, I'll be out in the car park at half past four."

"You'd better be," he says. "There'll be trouble if you ain't."

And there'll be trouble if I am.

Because if Spike don't have a go at someone soon, all his spots are going to go off zit. Why can't he leave it alone? And why do they have to light on me all the time? Maybe it's because I'm on the small side and I look like easy pickings. Well that's a mistake if ever there was one. I won't go down quiet, that's for sure.

Ken Cartwright

What is it with boys that they have to be fighting each other all the time? It must be inherent in their genes, stamped in their DNA. Perhaps there's an inalienable yet unwritten law of human nature that says they have a constant need to prove themselves, establish a territory or show they're top dog. Because they're forever at it. If they're not niggling each other in the classroom, they're outside somewhere with their sleeves rolled up ready to knock each other about. I've got a dozen of them in the workshops, not to mention another two in the garage, and there's enough testosterone boiling up between the lot of them to fuel a minor war. Why can't they live in peace?

I'm tempted to say it was different in my day – but of course it wasn't. Every so often one lout or another would spark off and something brutal would go on behind the bike sheds. It's still the same today. They tell me girls bitch (I wouldn't know about that) but it can't be as bad as this. It's so unbelievably wearing.

I thought that by putting Mullins in with Brown I could insulate him and keep him away from all that. He seemed like a decent lad and deserving of a better fate than to get mixed up with the others. And as far as the garage was concerned, my hand had already been forced. If I'd left Brown to the tender mercies of the mob, I'd have had a serious situation to answer for. He needed company and Mullins seemed the perfect solution. But once again, things didn't quite go according to plan, although on this occasion they turned out better than I could ever have imagined. Mullins, it seemed, neither needed my help nor wanted it – he was quite capable of looking after himself...

Barry

Come half past four and we're all out in the car park. All except Matty that is, and he's gone home already. No one else has left early though, they've all stayed around to watch, word having got out an' all. It don't take much in this place.

I figure on coming out last. I'm planning to make Spike wait a while, just to get his nerves going a bit. Besides, it ain't me that's picking this fight, it's him, so I don't see why I should be the one kept hanging about. I walk toward the door and he's already out there with his coat off, practising his jabs and bragging how he's going to put me down. Ain't nobody told him it don't work like that with me? I take a breath, then push open the door and go out to join him.

It's different out there. Colder for a start, there's a bit of nip already, pinching my cheeks, but that ain't what I mean. What I'm saying is it's a different world. It's like this is our place, our rules, our own space – somewhere away from the rest of them, somewhere where we can do what we want and they can't stop us. So for ten fleeting minutes we get to run our own lives, be who we really are – law of the jungle if you like. And whoever dares, wins. I just need to make sure that it's me.

They're gathered in a knot by the gate, all twelve of them. And as soon as I step out the old chant goes up, echoing round the forecourt – *Fight! Fight! Fight! Fight!* – like their tension's been building up and now they can let it all go. So any chance we might've had of keeping this to ourselves has gone out the window already. I reckon the whole neighbourhood's awake and watching, never mind Cartwright an' all. Bag down, coat off, I go through the usual procedure. Then the crowd gathers in, forming a circle. Nobody's getting away 'til this is finished.

No prizes for guessing whose side they're on. I can tell straight off from the way they're looking that I ain't got no friends. Then, just to make sure, someone bellows out, *"Crack 'im, Spike!"* So I know which side my bread's buttered.

Spike takes encouragement and starts pawing the floor like he's a bull waiting to charge. Fact is, he's got to have a go at me – he won't get no points for hanging back. Meantime, the spots on his face are boiling up red as a ripe tomato and any minute now I reckon he's going to start snorting.

Then I'm in the fight. And when I'm in the fight, there ain't nothing but the fight. It's like the fight is all of me and I am all of it. But this is Spike and if he's a bull then this must be a bullfight so I play it like one. But I ain't got no cape and sword, just a pair of fists, so I turn side on and drop my hands like I'm saying "Look, I'm giving you a chance. Come at me now while you can, it ain't going to get no better than this," like that's my red rag, my way of bringing him on. And maybe it's for the fun of it, maybe it's the devil in me, or maybe it's just the joy of the fight, who knows, but I just let him come at me, time and time again, 'til he starts getting tired. And every time he passes by, I can smell the animal in him, sweating.

So spot-ridden Spike comes roaring in like a railway train, like he's trying to knock me over rather than fight. But he can't get me, never will, and he just goes charging past. I let him have a few goes so's he can get used to it, but he don't get no better and soon he starts breathing heavy. Then I figure he must have had enough of it what with him wasting all that energy and so have I, it stopped being fun after the first couple of passes. So the next time he flies by I let him have one, smack on the side of the head – *WALLOP!* – and down he goes like he's been pole-axed. And all of a sudden the rest of them go quiet, like they're as stunned as he is, and you could cut the air with a knife. Nobody's shouting *"Crack 'im, Spike!"* now. Fact is, nobody's shouting nothing. Me, I just leave him lying there – they don't get up after one of those, trust me. But this time they can sort themselves out, I'm done with it, I'm off for my coat and my bag.

They all stand there watching while I pull my gear on like nothing's happened. I head toward the exit, the circle breaks and they draw aside to let me pass. Something's changed and they know it. Things won't be the same at Park Street no more.

I get to the other side of the gate and turn to look back at the office window. And sure enough, there's Cartwright's beady eyes staring out at me. So now I'm in trouble again.

I'll come down hard on anybody who breaks my rules. Do I make myself clear?

Yes, Mr Cartwright.

So you won't be doing any more fighting?

No, Mr Cartwright.

Do I have your word on that?

Three bags full, Mr Cartwright.

So what did he expect me to do, for Christ's sake? That I'm just going to stand there and take whatever they feel like dishing out? That I'm going to be the one that gets it instead of Matthew bloody Brown? Is that what he was thinking when he put me in the firing line? Fact is, it's all his fault anyway and he can't go blaming it on me when things go wrong. But he will, you can bet your life on that. They always do.

Ken Cartwright

I'm ashamed to say that I watched the whole of the proceedings from my office window. It was wrong of me I know, and as soon as I heard the chanting I should have gone outside and put a stop to it. But just for once I got tired of it all and besides, curiosity got the better of me so I stopped to look out into the car park and see who it was. One of the lads had his back to me, although I took it to be Jones because as soon as he stepped forward someone called out his nickname. Then, to my horror, I saw that the other boy was Mullins. But I needn't have worried because the blows Jones intended for him never landed. Even then I should have gone out and intervened, but something held me back as it dawned on me what I was witnessing.

I've heard it said that pugilism is an art. Well, if that's the case then there was no finer exponent of it than Barry Mullins. I did a few rounds myself when I was younger – and got into the odd scrap, I have to admit. But I'd never seen anything like this. There was a grace and style about his performance that defied description and each time Jones went in, Mullins turned to the side and swayed away. And as the danger slid by, I'm sure he could have reached out and hit him whenever he liked. But he held off – although when the end came it was swift and sure, a crushing right hook, the power of which made even me wince. Jones went down like a sack of potatoes falling off a lorry. I have to say I'd have cheered had the whole thing not taken my breath away.

The following morning I arrived at work early. I kept a look out for Jones and I wasn't surprised when he didn't come in. He'd done well enough to gather himself up off the floor of the car park and get himself home where he could nurse both his wounds and his battered pride. It took a couple more days plus the weekend for him to recover but to my relief he finally showed up on the Monday. After three days of unexplained absence I'd have had to send a report to the Authority and that was something I wanted to avoid. Despite the time off there was still an angry bruise high up on his cheek, although the black eye he'd sustained had moderated to a dirty yellow.

"Ouch," I said, as I passed him in the corridor. "That must have hurt. How did you come by it?"

"I walked into a door, Mr Cartwright," was his lame and predictable response.

"Hmm... Must have been some door," I said as I inspected the damage.

Mullins, on the other hand, was in the next day as if nothing had happened. I went to the garage first thing and when I saw him start work, an idea occurred to me so I asked him to come down to the office. He must have thought he was in some kind of trouble as he stood there with his hands behind his back looking down at the floor. I sought to put his mind at rest straight away.

"Barry," I said, as soon as I'd closed the door. "There's something I want to talk to you about. Have you ever thought about taking up boxing?"

Part Two

Laurel and Hardy

Albert

Barry Mullins? Of course I remember Barry Mullins – how could I possibly forget? I taught Barry Mullins everything he ever knew about boxing. Although strictly speaking, that's not entirely true – he knew most of it before he ever came to me. So where did he get it from? I haven't a clue, but the boy was a natural. He had reactions like a scalded cat and a right hand that could put you into the middle of next week if you didn't know it was there. And even if you did sometimes – he was simply outstanding. The cynics said afterwards that all I had to do was put him in the ring and let him get on with it and he couldn't possibly lose. But you know as well as I do, things are never quite as simple as that.

So how do I know all this? I'll tell you how. Because one way or another I've seen them all over the years in my time at the City Boys Club. Every size and shape you can possibly think of, they've all walked through my door. Right from little Johnny whose Mum and Dad wanted him to learn the noble art of self-defence, all the way up to the big eighteen-stoners who think that just because they've downed somebody with a lucky punch outside a nightclub on a Saturday night, they're destined to be the next Mike Tyson. Until they find themselves lying on their back that is, looking up at the ceiling with the feel of canvas on their shoulders and wondering why the stars are inside the building instead of out.

You see, it doesn't matter how big you are, it's what you've got inside that counts. It's like Mark Twain said. *It's not the size of the dog in the fight, it's the size of the fight in the dog.* So it's not merely a question of how much power you're packing – important as that may be – there's much more to it than that. Sure, you need to be able to punch your weight, but you need to do a lot of other things too. You need to be sharp, you need to be able to think yourself out of a tight corner, you need to be fit, and frankly, sometimes you need to be able to run backwards faster than your opponent can run forwards. You need a thousand things if you're going to succeed as a boxer, but most of all you need guts – and plenty of them. You need guts to get into a ring with somebody who's trying his best to beat the hell out of you, and guts to tough it out and win.

And Barry Mullins? He had all of that. He had all of that and more – he was a decent guy to go with it. Barry Mullins was the best boxer I ever saw and given a decent chance he could have been Champion of the World. But when he came to me, when he first walked through the door of my gym, he was just a small lad with a huge talent and big right hand. It needed someone to set him straight and it was me, Albert Hyde, who was the one to do it.

Barry

Following my contretemps with Spike there's a few changes down at the Park Street annexe. I don't get no more funny looks for a start – seems nobody wants to meet me eye-to-eye in case I take offence. Suits me. Plus, there's a vacancy come up as leader of the pack seeing as Spike ain't doing much in the way of public appearances at the minute. But that position ain't of interest to me. Well, not just now it ain't, at any rate. Either way, there's no more trouble from that corner.

Mr Cartwright lets me into the workshop two days a week. I get my own bench, a toolbox with my name on it in and a set of tools I have to sign for every night before I go home, same as the rest. He shows me how to use the machines – the drill, the lathe, the press and everything – and then he starts telling me what to do with the tools. Now anyone with a grain of sense would think a file was just a file and all you had to do was push it back and forth a few times and that would be that, but it ain't. Seems there's a right way and a wrong way of pushing a file and I have to be taught which is which. Before too long I can file for England and I'm dying to be back working on that engine. But I guess if you're going to use a file you may as well learn how to use it right, so I stick at it like I'm told.

The other two days I stay in the garage. Cartwright still keeps it locked up good and proper, only now I get a key of my own and I can come and go as I please. *It's not as if anybody's going to take it off you, is it Barry?* He ain't daft, is Mr Cartwright, he knows what goes on.

Meantime, Matty's decided to get up off his backside and come out from behind the cupboard on a regular basis. Which is real handy seeing as I need someone to pass me the spanners while I'm lying on my back under the casing. Pretty soon we get the bottom end finished off. I poke around a bit and find a crank handle in one of the cupboards.

"What's that for?" says Matty.

I show him where it goes. "Let's wind her up," I says. "See what happens."

I fit the handle and turn the engine over. First off there's a rattling noise like a skeleton shaking its bones. Then I try dropping a bit of oil down each cylinder and she runs smooth as silk. It don't impress Matty though. I reckon he'd still rather be sewing curtains.

A week goes by and Dad gets a letter. He don't say a word and I don't pry but I figure it must be from Cartwright because the next time Dad drops me off he comes in with me and goes down to the office. I'm locked up in the garage so I don't know how long they're in there gassing, but when I get out he's gone. The first day Dad's on early shift he's home from work when I get in and waiting in the hall.

"Come on," he says. "I'm taking you out somewhere tonight."

"Where's that?" I says.

"You'll see."

"So what you telling me?" I says. "It's a mystery tour?"

"No, there's someone I want you to meet."

Well it's a mystery to me. Ain't no one I'm looking to meet.

We have some tea and get in the car. Dad don't walk nowhere if he can drive these days on account of his emphysema. All that dust in his lungs, the doc reckons. Like I say, you grind the metal down, but it grinds you down too. Mother's always on to him about it but he don't listen. *You should get some exercise, sat in front of that bloody television the whole time.* But he just looks the other way and pretends he ain't heard. To tell the truth, he don't hear much at all when she's talking, does Dad.

The mystery tour is a ten-minute drive to a back street the other side of the railway. We park up, get out and have a look round. I've seen better places to be honest. I've seen worse too, but I've seen a lot better. Across the way there's a dim street lamp outside an old brick building that must have been a warehouse once upon a time. A frosted glass window looks out onto the road, one of the panes is cracked and above the narrow door there's a light over a sign with the paint peeling off. I squint my eyes and I can just make out the words. *CHELMSFORD CITY BOYS CLUB.*

"Here we are," says Dad. And he don't bother knocking, just walks straight in.

As soon as we get inside there's a smell catches me in the back of the throat, like a mixture of disinfectant and sawdust. The last time it got me was when Granny took sick and we all had to go down the hospital. That didn't end too well, as I recall. I hold my breath and follow Dad down a short corridor – grey lino, green walls and then another door with frosted glass. On the other side I can hear voices. We go straight through and it opens out into a big bright room laid out like a boxing gym. There's a proper ring with ropes, and in the corner a punchbag, gym ball, and some weights. It's full of young lads, just like the workshop down at Park Street, only this lot are wearing boxing kit and instead of filing, they're working out or sparring. Stood in the middle is this thin grey-haired old feller with a clipboard ticking names off a list. I say old, he's a lot older than Dad and Dad's over forty, I know that for a fact. He clocks us coming and looks across. *So what do you want?*

"I'm Derek Mullins," says Dad. "And this here's Barry," pointing at me. "You must be expecting us. Ken Cartwright…"

"Yeah, yeah, yeah," says the old feller, like we're interrupting something crucial. "Ten seconds." He turns toward a corner where a couple of the lads are mucking about. "Cut that out you two, and get on with something serious." Then he's back with us. "Little buggers, they do my head in. Now, where were we? Oh yeah, come with me a minute."

And he dives off into a tiny cabin with a fluorescent striplight and a desk all covered in papers. Across the top of the door, the words *ALBERT HYDE, HEAD COACH* are written in the panelling. But I reckon I could have guessed that anyway, seeing as how he looks to be in charge of everything an' all.

"There's a few formalities for us to go through first," he says, rummaging about. "Parental consent, indemnity forms, injury insurance, that kind of stuff. Where did I put it? Ah! Here we are." He finds what he wants then turns to look at me like he's giving me the once over. "Did you bring your kit?" he says.

I look at Dad. Dad shakes his head.

"Don't look like it," I says.

Now *he* looks at Dad. Dad shrugs his shoulders. So next up he leans out the cabin and shouts over the din. "Micky! Get this one some spare kit will you while I go through the paperwork."

I look round, a head pops up and Micky walks over. I say walks, but it's more of a waddle because compared to the old feller this one's half the age, half the height and twice the width. He looks like one of them wobbly toys you get for Christmas when you're little – you know, a ball with a weight in the bottom and a clown's head on top. Every time you push it over it bobs back up again. So every time Micky takes a step it's like he's getting pushed over and bobbing back up. And as he comes across I'm thinking *This here's a double act. One of them's tall and thin and the other's short and fat. It's Laurel and Hardy.* They're one of Dad's favourite programmes. I can't help but snigger out loud and Micky looks at me like he could cut me in half, but he don't make no comment. I suppose he must get used to it.

"Hands?" he says.

I hold them out for him to inspect.

"Hmm..." he says. "They're big. Wait here." He waddles off round the corner and comes back with an old pair of boxing gloves. "That's it," he says. "There's no more spare kit. So you'll have to stay as you are for tonight. But you can put these on to get started."

I hold my arms out. He pushes the gloves onto my hands, then ties up the laces.

Ever had your hands inside a pair of boxing gloves? It's real weird. You can't move your fingers and you feel like you've been cut off from the outside world. I ain't too sure I like it. I bang my fists together the way I've seen them do it on TV to see if it makes me feel any better. The bad news for me is it don't.

Meantime, Fat Micky's pointing across the room to where the punchbag's hanging in the corner.

"Go and get yourself warmed up for a few minutes," he says. "Albert'll come over as soon as he's finished going through the paperwork with your father."

I look over at Dad in the cabin. He gives me a smile as if to say *It'll be alright son, I'll catch you later* so I walk across the room to the punchbag. I've got my street clothes on, I'm wearing boxing gloves I ain't too happy with so all in all I'm feeling like a right prick. No wonder my head starts running off.

So whose idea is this anyway? Because it sure ain't mine. Who says I want go boxing? Maybe I do and maybe I don't but ain't nobody thought to stop and ask? There's Dad in the cabin signing his life away, or in this case, mine, and I'm stuck out here and no questions. Don't I get no say?

And all the time the bag's hanging there and I'm stood looking at it wondering what to do with myself.

Then things start boiling up inside. My head's banging off because I don't know one way or the other and I start shaking with it all 'til I'm fit to smack the first thing that comes along. But right now, there's only the bag. So I figure it's either that or I blow up so I start on it, a couple of taps at first just to see it move. Then it starts to swing, left and right, right and left, so I can give it one each time it comes across – *left swing, smack, right swing, smack* – then *tap tap tap* some more. I've stopped shaking now and I begin to breathe with the rhythm of the bag – *swing swing, smack smack, swing swing, smack smack,* faster and faster, *smack smack smack* – until *BANG!* I give it the big right hand and the bag stops dead. Then there's this voice behind me and it's the old feller, Albert, stood with his arms folded, watching.

"Nice work," he says. "I'm impressed." He comes up close and drops his voice to a whisper. "Tell you what," he says. "Let's you and me get in the ring together for five minutes and we'll see how good you really are."

And he turns to wink at Micky. Like it's a joke. Laurel and Hardy. Having a laugh.

Fat Micky waddles off to fetch some headguards, we strap them on and climb into the ring. Albert gets kitted out with a flak jacket and instead of boxing gloves he's got a pair of padded mitts.

"Right then," he says. "What I want you to do is try and hit me the same as you were hitting the bag." He holds the mitts up to show me where. "Don't worry," he says. "I'm not going to hurt you."

As if I don't know that already. It ain't me I'm worried about.

"Come on then," he says, and he squares up to me like we're going to have a fight. My guess is he's waiting for me to have a go at him and when I do, he'll play the clever sod and jump out the way. Because he's no punchbag, he's Albert Hyde, Head Coach, it says so over the top of his door. But I'm stood there stock still, arms by my sides, wondering what to do. He sees that and he drops his hands too. Then he puts them on his hips and looks straight at me.

"So are you going to try and hit me or what?" he says.

"Maybe I don't want to hit you," I says.

"Well we're not going to get very far like that," he says. "Don't you want to box?"

"I dunno," I says.

"What d'you mean *I dunno?*" he says. "What the hell are you doing here if you don't know?"

I don't know that either.

"Look," he says. "There's a dozen more boys like you in a queue wanting to get in here. I've got a waiting list as long as your arm, and you're only at the top of it because Ken Cartwright happens to be a friend of mine. I haven't got the time to waste with people who aren't interested because there's plenty more out there who are. Now, do you want to box or not? It's make your mind up time."

Now I figure I don't have a choice seeing as Dad's made the effort to bring me down here and I'm stood with a pair of Fat Micky's gloves on.

"Alright then," I says. "I want to box."

"Thank Christ for that," he says. "Now let's get on with it."

And he squares up to me again. Only I still ain't too sure. But then he starts hopping about, one foot to the other, and saying stuff like *Hit me then, hit me. Come on and hit me for Christ's sake, what are you waiting for?* as if he's trying to wind me up. Which he does.

So I hit him. And I hit him real good, the same way I hit Danny McGuire. And just like Danny, he goes sailing over backwards and lands in a heap on his backside with all the breath knocked out of him. We all stand around looking at each other for a second until Fat Micky comes rushing in with a towel and a sponge to clear up the damage.

Here's another nice mess you've gotten me into, Stanley.

And Albert's lying there, spluttering and coughing his guts out. "Jesus, kid," he says, rubbing his chest through the flak jacket. "Where did that come from?"

"Where did what come from?" I says.

"That punch."

"You opened up."

"What d'you mean, 'I opened up'?"

"When your shoulder came forward, your elbow lifted up," I says. "You left a gap."

Albert sits up and starts breathing better. "Oh I did, did I? Hmm... We can talk about that later. Meanwhile, you'd better put that big gun away before you kill somebody with it." And he

and Micky look at each other. Laurel and Hardy.
Only now they ain't winking.

Albert

It was all my own fault, of course – I should have known better. And it's all very well saying it now, but running a gym's a busy job. What with parents coming in and out, paperwork to do and upwards of a dozen boys to control, you can't turn your back for one moment or there's trouble. And just as usual, on that particular evening there was too much to do and too little time to do it in. So I only took my eye off things for a fraction of a second and slap-bang, it hit me in the back of the neck. Or as it was in this case, full in the chest. Well it certainly taught me a lesson. You can imagine how embarrassed I felt. There I was, Albert Hyde, Head Coach, sprawled on the seat of my pants in my own boxing ring, panting for breath. But that's boxing for you, I suppose.

I could hardly blame Micky for laughing about it afterwards. He caught up with me just before we locked up and went home for the night.

"Come and look at this," he said, and took me over to the punchbag. One side of it had split open and a river of sand was trickling out onto the floor. "He only broke the damn thing. He must have given it one hell of a whack. No wonder he turned you over."

We continued clearing up and as we were switching the lights off, I noticed there was still a smile on Micky's face. I knew exactly what he was thinking. *Is this what we've been waiting for? Is he going to be the one? After all these years?*

As for me, it was much too early to say. All I know is, my ribs weren't half sore the following morning.

Barry

So my boxing career don't exactly get off to the best of starts what with me having knocked Albert Hyde about a bit an' all. But sometimes, that's how it goes. I mean, I never meant to hurt the bloke or nothing but I get to thinking they won't let me join up on account of it. *We'd rather not have that kind of person in our club.* And I can't say as I'd blame them. But just how wrong can you be? A few days later Dad gets something through the post and he's telling me *You must have done alright the other night, son* because I've been accepted two evenings a week, Tuesdays and Thursdays, starting as soon as I like. It's a Friday and we celebrate. Mum sends Dad out for some fish and chips and he sneaks in a bottle of Bud each to go with it.

"Here's to it," he says, taking a pull.

"Yeah, here's to it," I says and I take a pull too.

Saturday morning we catch a bus into town to get some kit. We look around the sports shops and Dad buys me a neat blue vest and a light-grey tracksuit. I've got a pair of trainers at home and Dad says I'll have to use them for now. Proper boots and shorts will have to wait. *Let's see how you get on first.* But that's alright, I understand, he can't do it all at once. I count myself lucky to get what I've got.

Tuesday night at six-thirty I'm back down the Boys Club. It's just getting started and Laurel and Hardy are in charge. Albert ticks the names off his list while Fat Micky waddles over and clocks my new kit.

"Very nice," he says, raising an eyebrow. He must be impressed, which is fine because I'm going to have to blag those gloves off him again. He gets me the same pair as before.

"While Albert's doing the list," he says, "I'll show you the ropes."

"You can save yourself the trouble," I says. "I saw them last week, ha, ha, ha!" Like I'm trying to be part of the act. But he don't laugh. He must have heard that one a dozen times too.

He shows me round just the same. There's three sets of kit in the gym – the weights, the ring, and a special area with the punchbag, the gym ball and so on. The idea is we get split into three different groups, spend half an hour on each set, then move on to the next and that makes up your time. Micky works you out a programme on the weights, but in the special area you might have to share stuff, like there could be two of you on the punchbag at the same time. When I get on it I can see there's some new stitching. I work my way round and eventually we come to the ring so now we can get gloved up. I'm paired with another lad about my size and we do thirty minutes sparring but to be honest, it's just pit-a-pat and it all gets taken on the gloves or the arms. I keep the right hand buttoned up like Albert told me, it don't do no damage and I don't try nothing clever. Then they turn the lights off and we can all go home.

Next day at Park Street Mr Cartwright makes a point of sticking his head round the garage door. There's a smirk on his face wider than a Cheshire cat's and you can tell he's just dying to get something off his chest.

"Morning Barry," he starts off. "I understand you were a big hit down at the Boys Club the other night."

I'm filing the burr off an o-ring where it don't quite fit right. The back of my neck catches fire. "Oh," I says. "So you've heard about that then."

"Yes," he says. "I happened to bump into Albert the other day and he told me all about it. Whatever else, you certainly made an impression on him."

I'm too embarrassed to see the funny side. "Sorry, Mr Cartwright," I says. "I didn't mean nothing by it."

"I'm sure you didn't," he says. "Don't worry about it. You're not thinking of giving it up are you?"

"No," I says, "I ain't giving it up, not now. I'm all signed up, two nights a week."

"Good," he says. "I'm pleased to hear it. And by the way, how's that engine coming along?"

I show him how we've built up the bottom end and I get the crank handle out of the cupboard to wind her over so he can see it's all in working order. I even tell him how Matty's been helping with the spanners. But Matty don't want to play no part in this conversation and stays put behind the cupboard.

"Well done, Matty," says Cartwright, looking in his direction. "That's very good."

Like he's throwing a dog a bone. Only this dog ain't hungry. So it's back to me.

"What I'd like you to try next," says Cartwright, "is…"

"Let me guess," I says. "Strip it all back down?"

"Precisely," he says. "How did you…?"

"Never mind," I says. "Let's just say a little bird told me."

When he's gone, I turn to Matty in the corner. Now he's the one that's smirking.

"Don't you say nothing," I tell him, pointing a finger. *Smartarse.*

So I strip it all back down. I was going to do it anyway to tell the truth, whether Cartwright said so or not. Because I want to remember and see how quick I can do it. That's the way you learn, right? There's no magic about it, it's just hard work. It takes me four hours all told, would have been longer if everything had been done up solid, but it was only finger tight. And when I've got it stripped down and laid out on the bench, I start building it back up. And I do it again and again until I know the touch, the feel, the shape of every part – bearing, piston, con rod – I can tell them all with my eyes closed. And which cylinder they belong to. It's like every one's something I can trust and rely on. In the end I get it down to two hours – an hour and three-quarters if Matty's in the mood and helps me with the spanners. Then I start on the top end.

And every Tuesday and Thursday I go to the Boys Club.

I must be four weeks into it when Albert makes an announcement. Which is great seeing as nothing dramatic's happened up until then and it's all been pretty quiet. In fact it's just like Park Street, a routine you fall into, something that's there to get you through each day. Weights, punchbag, sparring – sparring, punchbag, weights. Round and round it goes. Much the same as that engine – build her up, strip her down, all in a day's work. And when it comes to the sparring, nobody's pushing the boat out. They don't bother me, I don't bother them. Pit-a-pat, pit-a-pat, it's all under control.

But somehow I get the feeling Albert's watching me. It don't matter what I'm doing, seems like every time I look round he's stood there with his arms folded, one hand stroking his chin like he ain't quite got me figured out yet, like he's trying to size me up. So come the day he decides to speak out, I'm all ears.

"MAY I HAVE YOUR ATTENTION PLEASE." He has to shout on account of everyone's yakking their heads off before going home. They soon quiet down. "Thank you," he says. "In a couple of weeks' time we're going to have some visitors. Colchester Boys Club will be coming over for the evening. I've agreed with their coach we'll have a competitive event so we'll be taking them on in each of the seven different weight categories. Junior ABA rules. I'll be putting a team sheet up next Tuesday. I'd be grateful if those who can't make it would please let me know as soon as possible."

That sparks some interest and suddenly the yakking goes up a notch.

Colchester? Those country boys? We'll take them on alright!

I'm just getting my bag packed when Albert comes over.

"Barry," he says. "Is it okay if I put your name down? I was thinking of the 69kg class. Are you alright with that?"

"Fine with me," I says. "I'm up for it."

You bet I'm up for it.

So now Dad's going to have to get me some boots and a pair of shorts.

And give him his due, Dad does the honours and I get kitted out. Only trouble is, this here's an ordinary club night so the match ain't open to parents and he can't come and watch. I don't mind that, there's still a buzz about the place what with the lads getting keyed up seeing as everyone wants to get on with it. They're all sat there in the locker room, jiggling their knees, and maybe I should be nervous too, but I ain't. It don't worry me none, fighting. After all, I've done this a few times before.

My bout's fourth on the list, and by the time we get to it we're down two matches to one. So far, and never mind what was said at the start, we ain't exactly turning these country boys over. The last thing we want is to go two behind so it's down to Barry Mullins to pull us level. No pressure there then.

"Just go out and do your best," says Albert and he pats me on the back while Fat Micky gives me a wink as I climb into the ring. So maybe they know something I don't.

And here's a thing. Just for once, seeing as it's all done by weight, the lad I'm up against is the same size as me. That makes a change – they're usually much bigger. We look at each other for the first thirty seconds and I wait to see what he's about. But he don't come at me like the others, he hides away behind a left jab and tries the occasional right cross. Which don't land of course, none of it does, I'm too good for that. But what I can tell is, I ain't in the fight. That's because he ain't in the fight either. Fact is, he's shaking like a leaf, he most likely spent ten minutes in the crapper before he came out and he shouldn't even be in the ring in the first place. Poor bugger.

End of round one, nothing's happened and I go back to my corner. Albert wafts a towel while Micky dabs a sponge. Like I say, it's a double act.

"How's it going?" says Albert.

"Alright," I says. "Why?"

"Well, you might try scoring a few points."

"Points?" I says. "What points? Nobody told me about the points."

But before I get an answer, Albert's had the stool away and pushed me back out.

So we're back into it, round two and it's much the same as before, a few little jabs and every so often a right cross, but he still can't touch me. And all the time I'm trying to think *The points, the points, what's this about the points?* when suddenly he opens up and before I know it I've let one go with the right hand as cool as you like and down he goes, thump, same as the rest, just as though someone's turned his lights out.

So I start crowing to myself. *Yes, Barry Mullins has done it! Two all with three to play and we're in with a chance.* But when I look round at my corner expecting a pair of happy smiling faces, there's Albert with his head in his hands and Micky looking up at the ceiling, whistling. Meantime, the other lad's out cold and they've gone to fetch the smelling salts.

Search me, I'm wondering, *so where did I go wrong?*

Albert

Alright, so that was my next mistake. Maybe it was too early, maybe I let the cat out of the bag a bit too quick and perhaps I should have held him back and given him some tuition first. A lot of things can happen with a boxer – you start them off fast, they have a few easy wins, then they get overconfident and start to think they're invincible. And no one's invincible in this game, believe me, not even Barry Mullins. All it takes is one lucky punch – I can vouch for that. But at some point you have to give them their head. You can't have talent like that and keep it bottled up for ever and a day.

Their coach came up to me afterwards. "Well you certainly kept that one under your hat, Albert. How old is he?"

"Fifteen," I replied. "I think." I couldn't quite remember the dates on his form.

"Really? Still on the young side then. But I guess you'll be entering him for the Divisional Championships, all the same."

How did I know that was coming? It had already been in the back of my mind but I still um'd and ah'd a bit. "Well, I'm not too sure about that," I said. "Maybe next year. I don't know as he's ready yet."

"You don't fool me, Albert, you're just being cagey. He looks ready to me."

Yes, I thought, *but you don't know what I do. You don't know where he's come from and how he got here. Ken told me he could fight, and now I've seen it for myself. He can fight alright. My job is to teach him how to box.*

Barry

I'm a bit behind getting down to the gym seeing as Dad's on a late shift and I've had to walk. So by the time I arrive Albert's ticked his list and I've missed the roll call. But he clocks me anyway and comes straight over.

"We've got a problem," he says.

"We have?" I says. "What's that?"

"This," he says. And he taps my right hand. "I thought I told you to put that away for the time being."

"Sorry Albert," I says. "I forgot. Besides, we needed the win."

"That's as maybe," says Albert. "But you can't rely on just the one thing the whole time. And anyway, this is boxing – not a roughhouse. You may not know it but there's more than one way to win a boxing match."

"Ah," I says. "Let me guess. You mean the points?"

"You've got it," says Albert. "The points. So just as a matter of pure technical interest, how many hands have you actually got?"

"Two," I says. "Last time I looked."

"Good," says Albert. "I can see we're making progress. Have you ever thought about using the other one?"

"Can't say as I have," I says. Fact is, I haven't thought about it at all. I don't think, it all comes natural.

"Well, how about we give it a try?" says Albert. He turns and shouts across the gym. "Micky! Take over the sparring session will you? I'm just giving Mr Mullins here a bit of one-to-one."

Fat Micky comes out of the cabin and waddles over to the ring. Then Albert's back with me. We go across to the punchbag. The same two kids are skylarking about again so he turfs them off onto some other piece of equipment.

"Now, here's what I want you to do," he says. "Put that right hand away. Behind your back. Go on, tuck it away."

I put my right arm behind me and fold it into the small of my back. But he can see I don't like it.

"It'll feel pretty strange at first," he says. "But you'll get used to it. Now, plant your feet, left foot forward and square up to the bag."

Which I do.

"Now pop out a straight left," he says.

I pop the left out and smack the bag. It quivers on the rope.

"That's good," he says. "But there's no need to leather it. All you have to do at this stage is tap it and you get a point. Now try two in a row."

I do two in quick time. *Tap, tap.* Two points. My right hand's still tucked up behind. It's awkward, but I can manage.

"Now," says Albert. "When you pull back out, you'll need to move left or right. You mustn't stand still or you'll be an easy target."

"You mean like this," I says, and I skip one way, then the other.

"That's it," says Albert. "Now let's see you put it all together."

I square up to the bag, right hand tucked. *Tap, skip, tap, tap, skip.* Three points.

"You've got it," says Albert. "Keep that up and in three or four weeks we'll be cooking on gas."

"Three or four weeks!" I says. "I can't wait that long. You never know what might happen in three or four weeks."

"Listen," he says. "If you want to be a boxer you're going to have to learn the hard way. Three or four weeks."

"And no right hand?" I says.

"And no right hand."

I go back to the bag. *Tap, skip, tap, tap, skip.* Twenty minutes' hard graft and I've collected more points than Mother's got on her clubcard.

Talk of the devil but she's the only one in when I get home. I say *Hi* and go straight up to my room. We don't talk a lot, Mum and me. I guess it's a man thing but to be honest we don't have that much to talk about. They don't exactly float her boat, boxing and car mechanics.

There's a mirror on my wall, but if I stand on the floor all I can see is the top of my head so I clamber onto the bed where I can box my own reflection. *Tap, skip, tap, tap, skip,* I'm back at it. Only problem is, it makes the bed creak. The sound must carry downstairs because as soon as Dad gets in, she's on at him.

"What on earth is that boy doing up there?" Her carping voice comes floating up from the kitchen. Two minutes later my bedroom door opens and Dad's head appears.

"What's going on then, Baz?"

Tap, skip, tap, tap, skip.

"I'm just lashing Sugar Ray Leonard up for the WBA Middleweight Championship of the World," I says.

"Well, do you think you could do it a little more quietly," he says. "Your mother's giving me grief." He pulls the door to, but as it's about to close he has second thoughts and sticks his head back round again. "And by the way," he says. "Sugar Ray Leonard was a welterweight."

Welterweight, schmelterweight – what's the difference? Either way, Albert's not around so I fetch the big right hand out and finish him off. Sugar Ray keels over and they count to ten.

Then I get changed and settle down to read Dad's manual.

I decide to take the manual into school. It can't do no harm now – them boys in the workshop ain't going to take the piss after what I done to Spike. And it ain't as though Matty's going to shop me either – he ain't interested anyway. All the same, it don't do to show that kind of thing around so I stuff it out of sight in my bag.

What I hadn't banked on is Cartwright having eyes in the back of his head and clocking it straight away. I'm leaning on the workbench having a read through, I don't hear him come in and suddenly he's behind me and looking over my shoulder.

"What's this then, Barry?" he says.

As if it ain't obvious.

Now I ain't got much choice but show him, and while he looks it over I tell him where it came from.

"You're pretty keen on motor mechanics, aren't you Barry?" he says.

"Yeah," I says. "You could say that."

"So what do you plan to do next?" he says, looking at the engine casing lying on the cradle.

I tell him about the top end and show him the workbench where I've got all the parts laid out ready. We talk about how it works and how to put it together and he tells me I'm going to need some special tool like a G-clamp for compressing the valve springs and so forth. Well, we don't have no G-clamp, somebody walked off with it, but he'll see what he can do. And sure enough, a few days later he turns up with one and spends half an hour showing me how to use it. And from the look of him I'd have said he'd have stood there and had a go at the job himself only he keeps looking at his watch and has to tear himself away. Even Matty starts showing a bit of spark. He ain't seen this bit done before and he comes over to help with the spanners.

Well, that top end takes us the best part of a fortnight to figure out. Not bad, considering I'm only in there two days a week. I say us, but it's me that does the figuring while Matty does the looking on. Same result though. And when it's all built up, I strip it down and build it back up just like the bottom end, again and again until I know it inside out. Then we get to tackle the timing gear, sprocket and chain and finally put the whole job together. Bingo. So eight weeks after I arrive, and almost as long after getting the manual, there's the three of us, Matty, me and Cartwright, stood in the middle of the garage, looking at the genuine finished article.

"What is it?" says Matty. Because he really don't have a clue.

"It's a fine working model of an internal combustion engine," says Cartwright. "Well done, Barry."

So he looks happy, even if Matty don't.

Nice job, I'm thinking. *Now you can have a blow.* But any ideas I might have about putting my feet up go straight out the window because Cartwright tells me we ain't hardly got going and there's a shed-load more for us to do. We might have an engine but we don't have no transmission for a start.

Anyways, seems Cartwright's got a friend that runs a scrapyard. Every other week or so, a pile of metal bits turn up in the garage and we're supposed to figure it out – clutch, gearbox, drive shafts, we get the lot. But I ain't going to let him beat me and he knows it. So every time he sticks his head round the garage door, the manual's open, the job's laid out and we're on with it.

Then one day, a month or so later, I've just pulled a set of disc brakes to bits and I'm wiping my hands on a piece of old rag when he walks in with another box of parts. Only this time I'm thinking, *My turn.*

"All very well, this lot," I says, waving a hand. "But what we really need is a chassis to mount it all in."

"You're absolutely right," says Cartwright. "D'you suppose I haven't thought of that already? I'd love to get us one, believe me, but the Authority wouldn't wear it. No," he says, shaking his head. "If that's the kind of thing you're after, what you need is a proper apprenticeship."

Ain't no chance of that though, is there? Not where I'm headed.

Ken Cartwright

That boy doesn't belong here – I've thought that right from the start. To be honest, I can't understand why they sent him to Park Street in the first place. As I said at the beginning, short of fighting in the car park I've never had any trouble with him.

Perhaps it was a mistake. People make them, I've made a few myself. I can just see how it could happen. At the time instruction was given, someone was having a bad day. They were on the point of picking up a file when the telephone rang and they got distracted. When they came back to it, they picked the wrong one. Or maybe they were running their finger down a list of names, miscounted, and ran that one name too far. You never know. So maybe there's someone out there, still in mainstream, causing havoc when they should have been with me, getting some discipline. In the meantime, an innocent boy suffers. But whatever the reason, it's a mistake. He shouldn't be here.

I could try calling the Authority but what good would that do? Not much, I should imagine – I've no brief to be interfering in the lives of my so-called pupils. Before too long Barry Mullins will be sixteen. And when September comes and the new academic year begins, he'll be cast adrift in the big wide world with no qualifications and no prospects. His file will be marked as "failure" and to tell the truth, they'd like to add "good riddance" to it too – the existence of such people on their records hardly enhances their reputation. "Not our fault the boy went bad," they'll say. "Not much we could do." Barry Mullins deserves more than that but what prospects has he got? None at all as far as I can see.

Barry

Tap, skip, tap, tap, skip.

It's like there's a tune inside my head and I can't get rid of it. It's there when I go to bed at night and it's there when I wake up in the morning. Tap, skip, tap, tap, skip, it just don't go away. And it seems like everywhere I go there's something to remind me of it. A door shuts, cutlery rattles on a plate or a car drives down the street, I can't hear nothing but what they all set it off the same, every minute, every day it comes pushing up from inside and my body moves to it, hands and feet, pounding, pounding, pounding. Tap, skip, tap, tap, skip. That's it, that's all there is, that's the rhythm of my life right now and just like a rapper's music, my head thumps to boxing's beat.

Three to four weeks, says Albert. I thought he was joking but he really meant it. Seems like forever and I'm doing the same thing the whole time. I've got my right arm tight up behind my back and all I can do is use the left – jab, jab, jab. Fat Micky don't exactly talk a lot but even he's got words on the subject.

"Can't you give it a rest, Albert?" he says. "You can see the boy needs a break."

"He can have a break," says Albert, "when he's good and ready."

Bronco busting, that's what I calls it – you'd think I was some wild animal he's got to break in. It's a straight month before he starts to look even the least bit happy.

"That's better," he says, arms folded, giving a slow nod. He's standing right next to me while I work the bag. "Now we can think about using that right hand again."

"Yes," I says. "If I ain't forgotten what to do with it."

"You won't have forgotten," he says. "You can trust me on that. Now, here's what I want you to do. Keep the left going, but every so often bring the right over. Mix it up a bit. Don't do it every time, mind – you'll need to keep 'em guessing. You'll know when, it's your call. And don't let go with the big one just yet. Keep that for when you need it. All we're looking for at the moment..."

"...is the points," I says.

"You've got it," he says. "The points."

So now I have to learn how to play a different tune. Ain't that just typical? As soon as you get one thing sorted, they land you with another. Only this time I get to decide on it myself and I can make it up as I go along. *Tap, skip, right – skip, right, tap,* it's whatever I want. It's like it's my own song, only this ain't no rap music with a steady beat, it's more like a piece of jazz with every note bouncing off the one before. I try it on the bag for a couple of minutes and it starts to flow. Albert's close by as usual, stroking his chin.

"Hmm..." he says. "Not bad. Let's go and try that in the ring."

Fat Micky fetches him the mitts but this time he don't bother with the body armour.

"Where's your flak jacket?" I says. "Ain't you bothered wearing it?"

"No," he says. "You're going to have to control yourself. Don't worry, I trust you."

We must be making progress.

It's better in the ring. With the bag you're tied to it, you can't go nowhere, but in the ring you've got the chance to move. Okay, so it's like there's four walls shutting you in and you can't go beyond them, but everywhere you look there's a space to slide into. So when Albert comes forward I duck and dive, then drive him back as I smack away at the mitts. *Tap, skip, right – skip, right, tap.* Before too long they're playing my tune as to and fro, Albert and me we dance the ballet of hard knocks.

Twenty minutes and Albert's puffed, so then he decides it's enough.

"That's good," he says. "Very good. A couple more weeks and you'll be ready."

"Ready for what?" I says. And as soon as the words leave my

lips I'm wishing I hadn't asked.

"Championships," he says. "Eastern Division."

Albert

I knew it wouldn't take him long, not a boy with his talent. I could see it in him straight away. And I don't mean when he knocked me over that time – that was just pure luck of course. I'm talking about when we started the one-to-one and I began to look at his style and movement. I could tell then that he wasn't just a small lad with a big punch – he was the complete article and what I had to do was bring it out of him.

And if I'm honest? Well, I needn't have pushed him as hard as I did, but I wanted to see what he was made of. You can't be a boxer if you're not prepared to take the discipline, if you can't buckle down and do the hard things that you have to do to succeed. And he passed that test with flying colours.

One hand behind your back for a month, Barry, and let's see how you get on. And while we're about it, let's make it the right hand, the big one, the one you rely on. Then we'll find out how good you are, how things are going to stack up.

But he never batted an eyelid and he took it on board as if it were the natural thing to do. If I'd told him to stand on one leg like the Karate Kid he'd have done that as well and not thought twice about it. And the funny thing is, he'd probably have won fights like it too.

It must have seemed like an age to him, that month, those four weeks when all he could do was jab, jab, jab and dance around – I could sense his frustration with every passing day. I was older and at a point where the years rush by, so for me the time passed quickly. But for Barry, a young man with his life in front of him and with a burning desire to explore his new-found skills, it must have felt like forever. It made a boxer of him though, all the same.

But I knew when it was over, when he'd learnt those first few basic steps, I could let him go out there and express himself. It didn't want to be much – as I said before, this game's tied to a long piece of string and you only let it out a bit at a time. I remembered to my cost what had happened the last time I'd let him off the leash. But I was confident he had enough about him at that moment to be getting on with.

And the Eastern Division Championship? Of course I was going to put him in for it – I'd never really thought otherwise, despite what I might have said. And if he didn't win it? Well then my name wasn't Albert Hyde and I didn't know the first thing about boxing.

Barry

So I'm almost sixteen and fighting in the Junior ABA Championships (Eastern Division, 69kg class). Only like I said before, this ain't fighting, it's boxing. *The noble art of* as Albert calls it in one of his poetic moments. *There's a big difference, you know.* He's right there – nobody gives a toss about the points when you're fighting.

I ask if I can use the big right hand. He shakes his head. I reckon I must have embarrassed him enough with that already.

"No," he says. "We'll keep that to ourselves for the time being. As I told you before, this is a boxing competition – not a bar room brawl."

"But what if I need it?" I says. "What if I get into trouble?"

"I'll let you know," he says. "Let me be the judge of that. Anyway, you won't get into trouble."

He's dead right. There must be three or four bouts before I reach the final and to tell the truth, I don't get no problems. Okay, so there's one lad taller than the rest with a longer reach like Danny McGuire. And just like Danny, I wait until I can get inside and I pummel his body for points. The rest are all much the same size and shape as me – but they ain't nowhere near as good. Some of them, the cocky ones, the ones who think they're it, they go all aggressive like they're trying to dominate. So I back-pedal and let them come at me while I duck, bob and weave and then, when the moment's right, I pick them off on the counter. The others stay covered up with their gloves in front of their faces and their elbows all tucked in waiting for me to get in close. So I stay out and work them round with the jab and the occasional right, picking up the points just like Albert said. *Tap, skip, right – skip, right, tap.* Any way I like. Then, once I get warmed up, I speed it up so my hands and feet work faster and faster until it's all a blur and I can do it quicker than you can blink.

And then I'm in the fight. And when I'm in the fight there ain't nothing but the fight. It's like the fight is all of me and I am all of it. Only now it ain't a fight, it's boxing, but it's just the same, never mind what Albert says. And all I can hear is the tune I'm playing, all the rest's gone quiet as I float above the noise. Laurel and Hardy are in the corner shouting their heads off but I don't hear a word they're saying. The boxing's got me now and I'm moving to its song, faster and faster and my feet are flying. I'm playing my tune and I'm dancing, dancing, dancing to the rhythm of the ring.

So now I'm a Champion, nobody's laid a glove on me and I've not yet used the big right hand. They even give me a cup to keep.

On my birthday we go into town and Dad buys me a smart new pair of gloves, red ones.

"Reckon you'll need these now," he says.

"Yes," I says. "Reckon I will."

I'm the best part of twelve months at Park Street, but then I have to leave. I ain't too sure I want to go, having just got used to it an' all. At least I get to finish that engine off. And there's plenty more to do after that, there's always something new to learn. But there's no way I can stay on.

"I'm sorry, Barry," says Cartwright. "I'd like to keep you here, but I can't. We only have so many places and the Authority wouldn't allow it. And anyway, you need to get out there and find out how to make your way in the world."

"I suppose you're right," I says. "So what are the chances of me getting a job?"

He sucks in air. "Not that good I'm afraid. Why don't you leave it with me and I'll see what I can do."

A couple of nights after school I wander into town and look in the job shop window. I can see what he's saying. There ain't a lot of demand for sixteen-year-old blokes with no qualifications and a bit of history. So things don't look too promising employment wise.

Then something turns up out the blue. Mr Cartwright's mate down at the scrapyard's got a position wants filling and I could be just the bloke he's looking for. Dad takes me down there one Saturday morning.

It's a weird place, the scrapyard. Looks like someone's parked a load of dead cars on a football pitch then piled them up one on top of the other. Some places they're four, maybe five deep. They all look smashed to bits.

The man in charge is Mr Jackson. If I didn't know better I'd swear to God he was Fat Micky's brother seeing as he's pretty much the same size and shape.

"So," he says, looking me up and down, "Ken Cartwright reckons you're pretty handy with motor parts."

"Yup," I says, "I pretty much am." I don't mind admitting it.

"I could do with someone like you around," he says. "Look at the state of me." He's got one of them pork-pie hats on and an old moth-eaten cardigan. He pulls it back so I can clock the width of his gut. "I'm in no condition to go clambering over piles of scrapped cars looking for bits any more. Gave that up a long while ago. I did have a lad until recent, but he had his hand in the till. He buggered off with a day's takings and I haven't seen him since." He leans over the counter so his face is close up to mine. There's a hairy patch under one of his chins where he forgot to shave. "Now, you ain't going to do that to me, are you?"

"No, Mr Jackson," I says, "I ain't." And I look him straight in the eye.

"Well, you seem alright to me," he says. "Ken told me I can trust you. You can start Monday week. How old are you?"

"Sixteen," I says.

He quotes an hourly rate. Which is Dad's cue to stick his oar in. "That's a bit on the low side, ain't it?" he says.

"It's minimum wage," says Jackson. "And you can take it or leave it. If you've got any complaints, send them to the North Pole. Because in case you hadn't noticed, this ain't Santa's workshop and I ain't Father Christmas."

It beats the pants off nothing so I decide to take it.

When we get home, Dad thinks it's hilarious.

"I'm forty-two," he says. "And I've managed to survive. But you, first job and you're on the scrapheap already, ha, ha, ha!"

"Oh, very funny," I says.

But I really ain't amused. A few days' time and I've got to start shinning up a pile of broken metal.

Back at Park Street, I say my goodbyes. Ain't too many of 'em, to tell the truth. Mr Cartwright and Matty are fine but no one else wants to shake my hand. Must be in case I feel like landing one on them I suppose. Matty thinks he'll miss me.

"What am I going to do when you've gone?" he says.

"How should I know?" I says. "You didn't do nothing when I was here."

That shuts him up. I still shake his hand though, even if it does feel like a wet fish.

As for the scrapyard, it ain't too bad once I get down to it. Most of the time the parts are easy to find and if the job looks dangerous, Jackson wheels a crane in and we get the car down to ground level. Then I can work on it and rip out the bit they want. After that I take it to the workshop and give it the once over to make sure it's okay. Ain't nothing I give out that don't work right.

Turns out Mr Jackson ain't such a bad bloke neither. He might talk tough but his bark's a lot worse than his bite. He's as tight as a duck's arse though and I never get much of a raise. But I guess I'm in no position to argue.

I'm there two years. Two years, the time flies by and I'm as happy as Larry. Five days a week in the scrapyard and two nights a week at the Boys Club. I win two more Championships (Eastern Division, 69kg class) and I get two more cups to put on the top of my wardrobe. My name's in all the papers – local ones, that is.

And that's it. I'm Barry Mullins, motor mechanic (of a sort), and would-be boxer – ain't no more to it.

Until I come across Ronnie Bent and Terry Bennett, that is. And that changes everything. As for Ronnie, he wasn't so bad. But I never did get on with Terry. No, I never got on with Terry at all.

Boxed In

Part Three

Fair Play

Ronnie

Don't let anyone ever tell you that selling second-hand cars for a living is easy. It ain't. I should know – I've been doing it for long enough. Or trying to, anyway. It's hard, bloody hard. I've got the scars to prove it.

Yeah, I know what you're thinking. You're thinking *Don't give me that crap, don't give me that old soft soap. Car dealers? They're a bunch of bleeding crooks.* Well that's nothing new, I've heard it all before. I get it every day, it's written on the punters' faces when they walk in off the street. If you sell second-hand cars, you must be crooks. Stands to reason, don't it? 'Course it does. And we are, we have to be to survive. So what? Every other bastard out there's a crook, it's a crooked bleeding world.

So let me broaden your education a bit and tell you how it works. There's a knock on the door, somebody's got a car to sell and a story to tell you about it. *It's been in the family for years. My grandmother used to own it. She hardly took it out of the garage except on a Sunday and that was only to clean it. 27,000 miles on the clock, we don't really want to part with it, it's almost a family heirloom.* And you, like a fool, believe them. Until you get it into the garage that is, and you discover that the clutch is knackered, the wheel bearings are shot and the general condition of it underneath suggests that Granny had a part-time career in stock car racing. And as for the 27,000 miles on the clock, that's what it says alright but you get the feeling it ain't the first time it's seen that number – second go round, maybe.

But by then it's too late and you're lumbered. You've parted with £1500 in hard-earned cash, the punters are back in Preston or some other godforsaken place at the other end of the country and the logbook's in the post. So now you've got no choice. Now you've got to turn it round, wave a magic wand and make that sow's ear of a motor into some kind of a silk purse and spend as little as you can on it in the process. So you replace a few essential parts, tart it up enough to get it through an MOT, stick £3250 on the windscreen and get it back out there as soon as you can. Then, if you're lucky, after about six weeks of sweating it out, some poor bastard starts sniffing round, they want to come in and talk turkey so you tell them the same story as got told to you. Only you happen to leave out the bit about granny's stock car racing habit because for some reason that don't seem relevant any more, you sell it for £2950 and everybody goes home happy. I say everybody but you've just got to hope you've made enough on it in the meantime to pay the wages, the Inland Revenue and keep the bank off your back so you can take whatever's left home to meet the mortgage payments and put some food on the table. Like I say, it ain't easy, that's for sure. But I suppose I must do alright, I survive. I'm still here, ain't I?

And whatever else, I like to look the part, I am a bit of a dresser. Well, you've got to be, haven't you? It goes with the job, that's what people expect – and I don't like to disappoint. A nice white shirt, clean on every day, a decent suit with a sharp crease pressed in and a good pair of shoes, hand-stitched Italian leather. It makes a man, don't you think, a decent set of clothes? It ain't who you are, it's who you look like you are, that's what I say. And I want to look like I am.

Besides, your average punter don't like parting with his money to some grimy bloke with a greasy collar and dirt under his nails. He wants to be made to feel good about it and do it all clean and comfortable. So I give him that opportunity, I make him feel good about it. When the selling's done and the price is all agreed, I take him to the office and we sort the finance out. We might talk about the weather for a bit and then if it's West Ham's or Charlton's turn to go down this year, but at some point, the crucial point, I slide the folded cuff of my clean white shirt across the polished table and we shake hands, clean hands, no dirt, no muck, and I take his money while he takes my motor. All clean and comfortable, in my office. And like I say, everyone goes home happy.

Sounds good, don't it? Sounds just the kind of thing you want – a good deal, money changing hands, all clean and comfortable. But it ain't always been that way. And maybe it ain't always that way now. You ask Terry, he'll tell you. He'll tell you everything you want to know – and a lot more besides. In fact, don't even bother to ask because he's going to tell you anyway. But don't ever let him tell you that selling second-hand cars for a living is easy. It ain't. And I should know – I've been doing it for long enough.

Barry

It's a bit of a shock when Mr Jackson keels over. I mean, I ain't had to deal with nothing like that before. And when the time comes, you don't really know what to do about it. True, Dad had a few dizzy spells a couple of year ago but he only had to sit down for ten minutes and he was fine. Low blood pressure, he reckoned, on top of the emphysema. Mr Jackson's a different kettle of fish. He's the other way round – the pressure's too high and he's gone off pop. One day, I come in from the yard, he's slumped in his chair and his face has turned a dirty grey colour.

"There's some pills in my jacket pocket," he croaks. "And fetch me a glass of water would you? While you're at it, you could phone for an ambulance. To tell the truth, I don't feel too good."

He don't look too good neither so I'm onto it straight away. It don't take more than ten minutes for the wagon to arrive and while the medics are carting him out, he hands me the keys to the gaff.

"You're a good lad, Barry," he says. "Look after the place while I'm away."

I manage to keep things going 'til the weekend. But when I turn up on the Monday there's a brand-new padlock and chain, and a notice hanging on the gate.

IN RECEIVERSHIP

Seems like someone ain't been paying their bills.

"What d'you think's going to happen?" I ask Dad when I get back home.

"If you're lucky," he says, "you'll get two weeks' pay and a thank you note."

"And if I ain't?"

He shrugs his shoulders. "Who knows," he says. "You'll have to wait and see."

I sit around for a day or so, twiddling my thumbs. But on

Saturday morning I get a letter from the Official Receiver inviting me to come in to work "at the earliest available opportunity".

"What d'you reckon?" I says.

"It's better than nothing," says Dad.

Though as it turns out, nothing ain't the only alternative.

Ronnie

Now every so often an opportunity arises. And when it jumps out in front of you, you either walk on by or you reach out and grab it with both hands before some other bastard gets it. That, as I keep telling Terry, is business. Push or be pushed, it's as simple as that. And that's how it was with Barry Mullins. An opportunity arose, a chance came up and I took it, quick as you like. It all starts on account of Brian Jackson having a heart attack.

"Well, that's no surprise," I says. "It's been on the cards for a while."

"You're right there," says Wally. "A man his size, shape and habits, it's no wonder."

Wally's one of my trusty lieutenants. Staff, employee, call him what you will, it ain't all down to me. But don't go thinking I'm running some vast multinational here, because I ain't. Fact is, there's just the four of us – and that includes the part-time cleaner and she's only in one morning a week. So when it actually comes down to it, it's me, Terry and Wal that does the business. Terry's out on the car lot with the punters while Wally's in the workshop doing the tarting up – and to tell you the truth, Wally's getting on a bit. Me, I stay put in the office with my feet up, counting the money and paying the bills. It's a tough job but somebody's got to do it.

"That's all as maybe," continues Wal. "The problem is, they've shut the yard and we can't get no parts."

Which is all a bit of a bugger seeing as the next nearest source of supply is a good twenty mile off and it's time and money I can't afford. But fortunate for us, it don't last too long. Seems like Jackson's up to his neck in debt the same as the rest of us and it don't take more than a week before the place is open for business again – only now it's in receivership and they're selling the parts off to pay the creditors. By which they mean the bank, naturally. You can always rely on a bank to pull a good man down. Banks? Don't talk to me about banks – I hate 'em, they're bastards. They're quick enough to lend you the money in the first place, but when the shit hits the fan they circle round like vultures waiting to pick the flesh off your bones.

I get the news off Wally what with him being over there every other day.

"Well, they're open again," he says. "But I don't know how long for. I just wonder what they're going to do with that lad."

"What lad?" I says.

"The lad they use in the yard," he says. "From what I gather he's pretty much running the place now. Barry Mullins, they call him."

"Barry Mullins?" I says. "That name rings a bell."

"Should do," says Wal. "He's an amateur boxer. His name was in all the papers – won some championship or another three years in a row."

And that's when I get this flash of inspiration, that's when I see the opportunity arise and a chance waiting to be had. Because if his name's in all the papers, it could be other places too. Like next to mine – in lights.

BARRY MULLINS – SPONSORED BY BIG RONNIE'S

That'd bring them in, that'd get the punters off the street and in through my front door. And right now I could do with some of that. Right now, we're struggling.

"He'll be looking for a job then," I says, "this Barry Mullins."

"I suppose he will," says Wal.

I mention it to Terry. He's against it from the start – somehow I knew he would be. He don't take too well to change, does Terry.

"What do we need Barry Mullins for?" he says. "We're alright as we are."

"The captain of the Titanic said that," I says. "And look what happened to him. Listen, Tel. You've got to take your chances in this game. Ain't no good just sitting around waiting for your ship to come in."

I make a few enquiries over the weekend. Monday morning, I call Wal into the office. "So, Wally," I says. "How old are you now?"

"Sixty-two," he says. "Sixty-three next month."

"Ever thought of retiring?" I says.

That makes his forehead wrinkle up.

"Why?" he says. "You planning to make it worth my while?"

No, I'm thinking. *But I can make it bloody awkward if you don't.*

Barry

So then I get this phone call.

I decide to tell Mr Jackson about it seeing as I'm going to visit him in hospital. He's lying there covered in tubes connected up to some machine or another and his face is still the same dirty grey colour. His eyes are closed shut and it looks like he's real tired as if this thing with the yard and his little health problem has sucked all the life out of him. He hears me coming and his eyes crack open. There's a trace of a smile but it's all weak and watery.

"Barry," he says. "Nice of you to drop by. How's things?"

"Alright," I says and I tell him about the yard, the padlock, the chain and the receiver (all of which he knows already), then about the phone call.

"Ronnie Bent?" he says. "Ha! I've known Ronnie Bent a few years, I don't mind telling you. Ronnie Bent owes me money. If it wasn't for the likes of…" But then he gets cut short with a hacking cough and I never get to find out what. It takes him a minute or two to recover. "Well never mind about Ronnie Bent," he says when he's done. "That's my problem, not yours. No, you go ahead son," he says. "You've got to take whatever comes your way – I'm not holding you to anything. Besides, I'm finished, what with the yard and the old ticker giving out. No, you take it and the best of luck to you."

He lays his head back down on the pillow, his face dirty grey against the white. I try shaking his hand before I go but he can't lift his arm off the bed.

"You look after yourself Barry," he says. Then his eyes close again.

"I'll try my best," I says. "You too, Mr Jackson."

But what with the yard and his ticker.

Never mind the tubes, suck suck suck.

Terry

I knew he was trouble from the start. Jumped-up little git. Who the hell does he think he is? He waltzes in here like he owns the place and expects some kind of special treatment just because he's a boxer and he's won a few fights. He ain't even turned professional for Christ's sake. It don't make no sense, what with Ronnie fawning all over him an' all. And in the meanwhile, I'm supposed to stand here and wave a flag. Bugger that.

"Barry Mullins?" I says. "What the hell do we need him for?"

"Publicity," says Ronnie. "We need some publicity. He'll bring the punters in. And this way we get it for nothing."

We're in the office, huddled round the electric fire. I've persuaded Ronnie to turn one bar of it on while he sits there in that camel bloody coat of his, chomping away on a prawn and mayo sandwich. I've only come inside because it's pouring with rain. I'm usually out on the car lot, selling.

"Look," I says, "it ain't the punters that's the problem. I'll tell you what's the problem – we ain't got nothing to sell them. I know what we need and it ain't the likes of Barry Mullins. What we need is a decent set of stock on the forecourt. You get me that and I'll shift it. You know I will."

Ronnie clamps his teeth and sucks in air. "It ain't as easy as that, Tel," he says. "You know that. Things is a bit tight just at present."

Ain't they always? Don't stop you from wearing a nice new shirt and tie though.

But that's always been the way of it with Ronnie. Flash clothes and a flash car, never mind whether we're making any money or not, he's got to look right. Now I know he's supposed to be a businessman but sometimes you have to wonder whether he makes the right decisions. Take Wally for instance. Though to tell the truth, Wally never counted. Wally was never in it so to speak, it was only ever me and Ronnie, and I have to say I didn't cry no tears when Wally left. You have to wonder about it though, here one minute and gone the next, just like that. And okay, he had to be replaced. But Barry Mullins? It just don't make no sense.

Two's company and three's a crowd, that's what I say. You see, Ronnie Bent and me, we go back a long way. And I ain't talking months here, or even years, it's more like a decade. Whichever way, it's been a long time. But that's how it was supposed to be, the two of us, we was always in it together. There was nothing ever written down, naturally – never any need for that (or so I thought), but it was always there, unspoken, understood between us. Maybe I should have done, got it set out proper like a partnership or some kind of business agreement, but I never felt I needed that. Not until now, anyway. Besides, we was always too busy trying to make a few bob, we never had the time.

And I never had the money – it was always Ronnie who had the cash, the bankroll that funded whatever happened next. And if I ever asked where it came from, he'd lay his finger down the side of his nose and say *Shush! No questions asked* like he'd robbed a bank or something and didn't want me to know. And the fact is, I still don't know how much he's got or exactly where it goes. Except for the suits, the shoes and a tidy motor that is – plus the handouts I get to keep me going.

Because if it wasn't for me, Ronnie Bent would still be selling watches out of a suitcase down the Old Kent Road. Don't laugh, it's cruel, but that's how he started – or rather he didn't because if I hadn't have come along he'd still be there. Fact is, Ronnie Bent couldn't sell a lifebelt to a drowning man, but me, I've always had the gift, a way with words, a way of moving stuff on. First it was the watches, then it was the Walkman, and after that there'd be some other piece of merchandise he'd manage to get hold of. He'd buy it (or find it – I never knew how he got it, that was always his secret), I'd sell it and he'd say *The first nine gets it paid for – every tenth one you sell, whatever you make, you get to keep,* and that was my incentive.

So we did the rounds, Ronnie and me, mostly on a weekend. In those days we worked out of the back of a clapped-out van – Chelmsford, Braintree, Basildon, Brentwood, and then into London and the East End markets. They were favourite, you could go there three months in a row and never be in the same place twice, never see the same set of punters. We'd get parked up, out would come the suitcase and I'd start doing the business. If we were lucky, I'd clear the lot, but if not we'd pack up and move on somewhere else. We never had much trouble – but Ronnie always kept the engine running, just in case. Then, if it was a Saturday night, we might just stay out and have one or two beers. Or three or four, depending. I lost count of the number of times we kipped in the back of that van.

We must have gone two years like that then all of a sudden things take off. It all starts with a batch of car radios, direct from Taiwan. We're on our way somewheres in the van (don't ask me where, I can't for the life of me remember) and what with Ronnie never being able to sell, I'm telling him this joke about how to do it.

So there's this young lad gets taken on in a general store and he asks the old guy in there how the job's done. Watch me, son, he says. A customer comes in and the old guy says, can I help you sir? And the customer says, yes, I want some grass seed. So he sells him the grass seed, then the old guy says, now sir, can I interest you in a lawnmower? Lawnmower, says the customer, what do I want with a lawnmower? Well, says the old guy, you've bought the grass seed, pretty soon you'll have a nice lawn and it'll want cutting. You're right, says the customer, and he buys the lawnmower. And that's how the job's done, says the old guy. Now it's your turn. Well, the next customer's a young woman, so the young lad says, can I help you madam? And she says, yes, I want a box of tampax please. So he sells her the tampax and the young lad says, now madam, can I interest you in a lawnmower? What do I want with a lawnmower? she says. Well, says the young lad, your weekend's ruined so you may as well cut the grass.

Now me, I'm howling my head off because I think it's real funny, but when I look round, Ronnie ain't laughing and his face has gone all serious.

"That's it," he says. "That's what we've got to do, sell them more than they bargained for. Here we are pissing around with all this small stuff when we should be in the big time."

"What d'you mean?" I says.

"You wait," he says, "and I'll show you."

And the very first radio I sell he stops the guy while he's giving change.

"So," he says, "now you've bought the radio, you'll be looking for a decent motor to put it in, ha, ha, ha."

And bugger me if the guy don't say, "Funny you should mention it..."

And that's how we got started with the second-hand car thing, Ronnie finding them and me selling them on.

But it was always Ronnie who took the cash, he was always the one as looked after the money. I just hope he's looked after my part of it, that's all. But it ain't as if I'm greedy. I just want it fair. And I can wait, I can wait for what he's put aside for me. *Don't worry Tel, I'll see you right. Come the finish and we get cashed up there'll be a good bit in it for you.* There'd better be, that's all I can say. Because Ronnie Bent owes me, he owes me big time and he'd best not be running out on me now. He's made a promise that one day I'll get what's mine, one day I'll get my share. Either that, or there'll be trouble – Barry Mullins or not.

Barry

So I decide to go and work for Ronnie Bent. Though to tell the truth, I ain't got a lot of choice, what with the yard closing an' all. *Ronald A. Bent, Car Dealer and Garage Proprietor.* That's what it says on his card, only you won't find it like that in Yellow Pages. *Big Ronnie's* is what they call it, and according to Dad it's never been called anything else. It's a fair-sized place on the Maldon Road on the way out of town. You can't miss it. Along the front of the car lot there's a string of tatty red and white bunting flapping in the breeze, and just so's you can't go by without looking, there's an A-board sat out on the pavement with great big letters on it.

BIG RONNIE'S
USED CARS
BOUGHT AND SOLD
FOR CASH

It's like a landmark. Everyone in Chelmsford knows it. In this part of the world, if you want the weekly shop, you go to Tesco's. If you want a second-hand car, you go to Big Ronnie's. It's a fact of life, simple as that.

The day I arrive he takes me into his office. Seems like everywhere you go they take you into an office. This one looks older than Steed's but there's no junk in it like Cartwright's. I clock the décor, a white wooden surround with the top half done out in frosted glass. Only this ain't '50s retro, this is the real deal.

"Sit down," says Ronnie, and he waves me toward an old leather armchair in the corner. The stuffing's spewing out of it and I figure it must have been there since they built the place. I don't recall feeling chilly but he's got one of them two-bar electric fires and he makes a point of turning it on like I'm some kind of special guest.

"So you're Barry Mullins," he says.

"Yes," I says. "That's right, I am."

I'm tempted to say, *so what?* but I'm learning when to bite my tongue. We sit for a minute while he looks at me out the corner of his eye, a bit like Albert, sizing me up, and then he starts off about the garage, the workshop and how I'm supposed to go about fixing the cars up an' all. But someone must have tipped him off because we ain't two minutes into it before he starts off on some other tack and you just know that this here's the subject he really wants to talk about.

"I gather you're an amateur boxer," he says.

"You gather right," I says. "I do a bit." Like I'm trying to keep it modest.

So now he wants to know the ins and outs of the boxing business, where I do it, who I do it with and how I got to be Champion. Seems to me we spend more time on that than we do on the garage, but at last he takes me out through the back of the office and into the workshop. It's pretty much what I expect. There's space for a car, some workbenches, a few cupboards, overhead lifting gear etc. In fact, it don't look that much different than the garage at Park Street two years before. I even look behind one of the cupboards to see if Matty's sitting there. He ain't of course. But I'm comfortable with it all the same, I can work there.

By the look of Ronnie's hands I'd say he's never held a spanner in his life, so I reckon he's going to leave me to get on with it. But I've just got my overalls on and I'm finding my way about when he comes straight back in again. He puts his arm round my shoulder like he was my uncle or something and I was his favourite nephew and he says, "Now then, Barry. I've got a little proposition I want to put to you," and he takes me out back to have a look at it.

Behind the workshop there's a bit of waste ground and parked on it are the wrecked shells of what must have been half a dozen cars. It's like a graveyard for dead motors. Even the ones down at Mr Jackson's were in better condition.

"So what are these?" I says.

"These," says Ronnie, sticking his chest out like he's proud of the fact, "are the ones that never quite made it. We do get them on occasion. We take them as trade-ins and for some reason we can't move them on. So we sort of lay them to rest out here..."

"...and then rob them for parts," I says.

Because like the bloke who lost his marbles, it's clear they ain't all there.

"Well, Wally may have had a few bits off them in his time, it's true," he says. "But that don't mean to say they ain't no use. Anyways," he says, trying to change the subject, "this here's the one I had in mind."

And he runs his hand over the top of the smallest pile of junk in the line-up like he's stroking a piece of silk. Only his fingers are going brown with the rust.

"And what was it?" I says. "Before it died?"

"This," says Ronnie, giving it a gentle pat like it was his favourite pet dog, "is a Mini Cooper S."

"U/S more like," I says. "So how long's it been stood there?"

Ronnie clamps his teeth and sucks in air the way people do when they're fixing to cook up a lie.

"Ooh," he says. "Three months, four at the most."

Months? I'm thinking. *Years, more like.*

"So where do I fit in?" I says. I get a funny feeling I know the answer already but I just want to hear Ronnie say it.

"What I want you to do with it," he says, "is get it up and running."

"Running?" I says. "You'll be lucky to get it to crawl, never mind run."

"Look," says Ronnie. "You're not quite getting the picture here, are you? I'm fixing to give you the bloody thing for Christ's sake, you could at least show a bit of enthusiasm."

"Give it me?" I says. "Am I hearing you right? You want to give it me? So what's the catch?"

Because there has to be one, right? There always is.

"There ain't no catch," he says. "It's all yours. But there is something I want you to do with it."

And when he tells me, it's that bloody simple I have to laugh.

When I get home, Dad's all for it.

"That's a gift horse if ever I saw one," he says. "And don't you go looking it in the mouth neither. When was the last time you got given something for nothing? You won't get another offer like that. You take it and good luck to you."

He's right, of course, I'd be a fool to turn it down. And besides, it's about time I had a motor, a young man like me, and I can't see no other way of getting one, not on my wages. So next night, after work, I make a special trip into town to buy the Mini Cooper manual. And when tea's finished, I'm up in my room reading it. It feels just like old times.

Ronnie

Week one goes by, the lad settles in and it all seems tickety-boo. Saturday morning arrives and I open up early in the hopes of catching a few extra punters. I'm in a good mood and I fancy a bit of a flutter so I've just settled down with a cup of coffee and a browse of The Racing Post when the outside door crashes shut and Terry comes barging in like he's fit to commit a breach of the peace. He's picked his moment seeing as the workshop's closed at weekends so Barry ain't about.

"What the hell did you do that for?" he says.

"What the hell did I do what for?" I says.

"Give him that bloody car!" he says. "I can't believe it! You gave him a car for Christ's sake. *YOU GAVE HIM A BLOODY CAR!* The bloke ain't been here ten minutes and he gets a leg up already. I've been here ten years and I'm still waiting. Somewhere along the line, something ain't quite right."

"Whoa!" I says. "Steady on, Tel, there's no need to get shirty. It's all part of my cunning plan. It'll work out, you'll see. It'll be fine."

"Cunning plan, my arse," he says. "You're just sucking up to him because he's had his name in the papers."

"Now that ain't the case at all," I says. "And you know it. It's business, strictly business, there ain't nothing personal in it. How many times do I have to keep telling you? It's an opportunity, and when an opportunity comes up you've got to take it. Besides," I says, trying to smooth things over. "It was only a scrapper for goodness sake. It ain't worth a light to start with."

"That ain't the point," says Tel. "It's the principle of the thing."

"Principle?" I says. "Since when did you acquire any principles? What we need is results. Somebody's got to make something happen around here otherwise we're all down the drain. Anyways," I says, "if you're so upset about it why don't you go out the back and take one for yourself. There's another half-dozen to pick from. You're quite welcome to choose."

"That's crap and you know it," he says. "Ain't one of 'em any good to me. I can't get them done up like he can."

"Then why don't you stop whingeing and get on with it?" I says. Out on the forecourt I can see a couple of punters sniffing round the family saloons. "Besides, you've got customers to talk to. You ain't going to earn a penny's worth of commission while you're stood here complaining."

That shuts him up and he heads back out to the car lot. He needs his ten per cent just like any other day.

So Terry don't like it. So Terry's going to have to lump it. Like I say, if somebody don't make something happen, we're all going down the drain. He must have noticed for Christ's sake, he ain't blind. Even if all he did was look in his pay packet at the end of the month, he has to see it. We ain't doing half as well as what we were, and even then it wasn't brilliant.

It ain't his fault. He'll sell whatever I put out there to whoever comes through the gate, I know that. Terry could sell a block of ice to an Eskimo. Trouble is, we ain't got no ice and there ain't no Eskimos. Don't nobody want to buy second-hand cars no more? He's right about the stock though, but I can't afford to put no more out there right now. The lease payment's due this month and once that's done we'll be clear for another quarter. At this rate we might just last until Christmas.

But whatever Terry says, Barry Mullins was a good move. Like I say, when an opportunity arises you reach out and grab it with both hands. It's cut my wage bill for a start. I ain't paying Barry nowhere near what I was paying Wally. Then there's the publicity, that's still to come. It'll work, it's got to bloody work. I've come this far, I've survived. I ain't giving up now.

Barry

So I start work on Ronnie's car. I say Ronnie's but it's really mine – he gave it me, didn't he? But I guess I can't call it that until I've earned the right. And there's a long way to go on it yet.

First job is get the brakes freed off. Stood outside for that length of time and they've seized up. Then I can get her pulled out of the line-up and sure enough, Ronnie's right, underneath all the muck and bullets there's a Mini Cooper S. Would have been a nice motor one time of day – nice that is if it weren't for the fact that somebody's run into the back of her, seeing as the rear end's stoved in an' all. But to tell the truth, if the only thing wrong with her is a bent back bumper and a dented boot, then I've got half a chance. The rest of her don't look that bad, apart from a few bumps and scratches. The mechanics I know I can handle, but bodywork? That's a place I ain't been to yet. But you've got to start somewhere.

As soon as the wheels are turning, I get her pushed round into the workshop. I clear a space down at the back where I can tuck her out of the way, then I can work on the customers' cars up front and the access is kept free. Garage work gets priority, but any spare time I get I spend on the Mini. It evens out around fifty-fifty, seeing as the customer side ain't exactly busy right now. But I'm happy enough, one way or another, messing about underneath a bonnet.

I decide to check through the mechanics before I start on the bodywork so I strip it all down then build it back up. It's just like being at Park Street. The engine wants a bit of tuning but she runs fine once I get her all fired up. Clutch and gearbox are okay and the transmission's alright, but she wants a couple of wheel bearings and there's two or three other parts could do with replacing. I get Ronnie to run me down the scrapyard.

There's a few changes to the place since I was there last. There's a brighter look about it for a start – a fresh lick of paint and such – like someone's made an effort to smarten it up. The padlock and chain have disappeared and all the old locks have been changed. There's a new notice hanging on the gate – *UNDER NEW MANAGEMENT* – so I ain't expecting to see Mr Jackson. Seems like the yard's been sorted, but in respect of his ticker and the tubes, I don't get no news.

Ronnie don't want to come in. He parks his car round the corner and sits there reading the paper while I go and do the necessary.

"You go ahead," he says. "I ain't got no business in there. Besides, somebody might recognise me and call me out for money. Speaking of which, you'll need some. Here, take this," and he gives me a hundred in notes.

As it turns out, I don't need it all as I get some parts on the sly seeing as I'm owed a couple of favours, so I blow the rest on a decent boot and a bumper. Which saves me fiddling around with the bodywork.

It takes me three months all told, start to finish. Ronnie's like a cat on a hot tin roof the whole time. He can't keep his nose out the garage and there ain't a day goes by but what he don't come wandering in to see what's going on. It's always the same.

"How's it going, Baz?" he'll say. And if I've heard that once I must have heard it a dozen times.

"Fine," I'll say, and while I get on with it I let him know what I'm doing. "I'm regulating the throttle," I tell him and rev the engine for effect. Or, "I'm lining up the headlights," and flick them on and off a few times. It's all a bit pointless – but it keeps him off my back, just the same.

As for the other one, Terry, he couldn't care less. He comes in the once to black his nose, takes one look around, fiddles with the change in his pocket, sniffs, and then walks out again. He's got some kind of a problem, has that man. And the longer we go on, the more I'm beginning to think it's me. He ain't hardly spoke to me since I got here.

I get most everything done myself, even down to the paintwork. There's a choice of colours – red or green – plus two white stripes on the bonnet. I fancy the red but Dad reckons I should go green what with it being British racing colours an' all.

"But I ain't racing," I says.

"Never mind that," says Dad. "It's part of the history."

In the end it's Ronnie's decision. He ums and ahs a bit, then comes down on the side of the green. "Let's have a bit of class," he says.

The only thing I can't handle is the signage. It must matter because Ronnie gets someone in to do it and he don't lay out cash unless he has to. He orders white lettering on both doors in big swirls.

BARRY MULLINS
SPONSORED BY BIG RONNIE'S
He's well chuffed.

"That," he says, dangling the keys under my nose, "is one smart motor. And I want to see it put about a bit. It's no good leaving it parked up outside your place the whole time, it wants moving around."

I take him at his word. I drive Dad to work in it and make sure we arrive just as everyone else does. I take Mum to the supermarket and wait in the car park while she does the rounds. I take it to the gym – and get a whole load of stick off Fat Micky and the other lads, but that gets it noticed just the same. And on long summer evenings I drive it round wherever, just cruising.

Then, one Sunday afternoon at the end of July, I park it in the Square and walk across to the Ice Cream Parlour for a coffee. And that's where I meet Tracey.

Sharon

If you was to ask me (which I suppose you are) as to how Barry
Mullins and Tracey Williams ever got together in the first place
then I guess I'd have to put it down to a combination of factors
– downright boredom for one, bravado for another and well,
Tracey just being Tracey for a third I suppose. And if you was to
go on and say *What on earth are we asking Sharon Roberts for?* then
I'd have to tell you it's because I know Tracey better than anyone
else, we've been best friends for as long as I can remember
besides which I was actually there when it happened.

You see, Tracey and I were born in the same year and in the
same street. Now that may not mean as much these days as it
used to but it's the kind of thing that sticks with you for the rest
of your life, well it does for us anyway. We grew up together, we
played together, we went to school together and now we go out
together. We don't work together thank God (you can have too
much of a good thing) and I don't mean that because there'd be
nothing to talk about after 5.30pm either, we'd find something
believe me but I'm in an office, she's in a shop and it just worked
out that way.

And after work we like to have a bit of fun – as you do, pubs,
clubs, we're always out on the town, we've had some laughs
over the years I don't mind telling you. And I suppose you never
really think about it much, but somewhere at the back of your
mind there's this nagging thought chipping away *How long is this
going to last? How long will things go on this way?* We're eighteen
now but will it be twenty, twenty-five, maybe even thirty, but at
some stage she'll meet some bloke or I will and that'll be the end
of it au revoir, arrivederci, goodbye, have a nice life. Because
that's really what we're trying to do, ain't it? Meet some bloke,
find the perfect partner, settle down and live the life we've
always dreamed of, la dolce vita, champagne and strawberries
and all that? And to tell the truth, hiding somewhere behind

the handbags, the shoes and the lipstick, we're just two decent hard-working girls looking for a future, well I am at any rate I can't always speak for Tracey, sometimes I look at her and think there's a lot more to her than meets the eye. But in the meanwhile, if there's a bit of fun to be had Tracey and I are there to have it, well we are Essex girls you know.

Now the thing about Tracey, especially when it comes to blokes (although in general really but blokes in particular), is that she knows what she wants and she's usually accustomed to getting it. I don't mean to say she's spoilt, she's not, she can't be, she lives on her own with her mother in a two-up two-down in Campion Street, her father hasn't been seen for years, joined the army went off to fight in some God forsaken place the other side of Suez and hasn't been heard of since. And pretty good riddance according to her mother, wouldn't have him back if he crawled in through the front door on his hands and knees and begged for mercy but that's another story. Which all means they don't have much to start with. And pardon my expression but their front room is like the difference between a six and two threes, there's nothing in it so no one in her family's got anything to spoil her with anyway and maybe it's that as makes her so determined to get what she wants in the first place.

Naturally, she's told me all about it. Of course she would, I'm supposed to be her best friend so if she can't tell me who can she tell? Sometimes it's all she talks about. There's a house (you'd expect that), a car, holidays in Spain, the usual stuff – like I say, champagne and strawberries – but somehow her champagne and strawberries have to be a damn site better than anyone else's, she won't settle for anything but the best will Tracey Williams. Take the house for instance. It's not going to be your ordinary place, the kind that everyone else has got – she's got it into her head that she's going to live in a palace at least six bedrooms three reception and a big terrace overlooking the sea and we're not talking Canvey Island by the way, most likely the Mediterranean or Malibu Beach. She even knows the colour of the curtains in the downstairs loo (never mind the dining room or the master bedroom) she's got it all planned out in detail. As for me, I'd be happy with a modest semi up at Bell Meadows with enough back garden for the kids to play in but that wouldn't be good enough for Tracey, like I say she has to have it better than anyone else.

Which goes a long way to explaining her choice of blokes. Because she has to have the best of it there too, she always gets first pick. So if we're out and about on the town – pubs, clubs, whatever – and there's a couple we're eyeing up, she'll say *I'll take the one in the blue shirt, you can have his mate,* never mind the fact that his mate looks like he's had a bad accident with the back of a truck. I'm stuck with it, no argument, I'm always second in line. But d'you know what? I don't really mind. And in some ways, it makes it easier for me. I'd be the first to confess I'm no great looker, so I just follow her, there's no squabbling and we all know where we stand. And if things don't work out for me, I just keep mine occupied while Tracey goes to town on hers. So I don't complain, I get my fair share.

So this particular day, the day I'm going to tell you about, this Sunday afternoon at the end of July, we're wandering round the city centre at a bit of a loose end. There's nothing on at the cinema (well, nothing we fancy seeing anyway), we've been to the park and gone on the boating lake only to discover that platform heels and rowing boats don't exactly mix, so we've come back into town for a bit of a nosy round the shops. Most of which are closed and the rest we've seen before anyway. Nothing new there. So we get down to the bottom of the High Street wondering what to do with ourselves, we come out onto the Square to see if anyone's about and there it is stood in front of us.

Well, I'm no expert on cars, I couldn't tell a Ferrari from a Ford Escort and neither could Tracey for that matter but this one makes you sit up and take notice, well it would do wouldn't it what with all that white lettering plastered down the side.

"Ooh," she says. "Look at this. And who's Barry Mullins when he's at home?"

"He's a boxer," I says. "Don't you ever read the papers? He was all over the back pages a few weeks ago."

"Don't be silly," she says. "I haven't got time to read newspapers, I'm too busy trying to get you fixed up, Sharon."

Which is her idea of a joke. I let it pass, I always do.

"Hmm... So he's a boxer is he?" she says. "Does that mean he's rich and famous?"

"Probably," I says. "And if he ain't now, then like as not he will be one day."

"In that case," she says, "I'm interested. Is he married?"

"How should I know?" I says. "I'm not his blooming keeper."

Not that it would make a scrap of difference if he was (married, that is). Tracey's a predatory animal when she puts her mind to it.

"Besides," I says, "you haven't seen him yet. Maybe he's not your type."

"I'll be the judge of that," she says. "Anyways, don't go confusing me with the facts, I've made up my mind."

Well, the next thing you know, we start scouring the place. There's two pubs open and they're both quiet so the obvious place to look is the Ice Cream Parlour. I peer in through the front window trying to catch a glimpse.

"There he is," I says, "sitting halfway down on the right. I recognise his face from the paper."

"Right then," says Trace and she hands me her bag while she fluffs up her hair, straightens her dress and checks her makeup, then takes the chewing gum out of her mouth and shoves it in a piece of tissue.

"Wish me luck," she says and before I can say *Break a leg* she's taken her bag back, pushed open the door and gone inside.

Now seeing as how we're best friends, we have a pact, most

girls do, it works like this. When there's just the one on their own (bloke that is) the other of us is supposed to make themselves scarce so's not to queer the pitch, and strictly speaking this is the point when I should wander off and let her get on with it. But I haven't come all the way into town on a Sunday afternoon just to catch an early bus home, so just this once I decide to break the rules. And it's not because I want to steal her thunder, spoil her act or anything like that, but I need a life too and you can get fed up playing second fiddle the whole time, so I reckon on picking up a few tips as to how it's done. Besides which, I'm curious as to how things might work out so I count to ten, follow her in and park myself a couple of tables away to have a listen.

And Barry Mullins? Well, he's supposed to be a boxer but he don't put up much of a fight as far as Tracey's concerned, it's like watching a rabbit getting caught in the headlights, poor bastard he never stood a chance, well no one ever does once Tracey gets going.

Barry

They say every man has a woman in his life somewhere along the line – even if it's only his mother. Well with me it was Tracey, there was never anyone else. Call me a sap if you like, but I fell for her hook, line and sinker the moment she walked in through that door. I fell in love with her then, and I guess I'm still in love with her now. It hurts, but you've just got to live with it.

You could say I was too young. You could say I wasn't prepared for it, that it jumped out at me when I wasn't ready. And to be honest, you'd probably be right. But it seems to me that life's like that, stuff happens when you least expect it and you ain't got no control. One minute you're walking down the street, right as rain, next minute, *BANG!* straight into a lamppost. And that's what it was like meeting Tracey – walking into a lamppost – the shock of it, I mean.

It ain't as if she was the first – there'd been a few others before. So don't you go thinking I sit home all the time reading motor manuals, or spend all my nights down the gym. I do have a life, but just because I ain't made no mention of it don't mean to say I ain't interested. There's a gang of blokes at the Boys Club and most Saturday nights they're off to a disco. I have been known to tag along. And you know what happens at discos, you get chatting with some bird and things move on from there. Or not, as the case may be. But up 'til now not one of 'em's set my house on fire. Then, out of the blue, along comes Tracey and it's burn, burn, burn.

So the door to the Ice Cream Parlour swings opens and in walks this black-haired goddess. I see her coming and I want to look at her but I daren't, if you know what I mean. Because for sure if I do, I won't be able to take my eyes off and it'll look like I'm being rude. So I stare at the opposite wall and pretend not to notice. But then I get the feeling she's headed in my direction and I can feel her eyes going straight through me like I'm pinned to the spot and can't move.

"This seat free?" she says, and without so much as a by-your-leave she plonks her little bag on the table, pulls up a chair and sits down.

Well I don't mind telling you, it's like someone's pressed my go-faster pedal because my motor's racing like an E-type Jag.

"You're Barry Mullins, ain't yer?" she says.

The answer to that is most definitely "yes" but somehow the cat's got hold of my tongue. I try to think up some smartarse reply but all I can come up with is something feeble.

"Oh…" I says. "Yeah…" I says. "But how do you know that?"

"A little bird told me," she says.

"I see," I says. "And what else did this little bird tell you?"

"That you're a boxer. Besides which, you was in all the papers the other week."

"You saw that?"

"'Course I did. Didn't everyone?"

"I suppose they must have," I says.

I can feel my cheeks going red as a beetroot so I nod a few times. It's like I'm confessing to some kind of crime. I tell myself I should have seen it coming but this ain't boxing where I can duck out the way – though if it is, she's got me on the ropes and I have to take every shot. Meantime, she's planted her elbow square on my table, her chin's resting on her hand and she's looking me up and down.

"You're not very big, are you?" she says. "I'd have thought a boxer would be all big and muscly."

"Ah," I says. "Well that's where you're wrong. Not all boxers *are* big and muscly." It's an uncomfortable truth and I'm embarrassed to tell it seeing as how she might be disappointed. Then I remember what Albert said and I try explaining. "You see, it ain't all about how big you are, it's about how big a punch you're carrying."

I watch as her big brown eyes flicker for a second and I see the question going through her head. *So how big a punch* are *you carrying?* But I can't answer that right now so it all goes quiet like there's nothing else to say – until she breaks in.

"You don't know much how to treat a girl, do you?"

"What do you mean?" I says.

"Well, I've been sat here over five minutes. Aren't you going to buy me a coffee?"

"Sorry," I says, and I jump up to do the honours – this ain't the time to be forgetting my manners. "How do you take it?"

"Black," she says. "And no sugar."

Because you're sweet enough.

The old chat line springs to mind. But I don't say it. We're past that stage already and besides, it just don't sound right. I get her coffee, plus another one for me, and when I get back to the table she's busy fixing her lipstick. She sees me coming, snaps her compact shut and drops it into her handbag, then blows across the top of her drink and takes a sip.

"So tell me, Barry," she says. "What's it like being a boxer?"

Now this here's pretty much the same question as got asked by Ronnie when we first met. I weren't too keen on it then but this time I'm ready for it. And of all the questions she could've asked, it just so happens that it's the easiest for me to answer. Because let's be honest, I could talk about boxing 'til the cows come home. So I tell her about how it got started what with the Game Boy and Parky and Danny McGuire, then about Park Street and Mr Cartwright and Spike an' all.

"You were at Park Street?" she says. "That must have been tough."

"Yes, I says, and I lay it on a bit thick. "It was."

Then I tell her about the Boys Club and Albert and Fat Micky and how the two of them are like Laurel and Hardy, and I guess I must tell it funny on account of it making her laugh. She starts choking on her coffee and I have to come round and pat her on the back to stop it. She don't complain, so then I know it's alright and I start telling her things I ain't told no one before, like how I'm going to win the ABA National Title, turn professional, fight Sugar Ray Leonard and become Champion of the World. Because that's what I want, that's where I'm headed and that's what it means to be a boxer. And she don't laugh or think I'm stupid and she sits there with her elbow on the table and her chin resting on her hand like she's taking it all in. But it's the first time I've said it out loud and that kinda makes it real, so now I know I'm going to have to stick by it and make it happen.

"So then you'll be rich and famous," she says.

"Well, yeah," I says. "I suppose I will. Anyways," I says, "you don't want to listen to me going on all the time. Ain't there nothing you want to do?"

So then it's her turn and she tells me about her Dad and how he did a runner when she was little and how she lives at home with her Mum but that don't mean she intends living there the rest of her life, she wants a place of her own. Only the place she wants ain't just any place, it's got to be special and she has this dream about it. Now this house, this special house, she tells me is six bedrooms, three reception with a big terrace overlooking the sea where you can sit and drink champagne and eat strawberries all day, and it's got to be the best house in the world. And believe it or not she already knows the colour of the curtains in the downstairs loo, not to mention those in the dining room and the master bedroom. And while she's talking I get this picture of me becoming Champion of the World and her having this house, so then it starts becoming my dream too and it's like a dream we're having together.

After a while things dry up like we're all talked out and I happen to glance at my watch. God knows where the afternoon's gone but we've been going near enough two hours and it's pushing five o' clock.

"Ooh," she says. "Look at the time. Chances are I've missed my bus and it's a long walk home. I don't suppose..." And she stares straight down at the set of car keys I happen to have left lying on the table.

"Why don't you let me..." I says. And being the gentleman I am, I don't think twice.

Sharon

It's a gift it must be, I haven't got it, I wish I did, I don't know how she does it, I swear to God I don't. I've sat here for the best part of two hours, kept well out of the way like I'm supposed to and listened to every precious word that's fallen from her pouty red lips, but I still don't understand how she gets away with it. So what on earth did she say that was so special? *Tell me Barry, what's it like being a boxer?* For crying out loud, do me a favour – where's the magic in that? *Chances are I've missed my bus and it's a long walk home.* You must be joking. Tracey Williams catch a bus? That'll be the day. Last bus she caught was the one home on the day she left school – it's been taxis ever since. As for him giving her a ride, she'll be taking him on one more like, somebody please tell me there's more to it than that, I can't believe it could be that simple.

Maybe it was the way she locked onto him, all gooey-eyed with her chin on her hand, lashes fluttering like a hyperactive camera at a David Bailey photo shoot. You'd have thought she'd been to RADA to learn that one – I've seen it done a lot worse on TV. But you've got to hand it to her, she gets results. She's walked in off the street, sat straight down with a bloke she's never seen before and they've barely said *Howdy Doody* but what she's got him eating out of her hand. Though I can tell you now he's on a very short string is Mr Mullins, it's threaded through his nose and likely to lead him up the garden path.

Which to my mind is all a bit of a shame because he seems like a really nice guy. You can usually tell, and in this case it's just as they're leaving when he opens the door to let her go first – and that don't happen too often. Meanwhile, she's flouncing out like she's the Queen of Sheba and just so no one's in doubt she slides her arm through his. She's even got the barefaced cheek to put her other hand behind her back and stick her thumb up to let me know she's pulled. As if I didn't know that already. Sometimes, if it weren't for the fact that she's supposed to be my best friend, I'd scratch her eyes out. Tracey Williams is the luckiest girl alive, she wants to be careful one day her luck doesn't run out on her, it wouldn't surprise me, nothing in this world ever does.

But what do I know? I'm just her hanger-on.

Barry

So that's it, Tracey Williams and me we start going steady, it's two or three times a week. I'd go for more only she says we have to keep things sensible. Tuesdays and Thursdays I can still go to Boys Club, though if she'd said those were her only free nights I'd have packed the boxing up, I'm that keen on her. But she knows how important it is to keep that going. Because without it, we ain't got no dream.

Ronnie still wants his pound of flesh so I don't get away before five. I'm home for five-thirty and it takes me an hour to get cleaned up, have something to eat, change and be out of the house. First night it must look like I'm panicking because Dad's stood in the hallway glancing at his watch. *What's all the rush for, son?* Meanwhile, I'm scrabbling through a pile of ironing looking for a clean shirt. I don't say nothing but they must twig. Maybe it's the smell of her on my clothes because next time, just as I'm closing the front door, they give each other a knowing look. *We'll leave the downstairs light on. Turn it off when you come in.*

I'm usually at Tracey's by seven. She says not to knock or come in, just sit in the car and wait 'til she's ready. Sometimes it's half an hour. I count how often there's a twitch in the neighbour's curtains. At a pound a time I reckon I wouldn't need the boxing, I'd be rich already. I mean, it ain't as if it's some kind of mystery for Christ's sake – here I am, sat in the middle of Campion Street in a green car with white stripes and my name plastered down both sides. They know who I am and they know where I come from. Maybe I should add a phone number so they can call me up and talk about it. But then Tracey walks down the path and we're off.

We go all over. I mention it to Ronnie, but he's okay with it.

"The further the better," he says. "They buy cars in Suffolk, don't they?" And he even sticks some petrol in the tank.

The evenings are light and we've time to get somewhere and

have a walk before it gets dark. We find we like the seaside best – Southend or Clacton if we want the bright lights, Maldon if we fancy it quiet. We park up, get out and stroll for a while or play the arcades, then, when the sky starts closing in, we find somewhere for a drink or a coffee. We drive home in the dark and I discover how good it is having her head on my shoulder. All of a sudden I've got a new life and I start wondering what I did before I met her. And d'you know what? I ain't too sure I can remember.

Summer flies by, we get toward September and one way or another things build up to a head. I figure it's to do with the tides. Because every time we're at the seaside, Maldon in particular, you can see the level's getting higher – 'til one night it spills out over onto the promenade. At the same time, me and Tracey, we're getting serious. It's like all that water's pushing us to something we ain't quite reckoned on yet.

It all kicks off at the Fair. And maybe that comes up with the water too, because one night the river rises and next morning Parliament Fields is covered in it – tents, caravans, sideshows and rides, all spread out like driftwood washed up on a beach. I guess it shouldn't come as a surprise what with it being the same every year, only this time things feel different. Last September a crowd of us from the Boys Club went down, a bunch of lads out for a good time. This year I'll be with Tracey. It'll be a whole new ball game.

The Fair lasts a week. They set up on the Monday and they're open Tuesday to Saturday. We wait 'til the Friday seeing as we'll both have been paid and we can make a decent go of it. I get mine in cash (Ronnie don't deal in nothing else) but Tracey gets hers from a machine outside the bank. We pool the money and we're ready to give it a go. It's our first big night out together.

So I'm waiting in the car outside her house just before seven, same as usual. The curtains start twitching next door, only this time they twitch a bit more than normal. Chances are they've noticed the little change I've made, namely the addition of a dark strip with white lettering at the top of the windscreen. It says BARRY on one side and TRACEY on the other. *That'll set your tongues wagging, won't it just.* Tracey clocks it too as she comes down the path. I've been working on it the last couple of nights and it's meant as a surprise. She looks at the windscreen, breaks into a smile, then gets into the car and gives me a peck on the cheek. Like I say, we're getting serious.

Ronnie reckons we should park on the Square and walk. *Don't go leaving it in the car park,* he says. *You'll get put at the back and nobody will see it. Stick it somewhere prominent where they've all got to go past.* It adds another ten minutes but it ain't as if Tracey's wearing high-heel shoes. This is Chelmsford Fair so we're both in jeans and trainers. We fall in with the crowd and head on over the bridge.

Now Chelmsford Fair is a bit of a beast, always has been. You can hear it a mile off and as soon as we step out the car we catch a wall of sound. There must be half a dozen barrel organs spread about, tooting and rattling, but it's the one by the entrance that stands out. I guess they put it there to attract. Tracey reckons there'll be a bloke stood there with a monkey on his shoulder, winding a handle, but turns out it's all automatic. Back in the day, Dad says the fair was run by steam-driven traction engines but now it's diesel generators and electric motors. Ain't quite the same, he says.

We walk inside the gate and get hit by the smell of food – burgers, chips, hot chestnuts and candy floss. Somewhere in the middle of it all there's the stench of warm oil and working machinery. It'll turn your stomach if you're not careful, so we steer well clear. I figure on getting Tracey on some rides to take her mind off.

"So," I says. "What d'you fancy going on first?"

She's already made up her mind on that one because she's pulling on my arm and we're heading toward the dodgems. I pay the man and once she's climbed in, it's difficult getting her out – she ain't happy 'til she's hit everyone else at least twice. I make a mental note not to let her drive the Mini.

For the next hour we do the big rides – the waltzers, the flying saucer, the pirate ship and last, but not least, the big wheel. By the time we get up to the top it's pushing nine o'clock, the sky's come over dark and you can look out over Chelmsford and see all the lights shining. We come down the other side and Tracey holds on tight like she's getting cold, so I put my arm around her. We get off and I fetch us a hot dog each, followed by some candy floss.

Then we start on the sideshows. There's a bearded lady (though I'm sure it has to be a bloke) which Tracey thinks is gross and says she don't fancy them proving it one way or the other. We see the Man with a Thousand Tattoos and then the Cat with Two Heads. That's pretty gross too but then we find a fortune teller. I ain't too keen on the idea myself, but Tracey wants to give it a go so the next time Madame Petulengro hitches up her bead curtain to let someone out, we duck inside. It's pretty standard stuff I suppose, crystal ball, tarot cards and a palm reading, and I sit and watch while this gypsy woman goes through it all. I'm a bit worried that if she starts on about a tall dark stranger I'm stuffed on account of being on the short side, but we get through that part fine. It's the fact she don't mention Tracey's big house that's the problem, ain't even a sniff of it. And that causes upset.

"Look," I says, once we're back outside. "Just because she didn't talk about it, that don't mean to say it ain't going to happen. It's only a bit of fun for Christ's sake, you shouldn't take it so serious."

But she ain't having it and I'm just thinking about getting on the rifle range to see if I can win her a teddy bear when we walk around the corner and there it is straight in front of us – the boxing booth.

Now I swear to God I ain't been looking for it, and I don't suppose Tracey has neither, we've just come across it unexpected. But to tell the truth, now I've seen it I've remembered how it's there and being stood outside it last year having a laugh with the lads from the Boys Club. Only then we was on a night out for a bit of fun and we wasn't looking to go into no boxing booth – we'd had enough of that two nights a week on our own account, not to mention the Championships an' all.

But like I say, this year things is different – now I've got Tracey hanging on my arm and she's still carrying that recent disappointment from the fortune teller's. She sees the booth and straight away her elbow's in my ribs. *You're supposed to be a boxer, ain't yer? Well, there's a boxing booth, why don't you go and box?* But like I said before, life ain't that simple, is it? I mean, what if my job was mending roads? Don't mean to say that every time I walk past a hole in the street I cross over and start digging into it for Christ's sake. But now ain't the time to be telling her that, not when that gypsy woman's just burst her balloon with no mention of a big house. So I figure there ain't a lot of choice and it's time to stand up and be counted – both for her sake and mine because without the boxing we ain't got no dream, house or no house. Besides, that question from the day we met at the Ice Cream Parlour still wants answering. *And how big a punch are you really carrying?* So this here's a chance to kill two birds with one stone and put that one to bed good and proper.

So here's how the boxing booth works. It's really just a big tent. On the outside they've hung up a punch bag and there's a boxer whacking away at it trying to make himself look good. Stood next to him is the MC dressed in a white shirt with a black dicky bow and holding a microphone, while above the pair of them there's a sign tacked over the top.

NEXT SHOW 9.45pm

Any minute now the MC will ask for some brave local lad to step up out of the crowd – three rounds, three minutes each round, ten pounds for every round you survive, fifty pounds if you can get through all three. And you can bet your bottom dollar someone always does step up because if nobody local's daft enough, there's a plant in the audience and they'll put on an exhibition bout. Then they charge you five pounds a head to watch the show and everyone goes inside. It's the same routine three or four times a night.

I'm just thinking whether I should go in for it or not when the MC starts his spiel.

"Ladeez an' gen'lemun," he wheezes. The microphone he's holding's shoved right up his nose and it sounds like he's on sixty smokes a day. "Can I have your attention, pleeez. We have a show for you tonight the like of which you will not have witnessed before in your entire lives. Because tonight, ladeez an' gen'lemun, for your delectation and delight, I'm pleased to announce that Fairground Promotions proudly present, a panoply of pugilism; a banquet of boxing; a repast of the ring; truly a feast of fighting. Introducing to you, all the way from the Russian steppes, The Incomparable, The Indestructible, The Mighty – Ivan the Terrible!"

At which the boxer stood out front gives the punchbag an extra-hard hammering then turns to face the crowd with his arms held above his head like he's some kind of superstar. Only he ain't, and chances are he's more likely come from Stevenage rather than Stalingrad. He still gives the bag a good smack though and I'm beginning to wonder whether this is a good idea.

Meantime, the crowd gives out a ragged cheer and the MC starts off once more.

"I thank you, I thank you. Now then, ladeez an' gen'lemun, to complete our entertainment for the evening we require a volunteer. Is there someone out there amongst you, a brave local lad willing to challenge..."

But before he can finish, Tracey's elbow's dug me in the ribs once more and my hand's shot up like I just can't wait. The

MC spots me and points a grimy nicotine-stained finger in my direction.

"Ladeez an' gen'lemun," he wheezes. "We have our volunteer!"

The crowd gives off another cheer and a few turn round to get a look. Some geezer I don't know is waving at me, and I guess he must recognise me from the paper because he starts calling out.

"It's Barry Mullins! Go on, Bazza, you can do it!"

A couple more join in and a buzz starts to circulate. I look at Tracey and she's all smiles of encouragement so I start peeling my jacket off.

"Here," I says. "You look after this while I go and sort Ivan out."

I hope she realises what she's let me in for. It's a good job Albert ain't here or he'd have a fit. Meantime, the crowd's started pushing like they can't wait to pay their five quid and get inside the tent.

I leave off with Tracey, walk over to the MC and make myself known. He looks me up and down a couple of times and sniffs.

"You're a bit on the small side, aren't you?" he says. "I hope you know what you're doing."

Maybe he thinks I ain't going to put up much of a fight. Bad for business an' all.

"You wouldn't be the first to mention that," I says. "Don't worry, I can look after myself."

"Fair enough," he says, and gives another sniff. He looks at me for a second like he's trying to work out if I'm tanked up or not and whether it's just the drink talking. But I must pass the test as he pulls back a flap and shows me into the tent.

We get inside and it's pretty much what you'd expect. In the middle there's a boxing ring set up on a platform three feet high with enough room round the edges for spectators five or six deep. In each corner of the tent there's a spotlight on a pole, so everything's lit up, but to be honest it's all a bit spit and sawdust as Dad would say. The MC takes me down the back to a changing room hidden behind a curtain. There's just enough space for a wooden chair but bugger all else.

"Shoe size?" he wheezes.

"Eights," I says.

"Gloves?"

"Twelves."

"Wait here," he says, and lets the curtain drop. I sit on the chair until he gets back with a pair of gloves, some boots, shorts and a gum shield. "Get yourself changed," he says, "and I'll be back to fetch you in about five minutes – then you'll be on. No need to worry about the first round, you'll get through that no bother so you'll get your ten quid and no questions asked. After that you're on your own. And no funny business, understand?"

I give him a nod. That's fine with me, I don't do funny business anyway.

"What did you say your name was?"

"It's Mullins," I says. "Barry Mullins."

"Well, good luck Barry," he says, and he holds out a hand for me to shake. "You'll need it."

The curtain drops again and he's gone.

He said five minutes but it feels more like thirty. It don't take more than two of them for me to get changed, then I'm sat on the wooden chair, waiting. I can hear the crowd filling up and their voices getting louder, and I can sense the ring, empty beneath the heat of the lights. And all I can do is sit there thinking *I wish Albert was here. He'll kill me when he finds out. If Ivan the Terrible don't do it first.*

Finally, out in the tent the MC starts wheezing into his microphone. As soon as I hear him begin, I get up off the chair and do a bit of shadow boxing to get warmed up.

"Ladeez an' gen'lemun," he breathes. "Good evening and welcome to Fairground Promotions boxing extravaganza. For your delectation and delight, our contest this evening is between... Introducing you to, in the Blue Corner, all the way from the Russian steppes, the Incomparable, the Indestructible, the Mighty... Ivan the Terrible!"

Ivan must already be up in the ring, doing his superstar impression – only he don't get much of a cheer, just a few boos.

"And in the Red Corner..." the MC goes on, his voice getting ever closer. "Presenting to you, from Chelmsford, a local lad with a big heart and a lot of courage... Will you welcome please... Mr Barry Mullins!" Until now he's right outside where I'm standing and with a sudden jerk he pulls back the curtain, somebody presses a button and an old stereotape player starts blasting out the Rocky theme. Tacky, but effective.

I head toward the ring, jabbing the air in front of me and dancing on my toes. I pull myself up into my corner and when the crowd can see me they let out a bit of a cheer. There's a few shouts of *Go on Barry!* and down at the back a chant starts up – *Bazza! Bazza! Bazza!* – but it's difficult to see over there on account of the light being in my eyes. I clock Tracey though, ringside on the right. She must be nervous seeing as she's chewing her nails, so I give her a nod just to let her know I've seen her. Meantime, Ivan's prancing about on the other side of the ring like a demented circus pony. The MC calls us together in the middle and gives us the usual spiel, *blah, blah, blah,* so I start to focus on what's going to happen next. A bell rings and he moves away, then the crowd shouts up, we touch gloves and we're off and running.

We start out real cautious, just circling round and eyeing each other up. Ivan's a good bit taller than me, but that's nothing new. Outside my weight range ain't none of them been smaller yet – except maybe Parky, and he was so easy it don't really count. And I know I'm going to get through the first round comfortable, so I take the time to suss him out. *Tap, skip, tap, tap, skip,* it's the same old stuff, boxing's dance routine. He's got a decent left jab on him and every time he throws it, I find I'm coming inside instead of away, so I need to watch out for his right. He don't throw it though, first round, and I repay the compliment. It's proper boxing, and Albert would be proud of me. The bell rings, nobody's caused any damage and we're back to our corners – though there's no one in mine except me.

Round two, I'm on my own and as soon as I get out there, the pace picks up a tad and Ivan starts using his right. But it's so predictable. Two left jabs and then it comes whistling over my head or my left shoulder. I duck, bob and weave, but he keeps coming forward so I start back-pedalling to keep out of his way – in and out the corners, off the ropes, he can't catch me. But I don't catch him neither – 'cept a couple of soft shots on the break. The crowd goes quiet, thinking I'm running behind. Fact is, I'm well ahead on points, but this ain't no boxing match, it's a survival course, and nobody's keeping score. All the same, the three minutes go by and I'm still in it.

Now this may seem strange to you, but I ain't doing this for the fifty quid – I've got other reasons. I don't deny it might come in handy, but you get the feeling it wouldn't buy a curtain pole in Tracey's big house, never mind the curtains to go with it. So I get to thinking that if it ain't me that wants the money, then it must be Ivan, seeing as there's just the two of us in it. Maybe it's his money anyway, and if he don't knock me down then he don't get to keep it. Maybe that's how it works, and maybe that explains why he comes after me so hard at the start of round three. To tell the truth, I ain't quite ready for it so the chase is on and I'm stepping backwards about as fast as I can go.

But he still can't get me, I'm too quick and all he's doing is hitting thin air after I've left it. One way or another we go on for a minute or so then all of a sudden he changes tack. He don't come after me no more, he just stands there instead and beckons me in. Then he starts mouthing off, just loud enough so's I can hear. *Come on then you little runt, why don't you stand and fight? You haven't got the balls have you.* Because what he wants is for me to go in there and mix it with him, it's the only chance he's got. But I ain't stupid, Albert's told me to keep out of that. I know what he's doing and I don't want no part of it, I'm too smart. Or at least, I think I am – but then he finds a way.

I've stopped back-pedalling now so the crowd gets up a bit and starts shouting me on. The boys at the back begin their chant again while down at the front I can hear Tracey calling. *Go on Barry!* she's yelling. Ivan picks up on it.

"That your girlfriend?" he says, next time we're up close.

"Yes," I says. "So what?"

"Thought I recognised her," he says. "I had her last time I was here. Shagged her brains out."

Now you know that ain't the truth and so do I. It's a lie and it's a dirty lie and it's meant to get me riled. But even though I know it's a lie, that don't make it any easier to swallow. I know I should ignore it, but I can't and it must get under my skin because then it's like something's snapped and I ain't in control no more.

The crowd disappears, there's a muffled roar, but it's soundless, I can't hear it. There's just the mist, a red mist falling like soft rain and all I can see is Ivan's mouth, his foul mouth with the dirty lie dropping out of it. I want to stop it, stop the lie, stop his mouth, his foul mouth so I hit him, his body, not his mouth that will come soon enough when I've beaten his body, pounded it like a piece of steak beneath a wooden hammer like he's some piece of meat my hammer's pounding, pounding, pounding. Then, when his body's beaten to a pulp, can I stop his mouth, his foul mouth and push the lie, the dirty stinking lie, back down his throat until he's choking on the lie and he can't say it no more. Then he's gone, the mouth, the body, the lie, all gone, buried deep beneath the red mist and I can hear myself breathe again.

Then I'm back in the world, the red mist has gone and I'm standing in the middle of the ring. I'm breathing hard and Ivan's lying on the canvas in front of me. He's fallen on his side and the part of his face I can see is a mushy red and there's blood dripping from his nose. The crowd's gone silent and for a second it's like everything's frozen. But then some woman starts screaming like an alarm's gone off and suddenly all hell breaks loose.

The MC and two of his mates come piling in through the ropes. The MC's got a bucket of cold water and a sponge but what good that's going to do I don't know, maybe they should fetch a doctor. Meantime, his mates look like a right pair of bruisers and they're heading straight for me. The crowd don't know what to do with itself, but then its mind gets made up. A whistle blows, somebody yells *Police!* and they all start rushing for the exits like you'd think King Kong was loose in the tent. The Kray twins have got hold of me by the arms and whether I want to go or not, they're bundling me out of the ring. I twist my head round to look behind me where the MC's bending over Ivan and sploshing water. I get the sudden feeling I'm being seen off.

"Oi!" I shout. "Where's my fifty quid?"

Because like it or not, I've done the business and I figure I may as well have it. And besides, I can't do with the idea of being skanked. The MC turns round and looks up at me with a face like *You must be joking*, then goes back to dabbing the sponge.

When I tell Dad about it later he reckons it's all a scam – the screaming, the whistle, shouting *Police!* an' all – just so's they don't have to pay out. So maybe it's Ivan as gets the last laugh. Only he ain't laughing too much right now.

Meanwhile, Ronnie and Reggie are shoving me out the other side of the tent in double quick time. To tell the truth, I ain't really struggling and I let the two of them dump me outside. They give me that *Don't even think about coming back* look. That's fine with me because the only thing on my mind right now is getting the hell out of it. Maybe it's the whistle, the word *Police*, or even that woman screaming, but all I want to do is get away as fast as I can. I shoot off down the alley between the backs of the shows, stumbling over cables and the uneven ground, heading towards the lights and the noise of a barrel organ. I make fifty yards then dive right where there's a break and collapse onto the side of a tent. I'm breathing hard again where I've been on the run.

Then it gets to me – the sheer bloody stupidity of it all. Here I am, leant against a sideshow tent somewhere at the back of Chelmsford Fair, panting my guts out. I've still got the boxing kit on (they ain't getting that back, by the way, I've already decided) and I've not had time to pull the gloves off – even my gum shield's still in my mouth. I take it out and stick it in a pocket.

So what am I running away from for Christ's sake? What have I got to be scared of? Okay, so maybe I whacked a bloke a couple of times too many. So what? He had it coming, I didn't break no rules. And even if the Police are after me (which I doubt), it ain't no good me trying to hide. I might just as well be on my way to a Fancy Dress Ball, kitted up like I am, they won't have no trouble finding me. So maybe it's my own shadow, maybe that's what scares me, makes me run. And maybe it's all stupid – fixing motors, boxing, Tracey even, the lot – maybe there ain't no point in any of it. That dream too, because it's just a dream, ain't it? And right now it ain't no more than that. You can't rely on it, you can't set no store by it, it's just a dream. And all the while Ivan's lying there with the side of his face stoved in and the blood dripping out of his nose.

Then I hear a voice calling. It's Tracey.

"Baz?" she says. "Where are you?"

I stick my head round the back of the sideshow and out into the alley. She clocks me and starts walking toward the break. I guess she's picked my stuff up from the boxing booth because she's carrying my shoes and street clothes in a carrier bag.

Now maybe it was the brutality, the power of it, watching one man destroy another with nothing more than the strength of his own hands, but something sure has lit her candle. She walks up, dumps the bag and the next thing I know her mouth's all over mine and her tongue's down the back of my throat. I want to hold her but I've still got the gloves on so all I can do is pull her close so we're touching.

"You need to get changed," she says. "Here, let me help you," and she makes like she's going to pull my shorts off but her hand goes straight down inside and she finds me where I'm warm and hard. I'm just nineteen for Christ's sake and Tracey Williams has got her hand down the front of my trousers behind the waltzers at Chelmsford Fair. It's more than a man can stand.

We're married within a year. Dad says I want my head tested. I tell him it ain't my head that bothers me. It sure ain't the part that bothers Tracey.

Part Four

A Fighting Chance

Ronnie

Now if your life's anything like mine (which I don't suppose it is for one moment, but still) it's full of ups and downs. One minute we're flat on our back and can't find a punter for love nor money, next thing you know we're flooded out with them. And one way or another it's all on account of Barry Mullins and that little scheme I cooked up with his motor.

True, things don't go so well to start with. But I can't blame the lad, I can't blame him at all. He's done all I asked of him – and more – and I can tell you he's certainly put himself about in that car. It's been to all four points of the compass and my mobile advert's been seen in just about every town from here to Harwich, so I can't complain on that score. And don't think I don't know the reason, it ain't entirely on my account, I am aware of that. My spies are out there, I get reports, I know what's going on. Okay, so maybe it stays parked up in Campion Street some nights a bit too often for my liking, but that can soon be fixed. Anyways, a young lad like that needs a bit of fun in his life, I know I did when I was his age. It don't help pay my bills though.

Then bugger me if I don't get a bit of a bonus. I'm just starting to think *What the hell can I do next?* when Barry comes up with a scheme of his own. And the beauty of it is, it don't cost me a thing. It's like a Buy One Get One Free from Tescos – I've picked the first and the next one comes for nothing.

They say there's no such thing as bad publicity. Which is just as well in this case because it's hard to see how you can squeeze good mileage out of the fact that he went OTT down at the Fair and hammered some bloke a bit more than he ought so the guy finishes up in Broomfield Hospital. Except that it's going to be all over The Chelmsford Gazette – which is right where I want it to be. I get wind of it a bit previous you might say, seeing as a good friend of mine happens to work on the Sports Desk. He tips me off on the Saturday morning.

"Have you heard?" he says.

"Have I heard what?" I says.

And he tells me all about it.

"Brilliant," I says. "Are you running it?"

"Of course we're running it," he says. "Front page."

"Even better," I says. "What's the headline?"

"Local boxer gets into fight."

"Hmm…" I says. "D'you know what? That's real inventive. Hardly news though, is it? That's what boxers are supposed to do, ain't it, get into fights? Can't you think up something more exotic? How about *Local garage employee in fairground fracas?* And while you're about it, you could mention the name of the garage."

"I take your point," he says. "I'll see what I can do."

Later on, I get a phone call. Can they come and take a photograph? *Is the Pope a Catholic?* I says. You bet your sweet life they can. I get Barry to line the Mini up on the car lot so you can see the white lettering on the doors with the garage behind. And there's me on one side and Barry on the other. Terry don't want nothing to do with it of course. He's camera shy, he says, and besides, there ain't enough room for three people in the photo. Which is all bollocks seeing as we had one much the same taken a couple of year ago.

So then it's just the two of us, "Big Ronnie" and "Barry Mullins". Don't half look good when it comes out in the Monday edition – though it's a shame it ain't in colour. *Never mind the story,* I says. *Take a butcher's at the picture.* And lo and behold, pretty soon after, the punters start arriving and where we once had a trickle it suddenly turns into a flood.

So he's kept his side of the bargain, has Barry. And I've kept mine too. It's his car now, ain't it? I gave it him straight and no strings, even if it did piss Terry off. And the smart bit about it is, it was a wreck, a scrapper, so all it cost me was Barry's time, a lick of paint and a few spare parts I picked up out of petty cash. Don't you just love it when a plan comes together? A risk, a chance, something for nothing? Only this plan ain't all together yet, not by a long chalk. We might be in the paper, but we still ain't in the money.

Then I get to thinking. There's three of us in this business – and I'm doing my bit and Barry's doing his. So if there's a weak link in our chain and anyone's in need of a gee-up, I guess it must be Terry. Like I said before, Terry's a salesman, he could sell books to a blind man, so maybe it boils down to incentive. Every salesman needs incentive, although what more incentive he needs beyond the fact that if he don't sell nothing he gets paid nothing, I can't rightly say. I'll have to have a word in his shell-like.

But I can't fault Barry Mullins. Barry Mullins is a nugget, a solid gold nugget. If I had ten more like him, I could be a millionaire. I just need to use him right, that's all.

Terry

Barry Mullins this, Barry Mullins that, it's all I get all day. I'm sick of it. You'd think the sun shone out of Barry Mullins' arse the way Ronnie goes on about him. He's only a boxer for Christ's sake, he's got fingers thicker than a Cumberland sausage and I'm surprised he can hold a spanner at all. Barry Mullins? I swear to God that if I hear his name mentioned one more time today I'll scream, so help me I will.

And just to make matters worse, now I've got Ronnie on my case – he's all over me like a rash. Everywhere I go, there he is hanging around the corner checking out every little thing I do. I can't even go to the pisser without he's stood there waiting for me as soon as I come out. He catches me just as I'm zipping up.

"So what's with you?" I says. "Ain't you got nothing better to do than follow me about?"

"Well," he says, "I was just wondering what you do with yourself all day."

"You never wondered before," I says.

"Never had to," he says. "But seeing as we ain't exactly selling a lot of motors right now, it got me thinking."

"Well think about this," I says. "Because now you come to mention it, the seat of my trousers has been wearing a bit thin of late and I need something on account."

"What do you mean?" he says. "'On account'. On account of what?"

"On account," I says. "You know, upfront, in advance. Do I have to spell it out?"

"Oh," he says. "You mean on account of the fact that you ain't sold nothing since England last won the World Cup and you ain't getting no commission."

"You can put it how you like," I says. "I prefer to think of it as a return on all the hard work I've put in over the years, a little bit coming back to me out of my share of the pot."

"Pot?" he says. "What pot?"

"The pot we're building up together," I says. "Or had you forgotten about that? We're supposed to be partners ain't we? Or don't that mean nothing to you no more?"

"Oh, that pot," he says, coming over all vague. He can act real ignorant when he wants to, can Ronnie. Then he slides that great big arm of his round my shoulder and starts off on his well-worn "I'm in business" speech. "You see Terry, it don't quite work like that. That 'pot' as you calls it, is everything you see around us, the yard, the stock, the garage..." and he waves his hand about to demonstrate "...and we can't go dibbing into it just like that. We have to be patient, we have to wait until the time is right before we go carving things up. And in the meanwhile, we have to sell the stock to pay for the upkeep. That's how business works, Terry, that's what makes it all go round. I buy the stock, you sell the cars, I pay the bills. It ain't exactly rocket science, is it?"

As if I didn't know this already – if I've heard it once, I must've heard it a hundred times before.

"Now what I don't understand," he says, chuntering on, "is why we ain't selling some of that stock right now. We've got plenty of customers coming in, Barry and me have seen to that. So what's the problem?"

I'm tempted to scream at the mention. But I resist.

"Customers?" I says. "You call them customers? They ain't customers, they're more like bloody tourists. They don't come in here to buy a car, they come here to black their nose. D'you know what I get asked most frequent these days? It used to be *Do you do part exchange?* Now all I get is *Is this where Barry Mullins works?* We've become a bloody visitor attraction, that's what's happened. It's cheaper to bring the kids here for the afternoon than it is to take them to Colchester Zoo. What we really ought to do," I says, standing up to Ronnie and prodding him in the chest, "is put Barry Mullins in a bloody cage and charge people to come and look at him. And while we're at it," I says, "you can dress me up in a white coat and I'll sell ice creams. We'd make more money that way than we ever will selling motor cars."

"Don't be daft, Terry," he says. "That's stupid."

"No it ain't," I says. "And don't you look at me like that, you know it's the truth. On the other hand, we could always call it Big Ronnie's Museum of Transport. Look at the stuff in here – they're practically antiques. How am I supposed to work with that lot? You tell me, when was the last time you bought any new stock in?"

That shuts him up, it usually does. His face wrinkles up like he's sucking a lemon and he don't say no more on that subject. Because I'm right and he knows it.

He forgets sometimes, does Ronnie. He forgets I've seen it all before, been through it all in the last ten years. It ain't the first time he's had a go at me and I don't suppose it'll be the last. And he forgets where it came from – the watches, the markets, the van, the trips up to London – and on occasion I have to remind him, bring him back up to the mark. I ain't going to let all that slip by without notice, not after all these years.

As for Barry Mullins, Ronnie can go kiss his arse as much as he likes for all I care. I ain't going to. But you know me, I hate the little bastard anyway.

Barry

We find a place to rent in Walton Terrace. It ain't much, I have to admit, just a small two-up two-down though given the state of the housing market, Dad reckons we're lucky to get anything at all. It certainly ain't the six-bed palace Tracey's been looking for and you can tell she's disappointed. I blame that gypsy woman, putting all those thoughts in her head that shouldn't really be there. But it's like I keep saying, what can you expect on our wages? What with her in retail sales and me on the tools in a garage. On top of which, it's Ronnie Bent's garage an' all, though I notice he's been a bit more generous of late.

"Look," I says to her, "you're just going to have to be patient, that's all. You can't have everything at once."

"So when can I have it?" she says.

Patience ain't exactly Tracey's strong suit. As I've discovered.

"We'll just have to work on it," I says. "First things first, we'll have to wait 'til I turn professional, then we'll see what happens."

"And when's that going to be, may I ask?" she says.

"It might take a year or two," I says. "I'll need to go for the National Title first, then we'll know where we are. Once I get that, they'll be queuing at the door to sign me up. Twelve months' time and it'll all be different. You'll see. Promise."

"It had better be," she says. "I'm not sure I can stand this much longer."

Trouble is, it's far too much like her mother's house for her liking – whereas what she really wanted was to move up in the world. Walton Terrace ain't no more than two minutes from Campion Street, and it's like as if she's walked round the corner from her old place and straight into another exactly the same. The only difference is her mother ain't come with her – and there's a lot to be said for that, by the way. I just wonder what would happen if her old man showed up right now.

"No chance of that," she says. "Not in a million years."

And to tell the truth, we don't get much in the way of visitors at all. Mum and Dad come round for a tour of inspection, but that's only natural – somebody's got to make sure their boy's doing alright. But you can tell they ain't going to poke their nose in too far because Mother don't put her handbag down during the whole course of the visit, she keeps it tight to her chest. We give them a good look round, every nook and cranny, and I manage to persuade them to stay for a cup of tea, but that's about it. Mother's barely done drinking hers when she gives Dad a nudge.

"Come along now, Derek," she says. "These young people need to be left alone to live their lives in peace."

And they're gone. So then it's just the two of us, me and Tracey, day in, day out, working it out together and waiting for the dream to start. In the meantime, I've got a Title to think about and I need to get down to some training.

Sharon

She's sold out on me has Tracey, I always knew she would as I said at the start I thought it might last 'til we were twenty-five, thirty at a push, but she's gone at twenty, perhaps I should be grateful that we at least made it to eighteen. And don't ask me why but I'd always imagined she'd marry a sailor, a Jack Tar, a tall handsome lad who'd sail in off the wide ocean on board a white three-masted schooner, leap out onto the quay, take her in his arms and carry her off to the South Seas where he'd dive for pearls and find a fortune while they lived like King and Queen on some Polynesian island. But it turns out he's a boxer and they get a house in Walton Terrace. I think she'd have preferred a footballer if she could have found one.

"Walton Terrace?" I says. "That's a bit of a come down, ain't it?"

"It's a sore point," she says. "Don't go there."

"Well, you did," I says, smirking. It's not often I get one over on Tracey Williams.

"Anyways," she says, "it's only temp'ry. Barry says we'll be moving on in a year."

Well it don't look temp'ry to me. The place must be a hundred years old and I get the distinct impression they're aiming to stay there just as long, the way he's done the place out for her it's really quite cosy – though it is small and nowhere near up to Tracey's standards. I keep thinking that when I get my house in Bell Meadows at least it'll be built this side of the Great War, there'll be enough room to swing a cat and it'll have somewhere I can hang my washing – and that's a lot more than you can say for Walton Terrace. So I'm surprised.

Then I get to thinking that if it ain't the house that makes her stick it out it must be him, Barry Mullins, Barry the boxer. He's a nice enough guy but I know why she went for him in the first place, I was there remember, that Sunday afternoon. Though

Trace don't suffer a fool gladly and if a man don't come up to scratch he don't get to stay around for very long – but this one's stuck like glue so you have to wonder why. Is it at all possible, I ask myself, is it conceivable that she's done what the rest of us are dying to do, what we'd give our right arms for but what in her case would be almost unimaginable, and actually fallen in love? Knowing Trace the way I do I doubt it, I don't believe she's got it in her. But he has that's for certain, fallen in love I mean, you can tell by the way he dotes on her, she only has to say she's cold and he puts the fire on or she's hot and he opens a window, it would be touching if it wasn't so pathetic the way he hangs around her all the time.

So if it ain't that, it must be money and there must be a glint of gold someplace. Maybe there's a bar of it stuffed down the end of his boxing gloves so instead of iron in his fists it's a slab of precious metal. It can't be the garage work – when was the last time you heard of a motor mechanic living in a six-bed mansion with servants and a sea view? It don't add up but you can bet your bottom dollar Tracey's got it all worked out, she always did have, from day one she knew what she was doing. And it must be money later because it sure ain't money now, not if the wedding was anything to go by. That was a low-key affair just a ten-minute tour of the Registry Office then back to her mother's in Campion Street for a plateful of prawn sandwiches – though I got lucky and bagged a ham and mushroom vol-au-vent. So maybe they're planning to wait a few years 'til he's rich and famous and they can re-affirm their vows on some beach in Acapulco serenaded by a Mariachi Band and with drinks from a donkey that serves tequila. What a day that'll be, I can't wait my bag's packed already.

"You've really pushed the boat out on this one, haven't you Trace?" I says, wondering if there's enough Black Forest gateau to go round.

"Well at least I'm married, Sharon," she says. "Last thing I heard, you was still looking."

Touché as they say in La Belle France. And that just about sums me up as far as Tracey (née Williams) is concerned, she may have changed her name to Mullins but she's not changed her views. *Sharon Roberts? Oh she's always one step behind, ever the bridesmaid never the bride.*

Albert

There was a time when we thought we might lose him, Micky and I, that Barry would pack the boxing in and we'd never see him again. We both knew he was courting – you can usually tell, we'd plenty of experience on that score. Young men have a sly look about them when it comes to being with women and in that period between the incident down at the Fair and his subsequent marriage it was written all over his face. Not only that, but there was a noticeable decline in his sharpness in the ring and the timing of his punches went awry – so much so that we decided to give the Championships a rest for the year. He still managed to drag himself into the gym two nights a week but more often than not he was the first to get away rather than the last. Something other than boxing was driving him and it didn't take much to guess what.

He wouldn't have been the first of my prospects to run out on me. History suggested that they usually did, it was hard to avoid. We'd find a lad with some talent, bring him on and then they'd "meet someone", get married and settle down – and that would be the last we'd see of them. There are occasions in a man's life when he comes to a crossroads and he has to make a decision. Most of the time he goes one way while his past goes another. It's like a snake shedding its skin and starting off afresh, beginning a brand-new life and leaving the old one behind. It could easily have been that way with Barry. There were any amount of reasons – you only had to take one look at his wife to see she could be something of a distraction for a start. I've seen bigger men than Barry Mullins go to pieces over lesser girls than her, believe me.

On the Monday after their wedding, Micky found some photographs in the paper. He brought them in to show me. There was quite a spread – hardly surprising seeing as Barry was something of a local celebrity.

"Jeez," he said, and whistled out loud. "She's a good-looking woman."

He held the paper up so we could both see the pictures better.

"Yes," I said. "And Barry's a good-looking man – don't forget that. Anyway, they certainly make a great couple."

Micky and I may have had our differences over the years, but on this occasion, it didn't take much for us to agree.

It was while I was looking at those photographs that I began to wonder. What is it that gets a man out of bed first thing in the morning when he could stay tucked up in it with a girl like her? Now, for most men the answer to that question is likely to be *Nothing much at all* and sometimes they don't even realise it's there to be asked – so in that respect it would have come as no surprise if Barry had gone the same way. After all, he was supposedly made of the same flesh and blood as the rest of us. But boxing isn't just about talent, it's also about temperament and we were about to discover that Barry's temperament was a bit different to everyone else's and if anything, his sudden marriage had pushed him in the opposite direction. So rather than leaving his past behind at the crossroads, it was as though it had now overtaken him and was helping to pull him forwards toward his future.

The turnaround began soon after he returned from honeymoon. Micky told me they'd managed to scrape enough money together to have a week in Tenerife and a few days later Barry walked into the gym and knocked on my door.

"Hello Albert," he said. "I'm back."

"Hello stranger," I replied. "We were wondering if you'd bother to show up again."

"Sorry. You may have heard – I got married and we've been away for a while."

He'd got those great big hands of his shoved into his pockets and he was looking down at the floor in that sheepish way he had. There was a tanned look about him that suggested he'd been lounging in the sun.

"Yes," I said. "So we gathered." Micky's paper was still on my desk and lay open at the events page. "Congratulations by the way."

"Thanks." He began shifting from one foot to the other as though there was something on his mind. Eventually he got to the point. "We didn't do Eastern Division this year. Any particular reason why?"

"Well," I said. "You'd won it three times in a row and I wasn't sure you wanted to do it again. You didn't seem to be up for it."

"Oh," he said. "I see." He could barely disguise his disappointment – it was as if he felt he'd let himself down in some way. Then, "What about the National Title though, is that on?"

"The National Title?" I must have sounded surprised. "Of course it is. You can go in for it any time you like, you've proved you're good enough. Why? Do you want me to put your name forward?"

"I do."

His voice carried a deep sense of seriousness. I don't know if he realised it but these were the same words he'd used barely a fortnight before and in the space of two short weeks he'd got married twice, once to Tracey and once to boxing. I knew then that this was going to be a hard road to travel.

"There's no problem submitting an entry," I said, "but you'll need to be on top of your game. You've had it fairly easy up until now in the Eastern Division – fighting at National level is something totally different. You are aware of that I suppose?"

"'Course I am. I know what I'm letting myself in for. Anyways, I'm ready for it."

"Well that remains to be seen. You'll need to get back into training – you look as though you've let yourself go a bit in the last few weeks. I'll put together a programme."

"I was thinking about that. Maybe I could come in a couple

more nights a week."

"That's fine with me – I'll set it up. How about starting on Monday?"

"Okay… But how about starting now?"

I could see he'd brought his kitbag with him and a spare towel. Given the circumstances it would have been cruel of me to say no so we got on with it straight away.

I don't think I've ever seen a man so keen to get into training. Most people have to be cajoled but Barry couldn't wait. He was desperate to get his hands and feet moving again and he'd taken his jacket off even before I'd said yes. Then he set to work, harder than I've ever seen anyone work before. He doubled up on the weights and spent twice as much time on the bag. He came in four nights a week instead of two, and whereas prior to the wedding he'd been the first to leave, now he was the last. It was almost as if he were living at the gym.

It wasn't long before the work began to show. He grew faster and leaner and although it was hard to believe, he was punching harder and more crisply than in the past. As you know, Micky's always been a man of few words but even he commented on the difference.

"What's got into Barry?" he said. "It looks like something's geed him up."

"Yes," I said. "Something has – and I'll tell you what I think it is. I believe our boy has developed a serious case of ambition. He's going for the National Title."

It wasn't something I'd seen in Barry before. Oh sure, he'd been keen to develop himself and enjoy his sport, but this was something different. Up until then he simply hadn't wanted to lose – now he desperately wanted to win. I'd always known he had the skill and the strength but now I knew he had the desire – and that's a combination that can make a man a champion.

But it can also make him vulnerable – as we were about to find out.

Barry

So we're off and running for the National Title – or in my case, up and running as I get into my jogging routine. Albert says I can have Sundays off so it's six mornings a week and my alarm's set for quarter to seven, though chances are I'm awake already and I catch it before it beeps. Tracey's still half asleep (she won't stir 'til she has to), I give her a kiss on the cheek but then I'm up and out of the pit. I pull on my tracksuit and trainers, drop down to the kitchen for a glass of orange and half a banana and I'm out of the door by seven and ready to get started. I've got a tape made up so I can jog to the beat, I plug into my music and I'm off to do my roadwork.

It's at least two miles, three if I'm up for it or if it's a Saturday and I've got that extra bit of time. I turn right onto the street, drop down to the bottom then go right again. It takes me a couple of blocks to get into the rhythm then I hang another right and I'm up into Campion Street. I check things out at Tracey's Mum's but there's nothing going on there this time of day. The curtains next door don't twitch neither, so I'm straight on by. Around this point I catch the milkman rattling his crates but then I'm up and onto the main drag, half a mile down the road and on into the park. It's quiet in there and there's no one about except a couple of dog-walkers, but I've got the music for company. Once round the boating lake gets me the two miles, twice round and an extra block on the way back home gives me the three. Either way it's all uphill for the last half-mile, so to reach Walton Terrace I have to push, push, push, and by the time I get there my heart's pumping nineteen to the dozen and I'm crying out for a lungful of cold morning air. But I'm always back by half past seven, come rain or come shine.

Tracey still won't be up yet. I make a pot of tea, take her up a cup then give her a nudge and we're off and into our normal routine – bathroom, breakfast and out of the house by eight-thirty. Only this time I'm in the car and I've got Tracey with me. I drop her down in town and I'm at the garage for when it opens at nine. And then there's a whole day's work in front of me, waiting to be done.

I must have been at it a couple of weeks when Ronnie starts taking an interest. How he can tell there's something different I haven't a clue – maybe it's the glow I get after running but whichever way, he's twigged it. I'm halfway into my overalls one morning when he's there, arms folded, leaning against the door jamb and I can see that something's brewing.

"So what's going on then, Barry?" he says. "You're looking fit."

"I've been doing a bit of training," I says. "Getting into shape."

"Well that's good to know," he says. "Any particular reason?"

"Maybe," I says. "Why, what's it to you, anyway?"

"I've heard a rumour you're going for the National Title this year."

"Oh really," I says. "And where did that come from?"

"Ah," he says, tapping the side of his nose. "Let's just say I have a strategically placed source."

"You mean a spy," I says.

"You can call him that if you like," he says.

He plays his cards close, does Ronnie, but it don't take much to guess. I reckon his source must work down at the Gazette seeing how quick they had that photographer here after that dust-up at the Fair.

"Suit yourself," I says. "It ain't no secret." I guess he must be wondering about his little investment now I've cut down on the travelling and his mobile advert don't do the rounds like it used to. "Anyways," I says, "I expect there'll be some publicity in it for you when it comes down to the finals, so don't you worry."

"Good," he says. "I'm banking on it."

Only what he forgets to tell me is exactly how much banking he's doing.

Ronnie

Lucky, lucky, lucky
I should be so lucky
In a rich man's world

I remember when I was little my mother kept telling me I was lucky. But it never felt like that at the time and I didn't understand why. Maybe now I do. *Ronald* she used to say (and as soon as I heard that I knew I was in trouble – if I was in her good books it was only ever "Ronnie"). *Ronald,* she'd say when I'd done something wrong, *you're lucky I don't spank your backside.* Or like the time I kicked that football through Dad's greenhouse window, *Ronald, you're lucky I don't tell your father.* And I could never see the luck in that – didn't think there was any – except if things had gone the other way, I suppose I'd have said different. So maybe I was wrong and maybe she did have it right after all, maybe Ronnie Bent really is a lucky bloke.

It all started when Barry dinged that Ivan bloke down at the Fair. Now I know it don't look that way in the beginning, what with that pack of tourists as Terry calls them rubber-necking an' all, but it had to come off in the end and sometimes you just have to be patient. Plus, that little word in his ear must have paid dividends because all of a sudden Terry bucks his ideas up and almost overnight – *overnight* I'm saying, mind – he ups and sells half a dozen motors. *Half a dozen.* Must be a world record. And don't laugh, but the best of it is I get paid the bulk of it in cash. Don't you just love cash? No hassle, no bank and what's more, no VAT (but please keep that to yourself). So here I am, feet on the desk, smoking a fat cigar and looking at a briefcase bulging with the green folding-stuff. Although to be fair, most of it's a dark shade of purple seeing as I tend to prefer it in twenties. It's a touch over ten grand. I should know, I've counted it – twice. Bada bing bada boom, ten grand, in my hand, thank you very much.

But it don't end there, oh no, and the cash is only the half of it. It's just like waiting for a bus – you're stood there for ages, nothing comes by, then all of a sudden two of them turn up at once. It's Monday morning and there I am, sat at the desk, gazing in wide-eyed admiration at the contents of my briefcase and wondering what to do with it all, when the phone rings and blow me down if it's not Honest John, red-hot racing tipster and my mate on the Sports Desk down at The Gazette. Last time he was in touch we finished up all over the front of the newspaper. So every time I hear his voice on the dog and bone it's like music to my ears.

"Morning Ronnie," he says. "How're you keeping?"

"Well enough," I says, lifting the lid of my case and taking another peek.

"We've been thinking about your boy Mullins," he says.

"Haven't we all," I says.

"He must be a good bet for the Title now. We've had the Standard on the phone from London already, wanting to do a feature. We'll be running one of our own in a week or two. You interested?"

"Interested in what?" I says, as I don't quite get where this is going yet.

"Getting involved," he says. "You know – you get us the access, we get you the publicity, that sort of thing. Much the same as before."

"Sounds good," I says. "But let me come back to you on that. I'll have to see how it goes."

Because suddenly I'm not listening anymore and my mind's somewhere else.

A good bet for the Title.

Then I realise what a fool I've been and I know what I should have been doing all along. The answer's right under my nose – I've been sitting on a gold mine and all the time I never knew it.

Terry

I think he's lost it, Ronnie, I really do. He's gone mental, gaga, off his trolley – it must be the earliest case of dementia on record. If you was to crack him open (which given half a chance I might) I don't believe you'd find a drop of milk in his coconut.

That man is just not on the same planet as the rest of us – well, not on the same planet as me, that's for certain. I've bust my backside trying to dig us out of the hole we've got ourselves into this last couple of months and somehow he just don't see it. Anyone could tell we were in the shit, it don't take another bleeding lecture from Mr "I'm in business" Bent to work that one out. Next to nothing shifted off that forecourt in the six months after Christmas, it all dried up. And you know me, but I couldn't sell a second-hand car for love nor money. Then all of a sudden, it's like a log jam breaking, the flood gates open and our ship comes steaming in. I've turned six cars over in next to no time but he's hardly said a dicky bird. His head must be somewhere else, that man, and it's either in a cloud or up his own arse because it sure ain't focused on the motor trade.

Just a word of thanks would have been nice, a pat on the back, even that great big arm of his round my shoulder, something for Christ's sake. But no, talk about being taken for granted, all I get is some spiel about keeping the pressure off the workshop and how we don't want to be putting too much work through there right now what with precious Mr Mullins gearing up for his big title push an' all. So Barry boy gets wrapped up in cotton wool while I'm out in the yard working my nuts off. There's something wrong somewhere.

"Jesus Christ, Ronnie," I says. "Are we running a business here or what? Or did I get it wrong and it's really a rest home for amateur boxers. What the hell d'you think you're playing at?"

"I'm protecting my investment," he says.

"Your investment?" I says. "Your investment, as you were

only too keen to tell me the other day, is everything we see around us, the yard, the stock, the garage. Remember all that, do you? And how we have to sell the stock to pay for the upkeep? Which reminds me – now we're in funds, you'd best be getting some more in because the rate things are going we'll have run out by the weekend."

"Ah," he says, and he screws his face up like he's sucking on that lemon again. "I'll give it some consideration."

"Some consideration?" I says. "What d'you mean, *some consideration*? That's how the business works, ain't it? That's what makes it all go round – or so you keep telling me. Or had you simply forgotten?"

"'Course I ain't forgotten," he says, only now he don't look me straight in the eye. "It's just that… Well, there's a few other things going on right now, that's all."

"A few other things?" I says. "What else could there possibly be, for Christ's sake? It's simple enough, ain't it? We ain't talking brain surgery here."

Then I clock the big black briefcase sitting on his desk. I've seen that before and I know what he does with it. What's more, he knows I do. He sees me looking and starts colouring up.

"Now steady on, Tel," he says. "Don't go getting the wrong idea, it's not what you might imagine."

"Nah," I says, shaking my head. "You don't fool me, I know what's in there, I've watched you count it. And don't even think about it, you know it won't work."

I keep pushing but he don't respond, he just sits there looking out the window like he's waiting for a miracle to happen. Me, I don't understand it at all. I've sold six cars in record time and we should be jumping up and down like kids on a trampoline. He's lost the plot has Ronnie Bent, big style, and there comes a point when you start to wonder whether you've hitched your wagon to the wrong horse.

Ronnie

So never mind what Terry says, I finally get to pick a winner – and I ain't used to that. It's about bloody time, Christ knows I've been trying long enough – there's a lot of money been laid out over the years and not much coming back. Oh sure, I've had a few successes, a couple of quid here, a couple of quid there, but nothing ever really big. Did a three-horse accumulator once, ten quid down, decent odds and I pulled in over three hundred. Blew it all the same night of course. Well you do, don't you, when you've got something to celebrate. Which I have, now that I've seen the light. But it won't be the same way this time, I'll make sure of that.

You see, there's something I ain't got round to telling you yet – what with everything going off down at the garage an' all, I just ain't had the time. I've got a bit of a confession to make – I'm a gambler. Yeah, that's right, a gambler, a punter, a man who risks money in the blind hope of personal financial gain. In other words, a sucker. It's an addiction I suppose, but so's breathing – in the end you just get used to it.

My guess is you knew that already, so maybe it don't come as a shock. Perhaps there was something about me that pointed you in that direction before I even mentioned it. Maybe it's the coat I wear or the ties I choose or even the way I speak, there's got to be a reason. My friends say it sticks out a mile once you get to know me. I say "friends" but I guess acquaintances would be a better description – I mean the blokes I meet down at the track.

So what if I do like a bit of a flutter now and again? A man's got to have a bit of pleasure in his life, to offset all the pain. And it ain't as if I'm breaking the law, is it for Christ's sake? Or that it's immoral for that matter, though some might see it different. I mean, I'm hardly causing undue amounts of suffering to starving children in Africa just because I happen to stick ten quid on the ponies in Billy Hill's on a Saturday afternoon.

Anyways, we're all gamblers, ain't we, every single one of us. Because life's a gamble, ain't it? It's a gamble which side of the bed we get out of on a morning; it's a gamble whether we've tied our shoelaces right; it's a gamble whether it's orange or grapefruit juice for breakfast; and it sure is a gamble crossing the road to get to work, everyone knows that. As for getting married, that's the biggest gamble of all. I should know, I've laid out money on that one twice already and lost both times. So we're all at it, one way or another, don't matter how you look at it. Fact is, you've probably taken more risks than me – only your problem is, you just don't know it. So don't you come pointing a finger at me saying *You're a bad boy, Ronald Bent.* At least I know what I'm letting myself in for.

So like I say, I'm a gambler. Saturdays I do the horses, either down at the bookies or if they're on the flat and the weather's decent, I might leave Terry in charge and treat myself to a trip up to Newmarket. It's a nice day out, the course is pretty decent and there's always something to shout about down in the betting ring.

Though generally speaking, I prefer the dogs. And on a Wednesday night, nine times out of ten that's where you'll find me. Walthamstow's my favourite track. I got real familiar with it back in the day when me and Terry used to stay up there overnight on one of our sales trips. I'll bet he's told you about that already. He don't come nowadays of course, he lost interest a few years back, so now it's just me on my Jack. It's an hour's drive, I park up, pay a tenner to get in and I sit with a bar meal looking out the plate-glass windows at the first couple of races. If there's something I really fancy I might have a punt but then I go down to the trackside and see who's about.

Now you never know who you might bump into at the side of a dog-track so I keep my eyes open. Jimmy, Lenny, Don – most Wednesday's there's a gang of us turn up. We have a few drinks, place a few bets and have a few laughs, then we go home happy

– or not, all depending. Then there's Mac of course. Now Mac is always there, he's never missed a night in ten years. Mac's a useful bloke to know – he's got a few contacts, keeps his nose to the ground so to speak and he's always on top of what goes on. So if you want something doing that's a bit out of the ordinary, then he's your man. Which is the whole point of this part of the story.

So this particular Wednesday, I set off for the dogs same as usual. Only this time I'm carrying the briefcase with the ten large stashed in it. I've enough laid out to keep the bank off my back so I reckon it's safe to fetch the rest out from under the mattress. To tell the truth I'd have fetched it out anyway, safe or not, it's got to that stage now. Well it comes to something when a man can't wear a clean shirt to work every day of the week, that's what I say.

I get parked up, pay my ten quid and go sit in the bar with something to eat. Only I don't take my usual seat, slap-bang in front of the windows where the world and his wife can see what I'm doing, I pick a table in one of the corners where it's nice and private. You can't see the far side of the track from there but that don't bother me none. I'm not here for the dogs – my eyes are glued to the near-side rails and who's walking the patch. The first two races go by and I don't even bother to bet, I'm too busy looking for Mac. Then I spot him in one of his usual haunts. I don't fancy going down there myself – well, not carrying that briefcase I don't – so I send out for him to come upstairs and join me. Won't be the first time he's been told there's someone in the bar wants to see him and do a bit of business, neither.

The door to the bar opens, he clocks me in the corner and makes his way over.

"Oh," he says. "It's you, Mr Bent. I had a message but they didn't say who it was from."

"Yes," I says, "it's me alright. Take a seat." I offer one opposite and he sits down.

Now the thing about Mac, useful or not, is he's a tad lacking in personal hygiene. For a start, they don't call him Mac without reason, ain't nothing to do with his name, it's what he's wearing. I don't suppose he's changed it in the ten years I've known him and right now it looks like he's slept in it for a week – which he most likely has. So he don't smell too fragrant neither and if it weren't for the fact that he's visiting someone, chances are they wouldn't let him up here. But never mind the aroma, he's the man I need sure enough seeing as how he knows all the right people – or all the wrong ones, if you see what I mean.

"Can I get you a drink?" I says.

As if I didn't know the answer to that already.

"Well," he says, licking a cracked lip, "now that we're here…" And he has a gander round at the bar while he rubs his chin – which I note he hasn't bothered shaving for the occasion. "I'll have a Campari and soda."

I raise an eyebrow, but it's his call. Next thing you know Meatloaf'll be on Dubonnet and lemonade, there ain't much surprises me anymore. I order it up and it comes in one of those silly glasses with an umbrella in it. You won't get a drink like that at the trackside so I guess he's making the most of the opportunity. Shame his dress sense don't match his taste in cocktails. He pulls the umbrella out of the glass, sucks the stick, then takes a sip.

"Well, this is very nice," he says, leaning back in his comfy leather chair, taking it all in. "To what do I owe the pleasure? Somebody's birthday is it?"

"No," I says. "It ain't. You should know me by now – I don't do birthdays, I keep losing count. Fact is, I've got a little job wants doing."

"Ah," he says, sounding disappointed, "a job…" Mac ain't the working kind – he's never had a proper job in his life and anything remotely resembling effort gives him the shakes. He rubs the bristles on his chin. "Hmm, well… You know me, Mr

Bent, a job's a job and jobs cost money."

"Don't worry," I says. "I ain't looking for no favours – you'll get something out of it. I want a bet putting on."

"Ah," he says, "that kind of a job... So why me? You can go down there and get that done easy enough." He nods towards the window and the track below.

"Not quite," I says. "This is different. It's a special bet." And I open the briefcase a crack so's he gets a whiff of the money.

"Jesus Christ!" he says. "I see what you mean. And you want to put all this on a greyhound? It must be one hell of an animal, that's all I can say, I ain't seen one worth that much yet. You could *buy* a dozen of the buggers for what you've got in there."

"Don't be daft," I says. "Do I look like the kind of bloke who'd come all the way to Walthamstow just to buy a dog."

"Well no, Mr Bent," he says. "I'd have to say you don't."

"Anyways," I says, "this has nothing to do with dogs. Or horses for that matter. It's boxing. I want to get a bet on Barry Mullins to win the ABA Title at the Albert Hall."

"ABA?" he says, wrinkling his forehead. "Never heard of it."

"Amateur Boxing Association," I says. I've been doing my homework. "Do you want me to spell it for you?"

"No thanks," he says. "I think I'll manage. Amateur boxing? I don't think there's a market for betting on amateurs. Besides which, like as not it's illegal."

"Exactly," I says. "Which is where you come in. Knowing you and your set of dodgy friends, I'm sure you'll find somebody who'll take it."

"Ooh," he says, rolling the idea around in his head. "I wouldn't count on it. It won't be easy, that's for sure." He points at the briefcase and sniffs. "So how much is there in there, anyway?"

"Ten big ones," I says. "On the nose, shit or bust, no questions asked."

"So what's in it for me?" he says.

I peel a purple job off the top and wave it under his nose.

"One of these for now," I says, "just to get you downstairs. Find me a punter and I'll make it a ton. Or you can wait 'til after and get double if I win."

"Hmm…" he says and he gives his chin another going over. "I'll see what I can do. Meet me back here in an hour."

I'm expecting him to shoot off and get started on it straight away, but no. He takes another look round to make sure he's in the clear, then puts the umbrella back in his empty glass and pushes it across the table.

"While we're on the subject," he says, clearing his throat. "Any chance of another one of these?"

So it's ten more minutes and another Campari and what-have-you before Mac's ready to go off and do the necessary. As for me, I stay put in my Little Jack Horner, one eye on the track and one eye on the briefcase. I won't be going nowhere 'til that's been sorted out. Down below I clock Jimmy lighting up under one of the floodlights. Any other night I'd go down and join him but this is private stuff and I don't want him poking his nose in. Plus, I'm too uptight to be thinking about the dogs so I sit out the hour, twiddling my thumbs.

Sixty minutes on the dot and Mac comes shuffling back – but he don't exactly look too happy. Fact is, he's got the shakes real bad so I get him his drink, umbrella an' all, so's then he can sit down and feel comfortable.

"Now," I says. "What's the story?"

"Story is," he says, "I can get it done – but I don't like it. Goldstrap'll take it."

"Goldstrap?" I says. "I ain't heard of no Goldstrap. Should I know this person?"

"You wouldn't want to, Mr Bent," he says. "Believe me, these ain't nice people."

Which is a bit rich coming from the likes of Mac.

"Nice people?" I says. "I ain't bothered whether they're nice people or not. Frankly, I don't give a toss just as long as their money's the same colour as mine."

"Ah well, that's it," says Mac. "Maybe it is and maybe it isn't. Anyways, he'll do it. A straight bet. You lose and it costs you the ten. Win and you'll get twenty back. In the meanwhile, I'll be keeping a hold on things. Purely as stakeholder, you understand."

There's a glimmer in his bloodshot eyes I don't quite like the look of.

"Well, you'll do for me," I says, and I hand over the briefcase. "But don't even think about running off with it. I'd come looking." Though I don't really need to tell him that. He ain't going nowhere with it because he ain't got nowhere to go. He just about lives at that dog-track, hasn't been off it in years, he'd never get as far as the nearest Tube station.

He puts the bag down and clears his throat.

"So, er... What about my ton?" he says.

I take another four twenties out of my wallet and put them on the table.

"Here you go," I says. "That's yours. Are you taking it now or waiting for it to double?"

"No offence, Mr Bent," he says, picking up the stash, "but I think I'll take it now."

While I still can. I can read him like a book.

He holds the notes up to the light, looking for those magic pieces of thin silver thread, then swallows hard and licks his lips like he's dreaming of how many Campari and thingummies he can get out of it. I see a thought occurring.

"Now we're here..." he starts.

"...you can get your own," I says. "You've had enough bloody drinks off me for one night."

So now we're done and he slopes off with the case. I make to leave too – there's nothing left for me to hang around for. This is the biggest punt of my life but all I can do is be patient and wait it out.

Goldstrap or not, I said Barry Mullins was a nugget, a solid gold nugget – I knew it from the moment I met him. Like I say, I just needed to use him right, that's all.

Albert

In all the years Micky and I spent together (and it must have amounted to over twenty), the period in the run-up to Barry's shot at the National Title was the best I can remember. It was certainly the busiest. We began by opening the gym five nights a week (up until then it had usually been three), primarily to accommodate Barry's desire for training. How much time he spent at home with that wife of his I have no idea, but if the hours Micky and I were down at the gym with him were anything to go by, not a lot. Some nights he'd be there before we arrived with the keys, waiting for us to open up. If he'd had the chance, I think he'd have had us in there on Sundays as well, but we had a home life even if he didn't and we had to draw the line somewhere.

At first it was just the three of us, but as things progressed and word got round we found ourselves attracting company. That all started when the sports columnist down at The Gazette decided to write a feature article and turned up at the door wanting an interview. He'd naturally brought a photographer with him. And rather than catch Barry in a static pose, could he take a snapshot of him in action with his sparring partner? There was a danger Barry might get carried away with the attention – and as his sparring partner at the time was me and I didn't want a repeat of what had happened the first time we got in the ring together, the answer to that question was an emphatic "No". But as time went on the pressure grew and we felt obliged to bring someone in from another club for him to spar with. Besides, Barry was in need of bigger challenges by then and I no longer fitted the bill. There was no shortage of volunteers. As a budding pugilist, being seen in the mix with Barry Mullins apparently did wonders for your street cred.

As Barry worked his way up through the rounds he grew steadily in both reputation and stature, and by the time he reached the semi-finals he'd become Chelmsford's Golden Boy of boxing. It seemed as though everyone wanted a piece of the action. Half the town wanted to come and watch him in training so we set aside an hour every evening when they were allowed in. Some nights queues formed at the door and the waiting list for membership almost doubled in the space of a few weeks. I soon found myself swamped with phone calls of one kind or another and the time I could devote to coaching Barry grew ever more precious as I fended off not only the press but prospective agents and promoters as well. Not that he needed me much, Barry was always good enough on his own, but what I discovered was that I wanted to be involved too and perhaps the same streak of vanity that ran in everyone else also ran in me. For a while it seemed that Chelmsford City Boys Club was the centre of the boxing world. This was our moment in the limelight and we wanted to make the most of it.

It was around this time, as the fights got harder and harder, that I began to have my doubts. Had I made a misjudgement? Was he as good as I'd thought? What if he ran out of steam? As it happens, I needn't have worried. For a start, there was still no one who could touch him. Sure, they could hit him, no boxer can avoid that, but it was always on the arms or up around his shoulders and never where it counted. And at the end of every fight Micky and I would look at him and then at each other in total disbelief, amazed at what we were seeing. There wasn't a mark on him, not a scratch, not a nick, nothing – in stark contrast to his opponents who'd come away with puffy eyes and blood streaming from some cut or another sustained in the heat of battle. But Barry? Clean as a whistle.

The semi-final was a classic. The opposition was good enough, that's for sure – Johnny McKeever from Liverpool. "Macca" had been around a good few years and knew what he was doing. He'd reached the semis a couple of times before but had never progressed to the final. Would this be third time lucky? Or would Golden Boy Mullins ruin his chances? The press were keen to play it up.

The problem we faced was that Macca was a southpaw so he led with his right rather than his left. It was a complication we could have done without and was bound to make things awkward. Believe it or not, Barry hadn't faced one before and not wanting to take the risk, we brought one in as a sparring partner for him to work on for the fortnight beforehand. Barry mastered the new technique in a flash and actually told me it was easier than fighting "lefties" since it made them more susceptible to his right – and that, as we know, was his preferred weapon of choice. And so it proved, as midway through the scheduled three rounds our boy whipped over a vicious right hook and Macca crumpled, dashing his hopes for the third time in a row. Micky and I were jubilant. Barry Mullins was the greatest thing since sliced bread, I was his coach and we were heading for the National Title. The world was at our feet.

None of us could have foreseen what was coming next.

Terry

Now as you might imagine, I ain't in the least bit interested in the progress of Barry Mullins' boxing career. It don't do nothing for me – quite the reverse in fact. And that's a bit of a bugger seeing as the whole of Chelmsford is gabbing on about nothing else and his face is plastered all over the back page of the paper. So now I've got no one to talk to and nothing I can read about without a mention of you know who. Which doesn't half piss me off.

One day he's going to get a pasting – and I'm so looking forward to that. As for this Title thing they're all going on about, I've written that off as a foregone conclusion so I ain't looking for the result of whatever fight he's been in and I only get to find out when Ronnie starts crowing about it on a morning. And on this particular Thursday the weather's brightened up, so I've gone out into the yard to polish a few windscreens when he comes out to find me.

"Heard the news?" he says, all bright and cheery. You'd have thought he'd have just won the lottery.

"What news?" I says. "Let me guess, you've had a sudden rush of blood to the head and decided to buy some stock in at last."

"Don't be daft," he says. "No, I mean the news about Barry."

As if I want to know.

"He's only gone and reached the final. Cleared his semi last night. Second round knock-out."

"Oh really," I says. "And what am I supposed to do? Throw a party?"

"You don't get it, do you?" he says. "Sometimes I worry about you, Tel. There's a bigger picture here and you ain't seeing it. I can't go into detail but the fact is, if he wins that Title it'll do us the world of good."

So what? I'm thinking. *So you can have some more lettering added to the side of that bloody motor car? Barry Mullins – ABA Champion. Give me a break.*

"Great," I says, polishing a bit harder. "I can't tell you how pleased I am for the both of you."

Only Ronnie's too made up to catch my drift and it just slides by. He gives up on me and heads back towards the office, humming that *I should be so lucky* tune to himself. He's been humming that a lot lately. As for me, I've got nothing to crow about so I just keep on polishing.

Anyways, what with selling those six cars plus a few more since, come the end of the month there's been a good bit in my pay packet of late. I decide a celebration's in order. So I'm out on the town, which is only natural seeing as it's a Friday night and I'm in funds. I invite Ronnie to join me but he ain't up for it. *I'll take a rain check, thanks Tel.* It's like he's waiting for something else but I don't know what and he ain't telling.

Now, out on the town ain't what it used to be. I tend not to do the clubs anymore, these days it's just the pubs – and in the interests of drinking efficiency, I've narrowed it down to two. They're both on the Square – The Bell and The Golden Lion. So the joy of it is, if I ain't in the one I must be in the other and I don't waste much time wandering in between.

Well, this particular Friday I start off in The Bell around seven. It's quiet, which is how I like it, so I play the fruit machine for an hour and get a couple of pints down the range. I blag a couple of small payouts but the machine ain't really talking my language so I decide to cut my losses and move next door. I ain't sold all those cars just to see my money wasted and no return.

There's a few more folks in The Lion but I still get my usual seat next to the window. Bernie the landlord says hello, I buy a box of smokes and a couple more pints so by the time it's nine o'clock I'm well on my way to my usual eight when this bloke walks in I've never seen before. Now I know I've had a few (though it's only four for Christ's sake) but my first reaction is *Did somebody die in here or what?* Because this guy looks like he's walked straight out of the undertakers. He's tall, thin, black shoes, black trousers with a long black overcoat and black kid gloves but the giveaway is his shirt – because that's black too and he ain't got no tie on. So he ain't come in here to measure nobody up. Not for burying anyway. And just by way of a contrast his hair's a silvery blond, thinning out on top but long and lank at the sides and hanging over his collar. It's weird. He has a slow look round then walks up to the bar.

Well it just so happens that Bernie is a mate of mine and I know he don't do chit-chat. So when I see the two of them stood there yakking for a couple of minutes, you can bet your sweet life that something must be up. Then they both turn round, Bernie points in my direction, and bugger me if Joe Black don't come straight over to my table where he pulls out a chair and plonks himself down right next to me.

Now I ain't looking for company and even if I was, his ain't the kind I'd choose – I prefer mine female and a tad more fashionable. So I ain't exactly overjoyed at the prospect of spending my Friday night with some bloke who looks like he's on his way to a funeral.

"Take a seat why don't you," I says, hoping he'll do just the opposite.

But Joe ain't in the mood to be put off. He makes himself comfy, then peels off his gloves and lays them down all neat and tidy in front of him.

"So you're Terry Bennett," he says.

Me, I want to burst out laughing. He must think he's as hard as hell but his hands are the same colour as his hair and my guess is he spends half his time in a nail bar keeping them clean. Though his voice is pretty sharp and it cuts through the air like a knife. Plus, there's a "don't you dare" look to go with it so I figure laughing might not be overly wise. I decide to keep it shut.

"Well maybe I am and maybe I ain't," I says, trying to keep things casual. "It all depends who wants him."

Which is all a bit daft because by the look of it, Bernie's already told him so there ain't no point in denying it.

"I've been making a few enquiries..." he says.

"So I saw," I says.

"...and I understand you work at Ronnie Bent's garage."

"You understand correct," I says. "So what if I do? It ain't a crime – I daresay there's a lot worse things to answer for."

"That's as maybe," he says, then turns down the volume and narrows his eyes to a slit. "So you'll know Barry Mullins then."

Well there's a surprise. It's what I keep telling you – Barry bloody Mullins is the only game in town and if there's one thing you can count on to wind me up, that's it. And there was me thinking that dear old Joe had come in to talk about buying a new motor.

"Friend of yours, is he?" he says.

Which is another turn up for the books seeing as he's just been speaking to Bernie and Bernie's well aware of my views on that subject.

"A friend?" I says. "You must be joking. Barry Mullins is no friend of mine. I'd love to show you what I think of Barry Mullins," I says, "but Bernie's moved his spittoon."

"I see..." says Joe, and he lifts his eyebrows to touch what's left of his hairline. "So you and this Mullins bloke ain't mates then?"

"No," I says, "we ain't. Whatever gave you that idea? Fact is, I hate the little bastard and I don't care who knows it."

"In that case," he says, "maybe we could do a bit of business."

"Business?" I says. "What kind of business?"

At which point he straightens the lapels on his long black coat like he's getting ready to make some kind of speech.

"Now as it so happens," he says, "I represent a certain party who, let's just say, have a financial interest."

"Oh really," I says. "I'm intrigued. But don't tell me, let me guess. This certain party can't bring themselves low enough to come drinking in my pub so they sends the likes of you out to do their dirty work instead."

Now if that ain't calculated to get under his skin, I don't know what is. At first he don't respond and he sits there as cool as you like, but then his thin lip starts curling up and I get the distinct impression that if we weren't in a public place, he'd like to be doing me some damage. Maybe I'm taking a risk but I've had one or two to drink and I'm in a Friday night kind of a mood – that's to say, provocative. But he's got a job to do has Joe, so just for the moment he's all restraint.

"Well now, ain't you the smartarse," he says. "I can understand why you and Mullins aren't mates. You don't exactly make friends easy, do yer?"

As if I want to be friends with him. I think not.

"Anyways," I says, "don't tell me you've come all the way here just to buy me a drink." Which, as yet, he hasn't – but I'm working on it. "So what can I do you for?"

And he resumes his official position with those bleached-white hands of his grasping his black lapels like he's chief negotiator for the bad-boys trade union.

"This certain party…" he says.

"The one you represent."

"Exactly."

"The one that don't want to come down here."

Another scowl. But he keeps things going just the same. "They have a proposal to make. Concerning Mr Mullins."

"I thought they might," I says. "But you go ahead, I'm all ears."

Joe takes a look around and then leans forward so he can be sure we're private. Now we're getting to the nub of it. His long white fingers go sneaking up to the inside pocket of his long black overcoat and he draws out an envelope which he drops onto the table in front of me.

"You look like the kind of bloke who could do with some extra cash," he says.

Now I ain't too sure whether this is a compliment or not. And just at the moment I happen to be in funds so I ain't that desperate. But it don't do no harm to get topped up so I pick up the envelope and look inside. It's stuffed full of tenners.

"No need to count it," he says. "There's two-fifty in total in there. You can keep that now and there's more the same after."

"After what?" I says.

And when he lays it out, it's so simple I have to smile. I sit there listening, watching the words drop from his lips, his sharp voice slicing the air, and I really like what I'm hearing. And once he's finished, I know I have to be in on it and it's like we've shaken hands on the deal already.

"And that's it?" I says.

"Yup," he says. "That's it."

"And there won't be no comeback?"

"Nope," he says. "None at all."

"Well I think I can manage that," I says. "It'll be a pleasure."

I take the envelope and shove it into my pocket. I get the feeling I shouldn't push it but I'm curious as to where it's come from so I try another tack. Besides which, I need to look out for number one.

"This certain party," I says. "The one you represent. They'll be coming to thank me in person then – after."

"No, they won't," he says. "What you've got in that envelope is more than thanks enough. But you play your cards right and I'm sure you'll get looked after. The boss'll see to that."

"The boss?" I says. "So who the bloody hell's the boss?"

"Goldstrap of course, that's who."

"Never heard of him," I says. "But I'll drink to him just the same."

And I down the last of my pint and set it on the table in front of him. But he don't take the hint and he just looks at me real steady like he knows I'm trying it on.

"Just make sure you're there," he says. "That's all."

"Oh, I'll be there," I says. "You can bank on it."

So now we're done and he stands up, buttons his coat and pulls his gloves on like he's dressing for dinner. Then he's gone.

I keep still for a minute and let it all sink in. But I can't sit for too long in front of an empty glass so I walk up to the bar and order another pint. Bernie's there mopping up and takes an undue interest. Maybe it's the smirk on my face but he's curious too.

"So what was that all about?" he asks as he's pulling my pint.

I sniff by way of reply. Which lets him know it ain't none of his concern.

"Just a bit of business," I says. "That's all. Private business." And I take the pint and go and sit back down.

Meantime, the place has been filling up and I ain't on my own no more. I budge up and make room but there's enough space in my head to go over what Joe Black was saying. I can remember it word for word so I let the thoughts play while I finish my beer. It's a long, cold pint, longest I've ever drunk, and I make it last because I ain't going to drink another one tonight. This ain't about a night on the town no more, this is about something different. And all the time there's a form of words that keeps running through my head.

Same wagon, different horse. It's got to be worth a try.

Barry

So this is how it happens. I get my semi out the way no problem and Ronnie gives me a couple of days off to recover. Thursday itself is alright. My body don't hurt too much and I go out for my usual run to stop things stiffening up. It's a day and a half before the boxing kicks in, so come Friday and I feel like I've been hit by a truck. Which is ironic seeing as how I'm supposed to spend the next couple of days of my working life underneath one. While I've been away Terry's sold a big four-by-four and it needs tarting up a bit before they can send it out. So first thing Monday morning I'm back to work and happy to get cracking on it straight away but Ronnie wants to spend time chewing the fat. The way he goes on you'd think he hadn't seen me for weeks, never mind a couple of days.

"Barry, my son!" he cries.

Which I ain't of course, but you get the general idea.

"How's it going?" he says, and he wraps one of those great big paws of his round my shoulder to give my arm a squeeze. Which ain't altogether helpful seeing as that's where I took most of the shots my opponent handed out the Wednesday previous. I wince and lift his hand off.

"All the better for you laying off," I says. "I'm still hurting thereabouts."

"Sorry," says Ronnie. "Give you a pounding, did he?"

"Yes," I says. "He did a bit." I may be good but there's no getting away from it, the boxing don't get any easier.

"You had him in the end though," says Ronnie.

"Yup," I says. "I guess I did."

And we go on like that for the best part of ten minutes, what with Ronnie wanting to know all the ins and outs of who hit who, how hard and when. I didn't think he did boxing but in recent weeks it seems like he's developed a real interest. He makes me give him a blow by blow account 'til I feel like I've done the fight twice over. Eventually I shake him off and get through to the workshop. One thing's for certain – once I'm in there, Terry won't be stopping by to say hello.

The truck's already in there, waiting. It's one of them big black buggers – wide wheels and done up boy-racer style. I wonder whether it's for work or for show because if it's for show then somebody's got a big wad of cash they don't exactly need. But that ain't my problem, my job's just to get it fixed up. Ronnie's left a worksheet of sorts on the bench – *MOT, oil change, Terry says there's a brake pipe leaking.* I take a quick look underneath and sure enough there's a few spots dripping out onto the floor. That looks like me for the day then.

I change into my overalls and put the radio on. I'm a Radio 2 man so it's Terry Wogan and a bit of chat, but I don't mind that first thing. I don't want it too loud in case the phone goes off and it's someone from The Gazette or maybe even The Standard or it could be some boxing promoter wanting to talk turkey. So I turn it down and keep the door open so I can hear anything coming from the office. Then I make a start on the truck. I decide to break myself in gradual so I tick off the easy jobs first. Crawling about underneath can wait until later. I get finished on the simple stuff then break for a coffee. By which time it's half ten so Ken Bruce is on and I'm stood having a listen when the phone starts jangling. Ronnie picks up the receiver.

"Hello?" he says. "Yeah, this is Big Ronnie's." He waits while the other party does the talking. "Sure," I hear him say, "I can be there in... what? Ten minutes?" So I know this ain't for me. Pretty soon his head appears at the workshop door. "Some bloke's got a motor he wants me to look at," he says. "But I've got to go out for it." Which is all a bit unusual seeing as they normally bring them in. "I'll be back in thirty minutes," he says. "Forty-five at the most."

Then he's gone and I'm left on my tod with Ken.

Now it's time to work on this brake pipe. This may be Big

Ronnie's but we don't run to a fancy lift so I'm going to have to jack it. I figure I'll need the big one for this job so I pull out the three-tonner, slide her into position and lever away. Hey-ho and up she rises. I make sure the handbrake on the truck's full on then I'm flat on my back and looking at its oily underside. Ken cracks a joke and I have a good laugh. You've got to – it ain't much fun where I am. And I've just nicely found the leak when the workshop door swings shut.

But it don't do that on its own.

"Ronnie?" I says. "Is that you?"

Maybe his punter blew him off and he's back early. No reply.

"Ronnie?" I call again.

Still nothing. I wait a minute. Then the radio goes dead in full flow.

"Who's there?" I says.

Still no reply.

But I know there's someone out there – I'm sure I can hear their feet shuffling. Only it ain't Ronnie. Because Ronnie don't shuffle. And it won't be Terry neither. So there's a stranger in my workshop and I'm stuck under a heavy truck. All of a sudden the back of my neck feels like there's an ice-pack stuck on the back of it.

I hear the shuffle moving. I look both left and right but I still can't see no feet. The ice on my neck turns to sweat and I want to get out from under but it ain't that easy. My hands are all tangled up in the suspension, the shuffle's gone behind me now and I try to turn my head. I start to panic. I free my left hand and try pulling myself out but I can't get purchase. The shuffle reaches the jack. There's a hiss as someone hits the fast release and I know I've just got seconds left – but the roof's collapsing in, there's a lurch as the truck comes crashing down, my body's out but my right hand's stuck and there's a pain shooting up my arm like someone's trying to cut my hand off. There's waves of it flooding into my head, again and again, until I feel the black ink coming.

I'm about to pass out when I get to see the feet, a pair of dark shiny shoes with gold buckles. But then the black ink gets me, good and proper, and I don't feel the pain no more.

Part Five
Boxed In

Ronnie

It's a real shocker, coming back to the garage and finding him lying there like that, all crumpled up unconscious and with his arm stuck underneath the truck. I've seen a lot worse in my time, I don't mind telling you, but that don't make it any easier. And I'm not in the best of moods neither, what with that stupid bloody punter having just let me down. He makes the call, I make the effort, I'm there on time and then the bastard doesn't show up. But that's punters for you I suppose – you just can't trust 'em further than you can throw 'em.

I get the feeling something's wrong the moment I walk in. You can always tell when it's your own place, can't you? All the doors are wide open for a start – and it's quiet, much too quiet. I'm used to the sound of Barry's radio humming away and for some reason I don't hear it. And it's not like him to keep it turned off.

"Baz?" I says. "Are you there?"

I look around the office. It's empty.

"Baz?" I shout, a bit louder this time in case he's gone out back. Still no reply. I go through to the workshop and there he is, sprawled out on the floor. His eyes are closed and he's completely out of it, but the good news is he's still breathing.

"Jesus Christ!" I says. "What the hell's happened here?"

I shake him by the shoulder to try and bring him round but all I get is a groan. And I can't pull him out as the truck's got him pinned up to the elbow. So I'm straight back into the office and looking for Tel. And where's he when you need him? On the other side of the yard, polishing bloody windscreens.

"Tel!" I call over. "Come and give us a hand – quick! It's Baz. There's been an accident." I know he's heard me because I see his ears prick up. But he don't exactly hurry. "For Christ's sake Tel," I says. "Get your skates on! This is serious."

But Tel can't get himself out of first gear. He ambles across like he's bringing up the field in a two-year-old handicap but at last I get the both of us into the workshop. I get him to try the jack while I haul Barry free. The jack comes up real easy, lifting the truck off slow and gentle, just like it should. No problem there then. And that's not so strange either seeing as I had it checked out no more than a couple of weeks since. Which is just as well now that Health and Safety will be all over me like a rash, poking their nose into every corner. So I begin to wonder, how the hell could that have happened? It's a mystery to me and no mistake.

And in the meantime, there's my strategic investment, my punt, my little trump card, lying on the deck in a pool of muck and bullets with his hand looking like it's been put through a mangle. So my big gamble is out of commission – there won't be any winners coming out of that particular stable for a while. Which is really a bit of a bugger seeing as it's all I had up my sleeve short of an arm.

I find a towel to wrap Barry's hand in, then I get Tel to call an ambulance.

Barry

Up, up, up out of the black ink and heading towards the light. No voices, just the rhythmic thrum of traffic passing by and a gentle swaying motion, like I'm floating on an air bed or lying in a hammock. My eyes crack open and the light floods in, bright from the long neon strip set into the flat white of the ceiling. It's quiet, almost peaceful, and I can feel my heart slowly beating.

Maybe this is what it's like when you're born. Maybe this is what it's like when you come into the world for the first time and everything's new to the touch. Only you don't remember it – you can't, it's beyond human recall. You haven't learnt how to yet, along with all those hundreds of other things you're still to discover, still to find out. So maybe this is it. Maybe I'm being reborn and it's like starting over. Only this time I will remember. Because this is the moment when everything changed. This is the moment my new life began.

I try sitting up but I only get so far before my head starts to swim and I sink back down again, dizzy. Everything's circling round so I close my eyes to stop it. I give it a couple of minutes, breathing deep, then try again, only this time slow and steady. I push myself up with my left hand but I don't feel nothing with my right. Somebody told me once that if you can feel the pain, the injury ain't that bad. But if you can't, it's serious. And I can't. I must have a right hand though because there's something sticking out at the end of my arm only it's all covered up in an old towel and I can't tell what it is. I clock the red patches, seeping through the fabric. But they ain't part of the pattern. So that's a worry. Then I notice the medic sat there with me, hovering.

"Here we go, he's conscious!" she shouts at the driver, then moves towards me, crouching. "Are you alright, luv?" she says and pats me on my good arm. She tries not to look too concerned.

That's a bloody silly question – of course I'm not alright. I'm in the back of an ambulance, my right hand's all busted up and covered in a blood-soaked rag and I'm starting to feel a bit queasy. The good news is that the siren ain't going and the van ain't speeding so I guess I'm not a basket case. Not yet, at any rate. I lie back down and find the flat white of the ceiling again. The light's hurting now so I close my eyes and rest.

"I'll be fine," I says, lying through gritted teeth. "No problem."

"Well done," she says, giving me another pat. "That's the spirit. Just a few more minutes and we'll be there."

Stupid bitch. What did she expect me to say? *Yes thank you, I'm having such a lovely time. It must be my birthday.* Then I remember. It is, second time round.

It takes a couple of hours to get me through A&E. But we are talking Broomfield Hospital here and in this part of the world people don't exactly rush about. To tell the truth, I've seen paint dry quicker. Good job it's first thing on a Monday and the place is almost empty. Christ knows how long they'd take on a Saturday night when it's packed full of drunks and self-harmers. I'd still be here come Sunday morning.

The medic wheels me in on a trolley and I get parked up in a corridor. Pretty soon I'm pig sick of staring at the ceiling and I decide I can't do with lying down no more. I sit up again, nice and slow, then slide my legs off onto the floor and try standing up. Only it's like there's nothing there for support and as soon as my feet touch the deck, I start keeling over. I stick a hand out to break the fall and halfway down I remember it's got to be the left – but the right still jars and the same sharp pain shoots up my arm again. I wince out loud. Someone must hear me because a minute later a nurse comes round the corner pushing a wheelchair. She helps me up into it.

"Don't play tricks like that on me, Mr Mullins," she says. "You're still in shock, you know. I'll fetch you a nice hot cup of tea. That'll make you feel better."

"Thanks," I says. "I could use one."

Only I'm beginning to think it'll take more than a cup of tea to get me through this. I mean, even Spike stood up quicker after I knocked him down, for Christ's sake.

I drink the tea and a debate starts up behind reception about what to do next – go straight for an x-ray or take the towel off and clean me up first. The towel and a cleanup win the vote and I get wheeled into a side room. Nurse reappears with a huge pair of scissors and a grin bigger than the Cheshire cat's. I start to worry again.

"What you planning on doing with them?" I says, pointing at the scissors. "You ain't thinking of cutting anything off, are you?"

"Don't be silly, Mr Mullins," she says. "Of course not. I'm just going to use them to remove the covering and tidy you up a bit before your x-ray, that's all." And all the time there's this huge smile on her face like she's trying to cheer me up. "I won't hurt you," she says. "Promise. But you might want to look the other way. Just in case."

Just in case of what? I'm thinking. Her cheer up routine don't fool me none – tea or no tea, I still don't feel so good.

I'm an hour and twenty minutes waiting for the x-ray results. I know it's an hour and twenty because I count it off on the big clock in the waiting room. *Tick, tick, tick.* It's actually an hour and twenty-two, but hey, I ain't going to make a fuss. What's a couple of minutes between me and Broomfield Hospital? Fact is, there ain't a lot else to do. I'd sit and twiddle my thumbs but one of them ain't working too well right now.

I'm just about to call someone when the doc comes in. He looks a bit on the young side but I guess it must be the doc on account of the fact he's got a white coat on and one of those listening thingies dangling round his neck. Besides which, he thinks he's important – you know the type I mean? He's carrying a clipboard with a brown envelope tucked under his arm.

"Mr Mullins?" he says, walking over to where I'm still stuck in my wheelchair.

"Yeah," I says, "that's me."

Well it can't be no bugger else, can it? Seeing as I'm the only bloke in there.

"You're the chap with the broken hand, I believe?" As if that ain't obvious, now it's all bandaged up and hung in a sling around my neck. "Here you go then," he says, and pulls the pics out of the envelope. "You might want to have a look at these."

Now I'm no expert on body parts and the negs are a bit dim, but I can at least tell my arse from my elbow. So if I've got it correct, then it looks like I've still got a right hand and it's still got the same four fingers and a thumb. Only problem is, they don't all point in the right direction.

"Hmm..." says the doc while he contemplates the damage. "It must have been quite a nasty accident. But first, the good news. You've actually been quite lucky."

Well it don't seem lucky to me.

"Your wrist is still intact. If that had sustained any serious damage, it might have been a different story altogether."

"And the bad news?" I says.

"You're going to require reconstructive surgery, I'm afraid."

"Oh really," I says. "And what's that when it's at home?"

"Well, Mr Mullins," and he starts off talking to me like I'm a five-year-old. "What that means is I'm going to have to rebuild your hand." He holds one of the negs up to the light and pretends to peer at it. "There's a few broken bones – here and here." He points them out with the tip of his pen. "Plus there's a couple of cracks – although they should heal up on their own. But as for the rest, that could take us a while – it won't be an easy process."

"So how long's a while?" I says. "All told." It don't take a genius to see what's coming next. I brace myself for the news.

"It's impossible to tell," he says. "But to give you a rough idea, we can probably get the surgery done in the next two or three days. You'll have a pot on by the end of the week. That should come off after a couple of months after which you can start the physiotherapy. All in all, to make a full recovery, I'd say a total of six months." He goes quiet for a moment but then picks up on it again. "Of course, that assumes you make a full recovery. Not all of these cases do..." Then he tries putting on the same cheery face as Nurse had – it must be something they practise. "So I'm sorry to have to tell you, but I'm afraid you won't be playing tennis for a while!"

Which is his idea of a joke. But that's okay with me because I don't play tennis.

Six months? I'm thinking. *Jesus Christ, I can't wait six months. I've got things to do, places to go, people to see. Then there's the small matter of the National Title. Not to mention that dream I'm supposed to be building.*

The doc must see I'm disappointed. "Tell you what," he says. "We'll get started on it straight away. I'll get you on my list for tomorrow. We should be able to fit you in some time in the afternoon. Nurse'll find you a bed. You might want to ask your family to bring in some overnight things."

I hate to think what Tracey's going to say about it all. I look at the negs again and shudder.

Terry

So Barry Mullins' big right hand is all smashed up and he's stuck in Broomfield Hospital. Don't look like he'll be doing much more in the way of boxing then. Oh dear, oh dear, now ain't that a shame, I'm so upset I could cry me a river. And no, I ain't got no regrets on the subject, I always said that jumped up little git had it coming – now I'm the one who made sure he got it. So what the hell did you expect me to do? Stand there and hold his coat while he buggers off and wins the World Championship? Not if I've got anything to do with it.

I weren't altogether happy when he won that semi, never mind anything else. But there wasn't much I could do about that, it was all done and dusted before they could get to him, before they ever asked me.

"What?" I says. "'You mean you and me? To tell the truth, I ain't used to that sort of thing and besides, I reckon Barry could be a bit of a handful. You know, what with him being a boxer an' all."

"No, no – you've got it all wrong," says Joe. "You don't need to get involved. The boss'll do whatever's necessary. We just need to provide an opportunity."

"Oh," I says, catching on. "You mean like opening doors."

"Exactly."

"And there was me thinking you were a hard case."

"Well that just goes to show why you ain't doing the thinking," says Joe. "You'd best leave that up to me."

"Okay," I says. "So what have you got in mind?"

"The garage," he says. "Monday morning. Quiet, is it?"

"Pretty much," I says. "Should just be me, Ronnie and that little bastard Mullins."

"Good," he says. "But we'll need to get Bent out of it somehow."

"Why don't you give him a ring?" I says. "Here's the number." I give him one of my cards. "Tell him you're a punter with a nice motor to sell, cheap. I know Ronnie like the back of my hand, he'll come *running. What do you want me to do?"*

He looks around, checking. But nobody's listening, the bar's half empty anyway.

"Just make sure the place is clear and there's easy access. Then, if you've got any sense, you'll stay well out of it."

"Okay," I says and I nod, slowly. So now I'm in on it, just as sure as if I'd started the whole thing off myself.

And that's exactly how it happens. Monday morning, I make sure I'm in early doors. I keep an eye out, looking, and around half ten the phone goes off and Ronnie comes out in a tearing hurry. Halfway across the yard and he's still pulling his coat on.

"I'm going out," he shouts. "On business. Back in half an hour."

I wait 'til he's disappeared then check around indoors. There's no one about apart from Barry and nothing's locked so I go back out to the car lot and start polishing a few windscreens. I figure they must be waiting somewhere across the road because five minutes later the two of them come walking in through the front gate, Joe Black and A.N. Other. A.N. Other's medium height, slim build but older with smooth silver hair. Smart dresser, same black coat and trousers as Joe, but given the cut of his shoes I figure he must be Goldstrap. I turn round and look the other way, pretending I ain't noticed. Like Joe Black says, I'm best off keeping my nose out.

But you know me, I'm curious, so I find a handy wing-mirror and tweak it round so's I can keep tabs while I'm facing the other way. Joe parks himself outside and minds the gaff while Goldstrap goes indoors, pulling his gloves on. Meanwhile I keep polishing. He ain't in there more than a couple of minutes before he walks out again, cool as you like. You'd think he'd just been into the dry cleaners or something on a Saturday morning. He could be someone's uncle. He could be my uncle for Christ's sake. But he ain't – he's Goldstrap. Then they're gone, out the front gate and away.

I decide on waiting for Ronnie to come back. I ain't going to be the first to go in there, no way.

They're calling it an accident and saying there must have been a fault with the machinery. As for me, I don't know a thing. Well, I wouldn't, would I? Seeing as I was outside in the yard at the time, polishing windscreens. But whichever way you look at it, Barry Mullins is dished, he ain't going to bother me no more. Busted hand, busted flush, that's what I say. Jumped up little git.

Come Friday and I'm back in The Golden Lion when Bernie calls me over.

"Here," he says. "Your mate from last week left you this." And he shoves a sealed brown envelope across the counter. I open it up and there's another bundle of them crisp tenners staring out at me. It ain't exactly a fortune but it's a darn sight more than that tight bastard Ronnie Bent's ever given me, that's for sure.

Barry

Clack, clack, clack, Tracey's high heels come tripping across the polished lino. She's first to arrive, her dainty little handbag swinging to and fro like a pendulum. Trouble is, she's come straight from work so she ain't been back to Walton Terrace and there's no chance she's brought in any of my stuff. She takes one look at the bandages and I can tell from the off she don't like it, it's written all over her face as soon as she walks in. I tell her to pull up a chair but it don't look like she's fixing to stay too long.

"So what's all this then?" she says, ending with a sniff.

"I've hurt my hand," I says. "But don't worry, it's nothing." I'm trying to keep it simple – I don't want to give too much away if I can help it.

"Hurt it?" she says. "That's a bit of an understatement, if ever I heard one. Broke it, more like."

"Oh really?" I says. "And where d'you get that from?"

"There's a bloke in a white coat wandering round reception with a clipboard," she says. "When he heard me give my name, we got chatting and he told me all about it."

"I see..." I says. So much for patient confidentiality at Broomfields. Maybe I should speak to my MP.

"So," she says. "How d'you manage to get yourself into this mess anyway?"

"Car jack fell on it," I says. "There was an accident down at the garage."

"Car jack?" she says. "What the hell were you doing messing round with a car jack?"

"It's part of my job," I says. "I'm a car mechanic, remember? It's what I do."

"I thought you was supposed to be a boxer?"

"That as well," I says. "Some of the time. Anyways, it's only a scratch. A couple more days and I'll be out of here. Give me a few weeks and we'll be right back on track. Promise. But it's like

I said, sometimes you just have to be patient, that's all."

"Hmm…" she says. "Well I ain't too sure about that. I don't see how you can box with your hand in that state."

"What state?"

"All mashed up like a ripe banana. And it's no good you trying to tell me different, I've seen the pictures."

"Hold on," I says. "You can't go blaming me." It's like the mechanic part of me's fighting back. "It ain't my fault. It was an accident, that's all."

I tell her about the truck and how it fell on me, though I leave out the bit about the bloke with the shoes because that don't seem relevant right now. I figure on waiting a while 'til I get to the bottom of that one. Besides, now don't seem like a good time to be opening up another can of worms.

She looks away and out the window, but she's muttering under her breath.

Bloody garage. I always knew it would get in the way.

Because she didn't marry the mechanic – she married the boxer. And right now the boxer ain't looking too good on account of the mechanic having screwed up. It's black or white for Tracey, there's no grey area.

"Anyways," she says. "I'll come back in tomorrow and see how you're doing. If there's anything you need you can leave a message at reception and they'll phone me at work. I've left them the number."

And then she's gone. No toothbrush, no flannel, no nothing – I don't even get a peck on the cheek. To tell the truth I'd have settled for some TLC, never mind the rest.

It's Mother as fetches my kit in. She and Dad turn up about seven having stopped off at our place on the way. And talk about going from the sublime to the ridiculous. Even if Tracey *had* thought about my toothbrush, if it don't fit in her handbag, she don't bring it. But Mother arrives with a parcel the size of God knows what and I get the full Red Cross treatment – shaving gear, three sets of clean underwear, a complete change of clothes and enough cake, fruit and biscuits to last me a month.

"Just in case," she says. "You never know, you might be in here a while."

Not if I've got anything to do with it.

But Mother never was one to look on the bright side. I reckon on getting Nurse to come and give her some cheering up lessons.

We chat for a while about this and that and then I show them my bandages – though to tell the truth there ain't an awful lot they can see right now. Which is probably just as well seeing as it's all a bit of a mess and I don't want to be looking at it myself. Ten minutes goes by and the conversation starts to flag. Dad ain't saying much anyway on account of he's puffed after walking up from the car park and besides, he don't get a word in edgeways when Mother's holding forth. So when she says *Excuse me* and slides off to find the ladies, I get the chance to talk to him on his own. I figure if I can't tell him, I can't tell no one at all.

"Dad," I says, when Mother's out of it. "This weren't no accident. I swear there was someone in that workshop, I know there was, I saw him."

And this is my Dad I'm talking to, and he's been my father for the best part of twenty-odd years and I ain't never told him a lie yet, never, not once in all the time I've known him, not even when telling the truth meant I was getting myself into trouble. And he looks at me with a face like he's the one in pain, like the emphysema's crippled him and he can't fight it no more, and he covers it up with a thin weak smile as if he's saying *Okay, have it your own way – but I think you must be crazy* and he pats me on my good arm just like the nurse and the medic.

"Don't worry about it, son," he says. "It'll be alright, trust me."

Only you can see he don't believe a word I'm telling him. Like I say, he never was one to buck the system, Dad.

Albert

I've never liked lying at the best of times – I suppose I'm like Barry in that respect. Mine was a traditional upbringing and I was raised to tell the truth – or at least, as much of it as I could be persuaded to give. In my day, if things ever became "difficult" they simply weren't talked about. Later on, of course, one discovered that expressions such as "Your Uncle's taking a long holiday from work" were designed to hide the fact that he'd gone to prison for a while, or that he'd run off with the scullery maid. And the one about John, "your long-lost cousin" was in reality an introduction to a child inconveniently born out of wedlock. That was the way things were done in those days.

If there was one thing this taught me, it wasn't that I shouldn't lie (I took that for granted) but that there was a world of difference between lying and not quite telling the truth. This may appear too subtle a distinction for most people but it's one that modern politicians exploit to their advantage – we all know that when occasion demands it, they can be exceptionally economical with the facts. My own ability to follow in their footsteps and tread the fine line between honesty and deception was to be put to the test in no uncertain terms in the weeks after Barry's accident.

It began on the Monday following his semi-final victory. We opened the gym as usual around half past six, and were surprised when he wasn't there waiting for us. By half past seven he still hadn't shown up, and sensing something untoward, I rang him at home. There was no reply.

By this time a small group of supporters had gathered in their usual position outside the front door seeking autographs and wanting to pass on their congratulations. Micky asked me what he should do about them.

"Tell them Barry's not training tonight," I suggested.

It was the first of many such attempts at evasion although this at least was true. He certainly wasn't training in my gym and I had no reason to believe he was doing so anywhere else.

The next morning I got a phone call at work from his father, and when Derek told me what had happened it completely took the wind out of my sails. My initial reaction was to shut the gym altogether and avoid any repercussions by hiding behind a closed door, but a frank discussion with Micky soon changed my mind. He rightly argued that such a drastic course of action would raise far more questions than we were presently capable of answering, so we decided to remain open. Until such time as things became clearer, we would put out the line that after such a hard fight it was in Barry's best interest to be rested so he'd been given the week off. That at least was credible and would buy us a much-needed breathing space.

On the Wednesday I left Micky in charge and went to the hospital myself in the hopes of filling in some of the blanks. As it turned out I'd left it too late to see Barry – he'd discharged himself an hour or so before with his hand encased in a plaster of Paris pot – but I was able to pick up enough clues from his consultant to come to some unwelcome conclusions. As far as I could tell, Barry wasn't going to be boxing for the foreseeable future and the likelihood was he might never box again. It put me in an awkward position – and one I found hard to resolve.

Boxing is a heavily regulated sport. A boxer has to be fit – and to be seen to be fit – before they can enter the ring. You can't let any old soul clamber between the ropes simply because they happen to meet the weight limits. You also have to be assessed as fit to be a trainer. I was lucky, I'd got my certificate from the Board of Control some years beforehand – without it, I wouldn't have been able to run the gym. My immediate concern was the report I'd be obliged to submit prior to Barry's next fight. If I didn't complete it, he wouldn't be allowed to progress. As his duly licensed trainer I was required to sign him off, and over the course of the next few days I must have read the relevant documentation through a dozen times, but try as I might I couldn't find that all-important loophole which would allow us to move on without actually telling a lie. The paperwork was laid out in black and white – there were no grey areas.

I did get as far as drafting a letter to accompany my report. It lay on my desk for days. *With great regret... Sorry to have to inform the Board... Based on information currently to hand...*

I showed it to Micky in the hopes of gaining some form of inspiration.

"Ouch," he said. "That's rough."

But that was all the help I got from that quarter.

An even more difficult task would be breaking the news to Barry. I was bound to speak to him first, and while misleading the Board of Control was one thing, not telling him the truth was quite another.

An added, and unwanted, complication in this regard was the press. It wouldn't be long before they got hold of the story, and faced with the prospect of a sensationalist front-page splash it was preferable that he heard things from me rather than read it in the newspaper. And so, with some degree of trepidation, I determined to grasp the nettle and speak to him sooner rather than later. It wasn't something I was particularly looking forward to.

Telling a boxer he's finished, be he professional or even just a good amateur, isn't the easiest thing in the world. The words "washed-up" instantly spring to mind. Oh sure, it wouldn't have been the first time I'd had to do it – there'd been a few occasions over the years. Like the time when little Johnny got his nose broken or when somebody worked one of the bigger lads over so badly that I had to put a stop to it and take them to one side and say *I'm sorry but this sort of thing isn't for you, you're just not up to it.* And then, inevitably, the tears would arrive, either from the hit they'd taken or the hurt I'd just given them by saying what I had to.

It wasn't going to be like that with Barry – although in some ways I wished it was as it might have made things easier. Because Barry had always been good enough, Barry was one of the best. In his case it was never going to be a lucky punch in the ring that would end it, it would be the men in suits, or rather, white coats, because that's what the Board would rely on, the opinion of the medical profession.

I wondered if it really had to be me to tell him or whether for just this once I could find someone else to do it. I even thought about asking Micky to talk to him – they were close in an odd sort of a way. But as we know, Micky was hardly a man of many words and besides, that wouldn't be altogether fair.

I racked my brain trying to come up with an alternative. Surely there were others in his life equally well suited? His father for instance, or maybe the doctor who'd performed his operation. Then there was always that wife of his – although she was an unlikely choice. But whoever I thought of, none of them seemed right. And so it would be me, Albert, good old Albert Hyde, laying it on the line, just like I'd always done, just like I always would. The reason? Because I was reliable and because I could be trusted. And sometimes that's a heavy burden to carry.

As for the paperwork, I got to the point where I'd pick up my pen with the firm intention of signing it off – but I found I couldn't bring myself to do it, so I opened the drawer and dropped both letter and report into Barry's file. There was no rush, I thought – that at least could wait. The decent thing to do was talk to him first.

So for all my attempts at prevarication, where did that leave me? In the firing line with nothing to fall back on but platitudes. Take those away and all I had to offer was the brutal truth.

Barry? I'm sorry son, but you can't ever box again.

Barry

So that's it, it's over, end of story, simple as that, I can't believe it. One minute I'm Barry Mullins, ABA finalist, a man with a future, in with a shout for the National Title – and the next I'm a nobody, a down-and-out, a has-been with nowhere to go. And a has-been that has been nothing in particular either come to that. Yeah, I know what you're going to say. You're going to say at least I never lost a fight – but there was a lot more to come I can tell you, I hadn't really got started. Okay, so I may have pulled a few punches in my time, but when it comes down to it Albert certainly don't. But that's Albert for you so I guess I shouldn't expect no different. Truth still hurts though all the same, no matter how you tell it. So what the hell am I supposed to do now?

I'm a week out of Broomfields, my pot's on good and proper so I figure on getting down to the Boys Club to see what's what. I push open the door, remembering to use my left hand seeing as I'm supposed to be looking after my right, ain't no point in causing more damage. But I always did lead with my left, ha, ha, ha.

Fat Micky's first to catch my eye. But not for long, just enough to say *Hi*, then he glances over at Albert. They exchange a look and it's like they're playing that old double act again.

Here's another nice mess you've gotten me into, Stanley.

Albert comes across, puts an arm around and guides me into his cabin, nice and gentle.

"Take a seat," he says, and nods toward a chair. Then he closes the door behind. Which in my experience ain't always a good sign. Bad things get said when you're sat in an office with the door closed. "So... Barry. How is it?" he says, pointing at the pot. But we both know he's really just being polite – he knows the answer to that one already.

"Alright," I says and shrug my shoulders. "It don't hurt me

none. Another five weeks and the doc reckons I can take it off. I'm just wondering what I can do in the meanwhile. You know, training-wise."

"Ah," says Albert, taking the opportunity. "I'm glad you've raised the subject. I need to talk to you about that."

And then he breaks the news.

You could say I'm shocked. *This ain't what I want to hear.* Though I ain't got no choice but listen. And read. He fishes about in the drawer and hands me a letter he's planning on sending to the Board of Control. I can see the words alright but they float around the page like it ain't sinking in. Me, I ain't got no words, I'm struck dumb. We wait awhile, wondering what to do next. Then he turns toward the window.

"I'm sorry," he says.

Which is just what I need him to say – now I've got something to push against.

"You're sorry," I says. "How do you think I feel?"

Sorry ain't going to buy no champagne and strawberries.

"You've still got a job," he says, like he's trying to make amends.

That's true at least, Ronnie's kept my place open 'til I can get back. But it don't seem like much consolation right now, it'll take more than that to get me through this. I sense things welling up inside. I'm just about starting to choke or sound off, one or the other, when Albert feels it too and cuts in again.

"You'll want to collect your things," he says.

I'm getting the message here – Albert don't like long goodbyes and he wants this done quick and easy. We go down to the locker room.

It's empty. The lads have all got changed and gone into the gym but you can still taste the sweat in the air. There's a towel been dropped on the floor and a pair of trainers left lying on a bench. I find my locker and start taking my kit out and stuff it into my bag. Right at the back, that pair of red gloves Dad bought me are hanging on a hook. There's a saying about old boxers – there comes a time when they have to hang up their gloves. Mine are hung up already. I leave them in there and close the locker door. I guess I won't be needing them no more.

Broken hand, broken dream. What the hell do I tell Tracey now?

Ronnie

So here's the situation. Barry's little accident has got me caught between a rock and a hard place. The bills are piling up and the £10k I might have used to pay them is all banged up in a briefcase currently residing somewhere between here and Walthamstow dog track. I just hope Mac's been looking after it, that's all I can say. Meanwhile, I've still got a garage to run – which is proving a bit of a challenge seeing as the total resources to hand are Terrence bloody Bennett and a one-handed mechanic. You'd think things couldn't get no worse, right? Well you'd be wrong – and here's the reason why.

A week's gone by and I'm wondering what to do about Barry seeing as he won't be back to work until goodness knows when. Like maybe I should call Wally and get him to come in a couple of days a week, only he might not want to talk to me on account of how I got shot of him in the first place. Anyways, I leave a message. Next morning I'm out on the car lot talking to Terry when the phone rings over in the office. I think it must be Wally calling me back, so I walk across to take it but it's some bloke with a voice I recognise but can't put a name to.

"Would it be possible to speak to Mr Bent, please?" he says, all smooth and syrupy like he's got a mouthful of toffee. But I still can't place him.

"And who could I say is calling?" I says, fishing for a name.

"The name's Smithson," he says. "Barclays Bank, Chelmsford Branch."

Then the penny drops. *Oh bugger, now we're in the shit.* Well, you know how I feel about banks – they'll screw you over as soon as look at you.

"Just one moment," I says, "I'll see if he's available." And I put the receiver back down on the desk and take a few deep breaths.

I start wishing I hadn't picked the phone up in the first place but hey, it is what it is and sometimes you've just got to deal with it. I could tell him I ain't there but that's just putting off the inevitable. The bastards'll get you sooner or later, they always do, so I figure I might as well face the music now rather than let things fester. I decide to put on my posh speaking voice and pick up again.

"Hello?" I says. "This is Ronnie Bent. Can I be of assistance?"

"I'd like to make an appointment to see you, Mr Bent," he says.

"Why?" I says. "Are you looking to purchase a second-hand vehicle?"

Which is a real joke because the only place someone the likes of Smithson is going to buy a second-hand car is in one of them shiny steel and glass showrooms on the industrial estate next to the furniture warehouse. And my best guess would be the Mercedes dealer but one way or the other, he's not going to be seen dead on my car lot. And he ain't the type to laugh much neither so all I get is this thin hint of a smile coming down the phone line.

"Very amusing, Mr Bent," he says. "But that's not quite what I had in mind. There's a serious matter I should like to discuss with you."

I'll bet there is.

"Oh please, discuss away," I says, gritting my teeth while I wait for the crunch.

"It would be inappropriate for me to talk about it over the telephone," he says. "We really need to meet face to face. Would you be able to come and see me in my office on Friday? Say two o'clock?"

I think about this for a second. Friday gives me enough time to leave the country.

"Fine with me," I says, and I stick it in my diary.

We get to Friday but I still haven't booked a plane. I tell myself I've been too busy, the flight times are wrong and I wouldn't get a seat next to the window – but the fact is I've got nowhere to go so I might as well keep the appointment. If I've got to bite the bullet, I figure I'd rather do it in Smithson's office than have him come sniffing round the garage. Which he will, trust me, I know the type.

Bloody bankers, I hate the lot of 'em.

Barclays Bank (Chelmsford Branch) is a listed building smack in the centre of town. It's one of them places I chose not to go to. I like to deal local – you know, close to home, head down, low profile, that sort of thing. Plus, there's none of your tubular chairs and stripped pine tables in here, it's all mahogany and walnut, real old woods. So Smithson's office is done out pretty nice, thank you very much. His secretary shows me in and he's sat there behind his polished desk just as I'd imagined he would be, dark suit, real condescending, no nonsense, pens and pencils all set out in a neat line. I take one look at him and I start thinking I should have shoved a book down the back of my trousers. He don't bother getting up.

"Ah, Mr Bent, do come in," he says, waving me into a chair. "Take a seat. Can I get you something? A cup of tea, perhaps?"

A scotch would be nice, only the last thing he's thinking about is my welfare. It's just a convention, like I'm being offered a last cigarette in front of the firing squad. I take the tea though, all the same – in this world you never know when you might get another.

"We can dispense with the formalities," he says. "I'm sure you know why you're here." There's a smarmy look about him which says he must think he's got all the facts. Only I know a few things he don't. So I decide to play the innocent.

"No," I says. "I haven't a clue. Go on, surprise me."

It's a lie of course but I tell it like I mean it.

He pauses a second, then comes back at me with that thin smile of his. It's the same one I got down the phone but you can see it's got a cruel edge to it.

"I've been looking through your books," he says, tapping a pile of papers on the side of the desk. "And the fact of the matter is, Mr Bent, there's a hole in your accounts."

"A hole?" I says. "What do you mean, a hole? Like somebody's poked their finger through one of the pages? Ha, ha, ha!"

Another of my little jokes. But he don't laugh at this one neither and this time I don't even get the thin smile, just a cold sneer.

"Please don't be facetious, Mr Bent," he says, "it doesn't become you. This is not the time for flippancy, it's a very serious matter. I think you know what I mean."

That's the thing about people who've had the benefit of a university education – whenever they get annoyed, they start using long words the rest of us can't understand. Meantime, he's put his glasses on and he's flicking through my papers.

"If we start from your last end-of-year balance and work through the latest set of quarterly returns, it would appear that somewhere in the region of ten thousand pounds is unaccounted for," he says. "Do you have an explanation for this? Or am I mistaken?"

"Oh really?" I says. "Ten thousand pounds? Well, that's the first I've heard of it. I'll have to speak to my accountant. Chances are he's on holiday in Bermuda at the moment, soaking up the sunshine – maybe he took it with him." Only I know for a fact that he ain't, he's holed up in Brentwood suffering from a nasty case of embezzlement.

"Mr Bent," he says, "please don't try my patience. You must understand that the Bank cannot tolerate these kinds of irregularities. Not to mention the fact that it's potentially fraudulent. However, I'm going to give you the benefit of the doubt for the time being and let you have three months to sort it out. Your accountant should have returned by then. You've got ninety days to get your affairs in order, Mr Bent. Do I make myself clear?"

"Oh yeah," I says. "You've made yourself clear. I understand alright."

You bet I understand. Ninety days and they'll shut me down, start proceedings. Give me a decent break and I could get it sorted by Christmas but you try telling Smithson that. Ninety days and it's costing me ten grand. I could have gone drunk and disorderly for a fraction of the price and still got the same amount of time. But ninety days is better than nothing. And right now, nothing's all I've got.

Then a thought occurs.

"While I'm here," I says, "I don't suppose you feel like extending my overdraft by a couple of thousand? I'm a bit strapped at present."

But Smithson ain't in the habit of giving marks for cheek. He looks back at me in disbelief over the top of his glasses, then snaps my books shut with a crack.

"Ninety days," he says. "That's all I'm giving you, Mr Bent. Ninety days!"

Well, at least I tried. And I did manage to screw a cup of tea out of the old bastard. I should be thankful for such small mercies.

So it looks like Ronnie Bent's going to have to make a few economies – maybe I'll have to try living on black bread and water for a while. And if it wasn't there before, that trip to Walthamstow just moved right up my agenda.

Sharon

Well you'll never guess who I bumped into (literally) the other day walking down Chelmsford High Street bold as brass, Tracey Mullins (née Williams as I recall) one-time friend, confidante and general childhood companion. And when was the last time I saw her you have to wonder, it just don't bear thinking about, must be all of twelve months or more since the wedding, my doesn't time fly when you're having fun.

So I've just come out of the Post Office after collecting the child benefit (second Monday of the month), my head's in the clouds thinking about what to get my Martin for his dinner when *BANG!* I run straight into her with the pushchair. Now I'm not saying it was her fault or mine for that matter but somebody wasn't looking where they were going and before you can say Jack Robinson, she's turned round and she's snapping at me like I must be blind or something.

"Can't you be more careful?"

Only it's her that can't see because it's clear she don't have a clue who she's talking to, but I know her straight away.

"Tracey?" I says. "It's me, Sharon."

Which stops her dead in her tracks. And while she's looking at me with her puzzled frown, I can tell she's thinking *Sharon who?* but then the penny drops.

"Sharon?" she says. "Is that really you?"

And I suppose I can understand her asking seeing as I don't look nothing like I used to on account of having had the baby (Amy three months and just starting the bottle) and with another one on the way it's no wonder she don't recognise me straight off, it would have been a miracle if she had. I turn the pushchair round and we pull off to one side to settle down and have a natter. And the first thing Tracey does is fetch a box of smokes out of her handbag and light one up.

"Oh," I says. "And how long has that been going on?"

Because as I remember we hardly ever touched the damn things, tried them once on the way back from the cinema one night, coughed our lungs out and gave it up as a bad job.

"Don't ask," she says. "Want one?"

"No," I says, "I don't, thanks. Especially not when I'm carrying."

And I pat my stomach just to let her know what I mean. So she looks at me and then looks at Amy in the pushchair while she takes it all on board. Me, I'm figuring out which way the breeze is blowing and trying to keep the smoke out of the baby's face.

"So," she says, raising a well-plucked eyebrow. "No need to ask what you've been up to since we last met."

And I suppose there isn't really seeing as it'll soon be sticking out a mile.

"Yes," I says, "Martin and me," (that's my Martin, Tax Inspector, Civil Service Administrative Grade 4), "we decided to start a family straight away, he's been doing so well at work promoted twice in the last twelve months you know." Well it wasn't quite like that but you know how these things happen. Then I remember how long it's been. "You haven't met Martin, have you?"

"No," she says. "He's new on me. I don't believe I've had the pleasure – but you obviously have, Sharon."

Which is a bit cheeky seeing as I'm the one doing all the work here but then she always did have the smartarse lines, did Tracey.

"Well," I says, "we must have met around the time of your wedding. We've got a nice place now up at Bell Meadows. You and Barry ought to come over and see us sometime. We'd come to you only it's difficult what with the baby and everything." And I wave my hand vaguely in the direction of Amy and the pushchair. Only I can tell she don't have a clue what I'm talking about babywise, so I try another tack. "Still in Walton Terrace are you?"

But if there's one question Tracey wants to avoid then I guess that's it so she harks back to my original invitation.

"Well," she says, "Barry and me... We ain't exactly..."

"Ah," I says, pretending I had no idea. "I'd heard he'd had an accident." And that's not all I'd heard either but that's Chelmsford for you, it's a small town, news travels fast and you don't always have to go looking for it especially if someone knows you're interested then it'll come looking for you. I keep my eyes and ears open I can tell you. "Bad one was it?"

"Bad enough," she says. And she drops her half-finished tab on the pavement and grinds it out with a twist of her pointy shoe.

So you won't be getting your big house just yet then.

"Anyways," she says, looking up and down the street. "There's plenty more fish in the sea."

Well I'm not too sure what she means by that but I can take a guess and it's nothing to do with the idea she might be having kippers for tea which reminds me I need to sort something out for my Martin.

"Well," I says. "Got to go, things to do, demands of a family life an' all – you know how it is." Though I'm sure she don't but maybe she'll find out for herself one day. "It's been nice seeing you, we must get together for a coffee sometime."

"Yes," she says. "Nice seeing you too."

But she don't pick up on the coffee thing and next thing you know, she's gone clacking off up the street in her high-heel shoes, never even waved goodbye to Amy.

All of which leaves me wondering. She's a dark horse is that Tracey Mullins (née Williams) she always was and I'm not talking about her hair colour neither. A pound to a penny she's up to something sure as my name's Sharon Miller (née Roberts) and if I'm any judge of character then Barry'd better watch his step.

She can turn can Tracey, there's no trusting her. I should
know she dropped me like a hot potato, she can just as soon drop
another, well you wouldn't put it past her would you?

Ronnie

It don't take much to knock a man down in this life – a throw of the dice, a bit of bad luck – anything can happen and sometimes you just have to take it on the chin. Win some, lose some, that's what I say, it's all a bleeding lottery. But £10k is £10k and that's a whole lot of money in my book so I can't give it up without a fight. Consequentially, I'm back at Walthamstow, seeking salvation in the form of a black briefcase stuffed with readies and last seen in the possession of a tramp in a dirty raincoat. I'm really looking forward to that, ain't I just.

The Wednesday I choose turns out pretty wild – weatherwise it's lashing down and the wipers are on the whole way there. As a result, I'm ten minutes late but the car park's all but empty anyway. Let's be honest with ourselves, there ain't that many people sad enough to want to watch a few half-starved dogs run round a dirt track in the pouring rain. But I haven't come to see the action this time, I've come to limit the damage, so I pay my tenner and take the meal deal just as usual.

And same as before, I pick a table off to one side instead of in front of the windows. If there's any arguing to be done, seems to me I'd rather be doing it in private. I watch a couple of races but I ain't in a gambling mood so I don't lay nothing out. To tell the truth, that last little episode's put me off for the time being. What's the point of chancing a couple of quid when you've probably just lost thousands? I keep an eye out for Mac and they've all but set off in the third when I catch him at the trackside, standing against the rain slanting beneath the lights. I send down for him, but it's as much out of pity as anything else.

The door swings open and he shuffles into the bar. He's all hunched over, dripping wet and with his hands shaking from what looks like an attack of the yips. It's not the first time he's been drenched in that coat neither, there's a tidemark just above his knees, you can see it a mile off. And he still ain't got into the habit of shaving since the last time I saw him, so all in all he's a pretty sorry sight. All of a sudden it don't seem right having him up here – down at the trackside he blends in but now he sticks out like a sore thumb. I get him over to the table real quick so's not to attract attention. A Campari and soda, complete with fancy umbrella, is waiting to smooth the path.

"So how's it going, Mac?" I says by way of an opener.

"Thanks for asking," he says, "but times is 'ard, Mr Bent, very 'ard."

Tell me about it.

He tosses his cocktail off in one, then wipes his mouth on the back of his sleeve, though this time he don't bother licking the stick of his brolly. I guess he must be looking for sympathy so I give him a line to keep him happy.

"I'm real sorry to hear that," I says.

As if I'm concerned, I've enough problems of my own.

Then I notice my briefcase. Or rather, the lack of it seeing as it's conspicuous by its absence. Just as I feared. Plus the fact that Mac's looking shifty. Anyways, we're done with what passes for pleasantries so now I can cut to the chase.

"So, Mac," I says. "What've you done with my money then?"

"Money?" says Mac. "What money?"

As if he don't know what I'm talking about.

"Don't come the innocent with me," I says. "You remember – that little bet you arranged. You know, that thing about Barry Mullins winning the ABA Title an' all."

"Oh, that money," he says, rubbing the side of his nose. Then he gives a sniff like he's suddenly developed a cold and starts clearing his throat. "There's been a bit of a problem."

Don't I know it. The last time I saw it, it came in the form of a three-ton truck.

Meantime, he's faced the other way like he don't want to look me in the eye.

"Problem?" I says. "How can there be a problem? You must

have seen the papers – the boy never got to the starting line. The bet's off, that's obvious. Now I want my stake back."

But Mac's not responding. There's a sinking feeling in the pit of my stomach.

"It ain't my fault, Mr Bent," he says. "They made me give it to them – there was nothing I could do about it, honest. I told you they wasn't nice people."

"I don't care whether they're nice people or not," I says. "Rules is rules – you know that as well as I do. If a dog don't make it to the trap, it's money back and no questions asked."

"Ah," says Mac. "But this is their rules. And by the way, in case you hadn't noticed Barry Mullins ain't a dog, so the argument don't apply. They said for me to give you this instead."

He rummages round in one of his coat pockets and pulls out an envelope. When it first saw the light, it might have been neat and tidy but now it's all crumpled up and grubby. *Maybe it's a cheque,* I'm thinking. *Maybe they banked it and they don't have the cash. That must be the problem.*

I tear it open and pull out the contents. There's no cheque, just a plain white sheet of paper with a few words scrawled on it in a thin spidery hand.

£10k. Lawyers' bet. No win, no fee.

I scrabble round inside to see if there's something else, but there's nothing there.

No win, no fee? What the bloody hell is that supposed to mean? That's no good to me – I need my money and I need it now.

Any day soon and Smithson'll be back on the phone, breathing down my neck. *Ninety days, Mr Bent, ninety days.* And we're thirty gone already.

Bloody Goldstrap. I've been skanked and I'm that cold my teeth have started chattering.

I drive home like a greyhound, tail between my legs.

Sharon

Well it's two weeks to the day since I met Tracey Mullins (née Williams) I know that for a fact seeing as I was two months gone at the time and just missed another period, nearly took the toe off one of her pointy shoes with the pushchair outside the Post Office. Then surprise, surprise, she calls me out of the blue. God knows how she got my number, must have rung my old one and my mother will have given it out – you've got to watch her sometimes, it's all very well being a proud grandparent but she could be a bit more discreet on occasion. Not that I'm complaining mind but you know what I mean. Because she didn't take it at the time (Tracey that is, my number), not when we first met and I suggested coffee, she wasn't interested but for some reason she is now. So we fix things up for a get-together.

Now it's no good her trying to trawl all the way up to my place. The buses aren't great and she's got no transport so I suggest a day when I'm back in town and we can meet in her lunch hour. Besides which, Bell Meadows ain't exactly her cup of tea, she wouldn't be seen dead up there if she could help it. So it's down to me and I'm careful where I choose – I need somewhere to change Amy and it's got to be no smoking so Starbucks is out but I know a nice little place just behind the Town Hall. I arrive there first and get myself settled in, it's a five-minute wait then Tracey shows up with a cig dangling from her lips. She reads the sign on the door, drops her tab on the pavement and crushes it like before, then walks in. At least I got that one right, didn't I.

"Well, this is nice," I says. "Seeing you again an' all."

"Yes," she says. "Ain't it just." And she pulls up a pew and has a good nosy round. "It's a bit different to the old Ice Cream Parlour."

Which is well true as there's no one under twenty in here. I can see she's curious so I tell her how I found the place (it being recommended by Mothercare an' all), so when she says

Who's Mothercare? it don't take long to find out she's about as interested in babies as I am in football. So then we get down to having a good chat, it's mostly the fashion industry and the latest goings-on at Dorothy Perkins. All of which goes right over my head until I remember this was how it used to be, her talking shop and me talking office all before she met Barry and I found Martin, it's hard to believe that's only two years ago, it seems like part of another life, my doesn't the memory play tricks. Me, I'm glad of remembering the old days. It reminds me there's a world out there somewhere beyond the shopping, the cooking and that great big pile of washing in the linen basket. So when she makes her suggestion it's like I'm prepared for it, already primed and waiting, and all she has to do is come up with it and I'll agree. Because I know Tracey of old. She hasn't walked a hundred yards without good reason, especially in her lunch hour and it's not just to meet an old friend, there has to be a purpose and eventually she gets round to it.

"So," she says, fiddling round with the contents of her handbag. "We should do something together. Go out a bit now and then."

I thought I'd suggested that already. Maybe she meant couples. I could ask Mother to babysit. Either that or there's always my sister Karen.

"What?" I says. "You mean the four of us?"

"Christ no," she says and laughs, shaking her head. "Just you and me. Once a week, just like we used to, girls only."

Well it's a good bit more than I'd bargained for that's for certain. She seems to forget I've got responsibilities to attend to and I'm thinking it could be a bit awkward what with one in the pram and one in the oven but I can see it's got its attractions. A girl's got to have a bit of fun sometimes and Martin's forever telling me I should get out more, maybe I won't get another chance.

"Oh," I says, slightly taken aback. "You mean *just* like we used to?"

"Well," she says, giving me a knowing look. "Perhaps not quite like we used to. But pretty much, I guess."

I'm a minute or two taking this on board worrying how Martin might manage. Now I know he's a proper twenty-first-century man, my Martin came complete with his own pair of rubber gloves and an apron, you've only got to show him the iron or the hoover and he does the business – but leave him on his own with a baby for any length of time and you start to wonder whether he'll cope. And I'm just turning the idea over in my head *Shall I, shan't I?* when Amy sets off bawling fit to bring the place down just like she's done every two hours since the day she was born and I'm thinking *Give me a break for Christ's sake just five minutes would be nice never mind a whole evening* and I guess that's what tips me over the edge.

"Oh, go on then," I says. "What the hell, I've got nothing to lose."

And that sets Tracey grinning, you can see she's well made up.

"You'll let Barry know then?" I says.

And yes, I have to admit I'm fishing seeing as he's the only one of us that ain't been mentioned yet. But Tracey's come over all vague, like her mind's wandered off somewhere else already.

"Barry?" she says. "What on earth do I want to tell Barry for?"

And she's asked the question but left the answer hanging, like it's obvious, like I should know without her needing to spell it out.

Barry? Barry can come and go as he pleases. Well, he ain't going to be changing no baby, is he?

Like I say, she's a dark horse, Tracey, always was.

Barry

I come home late on account of Ronnie's been keeping me behind. I've been back at the garage a few days now. It's earlier than intended but Wal told Ronnie he could stick his job where the sun don't shine and things have been piling up so I've been working over to catch up. And what with that bloody pot getting in the way all the time, it takes me twice as long as usual to get any damn thing done.

I wonder what the chances are of getting something decent to eat. Last week Tracey discovered she'd gone up a dress size and there's been nothing in the food department in our house except brown rice and yoghurt ever since. It's driving me up the wall. Sometimes I wake up in the middle of the night dreaming of a nice roast dinner, meat and two veg.

I turn the front-door key and the light's on in the hallway. The one on the landing's on too so I know she must be home somewhere. There's no light on in the kitchen though and the oven's stone cold – so if there was anything hot in it to start with it ain't hot now that's for sure. I decide not to bother looking.

I figure she must be watching TV so I stick my head round into the front room. It's empty. At the top of the stairs I catch a breath of warm steam and a whiff of that scented soap she uses, so I start thinking she must be in the bath. Turns out she's in the bedroom sat in front of the dressing table. She's got a red dress on, brand new, cut low at the back, and she's busy fixing up a pair of silver earrings.

"You're looking nice," I says. "What you doing?"

"What does it look as though I'm doing?" she bites back.

"Looks as though you're going out," I says.

"Well that's probably what I'm doing then," she says.

A bell rings somewhere and it feels like the end of round one. I guess I should go take a rest so I sit on the edge of the bed for my thirty seconds. I start wondering whether I'm missing something here – like maybe we were supposed to be going out somewhere together and she's pissed off because I've forgotten. But I don't want her to know that and I figure on trying to find out. So then I'm back up and at it again.

"So, er... Where you going then?"

"We just discussed that," she says. "I'm going out."

"Okay," I says, breathing deep. "Anywhere nice?"

"No," she says, "I'm going somewhere crap so I can sit and be miserable all night. What do you think?"

The bell sounds again and it's the end of round two. I'm seriously behind on points here and this time I wander round with my hands in my pockets for my thirty seconds. If I'm supposed to go with her, I reckon she'd have told me by now so my guess is I'm staying at home. But I still don't give up on it that easy.

"Need some company?" I says, polite as I can so's not to sound pushy.

"Nope," she says. "It's all arranged. You remember Sharon? We're off out on a hen party."

"I see," I says. "So, um... What time will you be back?"

"When I've finished being out."

She's done with sparring now and she lands the blow clean and straight off instead. As for me, I don't have no counter. Trouble is, when it comes to fighting at home, I lead with my chin every bloody time and I just stand there waiting to be hit. It's time I threw in the towel so I decide to go back downstairs and stick the TV on. There's some silly game show or another with big prizes but I'm not really watching what's happening.

Sometimes I feel as though I should give her a really good slap and tell her not to be so bloody stupid. But she knows I'm not going to do that, never have and never will. It don't stop me from feeling like it though. Okay, so she's started a diet and wants to go off on a night out with Sharon. So what? Nothing wrong with that. She may have put on a couple of pounds (haven't we all) but she still looks as good to me as the day I met her – that's one thing that hasn't changed.

So what did you expect me to feel? She's still my wife, for Christ's sake.

Terry

Now Friday evenings in The Bell and The Lion ain't exactly been a ball of fun in recent weeks so I decide on making a change. Plus the fact that I'm in funds. I've saved up the contents of them little brown envelopes so I've got quite a stash and I figure on having a good night out. It's about time Terry Bennett went upmarket now he's got something behind him and can afford to splash out a bit. Let's face it, The Golden Lion is past its sell-by date, it's all Old Spice and brown ale, when what the modern man wants is Givenchy and a Bacardi Breezer. So bugger it, I says, let's do something glitzy, like a cocktail bar and a nightclub and give ourselves a treat. I mention it to Ronnie but he's still down in the dumps about something or other.

First things first, I need to get kitted up. I buy a nice Italian suit (brown, pinstripe) and a decent looking shirt to go with it. I get a fashionable pair of shoes (nothing practical, I wear them all day long) so when I put the job lot on and stand in front of the mirror, I feel like a million dollars. Ronnie Bent ain't the only bloke around here knows how to dress up, we can all do it if we try.

I call in at The Lion on my way out just to say hello and pick up any messages. I walk up to the bar and Bernie does a double take, it's like he don't know me from Adam.

"Bloody hell," he says. "What's all this? Got a wedding to go to, have we?"

"Less of that," I says. "Let's have a bit of respect, if you don't mind." And I make a show of pulling out my shirt cuffs and straightening up my collar. There's no tie because where I'm headed it's going to be hot, hot, hot. "I thought I'd treat myself to a night on the town."

"Looks like it," says Bernie. "And the very best of luck. You should take care wearing that lot – it's so sharp you might cut yourself."

I hit The Lizard Lounge around nine-thirty. It's just what I'd expected – bright lights, dark corners, glass tables with steel legs, real noisy and packed with shiny people. First up I get a drink, then look round for somebody I know – there's bound to be a few of the lads out and about on a Friday night. So I'm up at the bar, I've got my wallet open and I'm waving a ten-pound note around in the hopes of catching the bar keep's attention, when I realise I've caught somebody else's. She's stood right next to me, five foot five, black hair, platform heels and a pair of legs that go all the way up to the top. I know that because the little red dress she's wearing is barely covering what it's supposed to, if you know what I mean. And every time I move the tenner her eyes follow it like she's hypnotised, so I play with it a minute while I dance it up and down to keep her dangling. Then I twig who it is and I put the note back in the stash with the rest.

"Well, well," I says. "If it ain't Tracey Mullins."

"Well, well," she says. "You're spot on there and it ain't – that's a name I've given up using. It's back to Tracey Williams these days if you don't mind."

I don't mind at all and when I look at her (third finger, left hand) I can see there's no ring either. Well if that ain't a clue, or a hint, or both, then I don't know what is. So that sets me wondering what the hell is going on. Meantime, her head's cocked to one side and she's giving me the once over.

"Don't tell me," she says. "But ain't you from Ronnie Bent's garage?"

"I might be," I says. "So what? A man needs a job of some description."

"Spot on again," she says. "Thing is though, it's got to be the right job."

"Has it now?" I says, wondering what she's on about. "And the name's Terry, by the way. But now we're acquainted, you can call me Tel."

"Oh I can, can I?" she says. "Well, that's damn decent of you."

"Yes," I says. "Ain't it just. So, er... You on your own then?"

And I have a good scout round to see if she's got company.

"Not exactly," she says, and she waves a hand in the direction of what I assume must be her friend, stood in the corner with her finger in one ear and a mobile phone in the other, engaged in what looks like hot debate. "Sharon's got a bit of a domestic on at the minute."

"Oh right," I says. And I nod, wisely, as if I understand. Which I don't.

Meanwhile, Tracey's clocked my stash and she can't take her eyes off it. It's like a moth flitting round a candle. But if that's what floats her boat, then it's okay with me. I can play that game as long as you like.

"Looks as though you could afford to buy a girl a drink," she says.

"I could afford to buy a girl a lot of drinks," I says.

"Well that all depends on whether a girl fancies drinking them," she says. "But now you're here, you can get me one to start with."

I don't see the point in fannying around so I pull out a fifty and get served straight away.

"A bottle of champagne please," I says. "Best in the house."

And as soon as I say it, her eyes light up and I know I've pressed the right button. It's like playing the fruit machine down at The Bell, only now I've pulled three cherries and hit the jackpot. The bubbly arrives, I pour out and we chink glasses.

"Cheers," I says, taking a sip.

"Cheers," she says. "Down the hatch."

And before you know it, hers is gone and I'm pouring out another. But that's just the start of it – we're in for the long haul and I don't get home 'til 3am. Next morning I've got a head like a block of concrete, my mouth feels like the bottom of a parrot's cage and her mobile phone number's written on the back of my business card.

Something tells me I've pulled.

Sharon

She's done it again, buggered off and left me has Tracey Mullins (née Williams) or whatever she calls herself these days I don't know, the only thing I can be sure of is my name's Miller and I'm sticking to it, it's a case of having to I suppose. Or maybe this time it was my fault what with having to rush off home in the middle of it all on account of my Martin getting slightly overwhelmed, poor man. Either way I'm the one that gets left holding the baby – literally speaking in my case.

We meet up at Barnaby's at half past seven. Which in my view ain't at all unreasonable seeing as Martin don't get in 'til half six and that gives him an hour to have his tea and get prepared. I leave him with two feeds already made up and half a dozen nappies just in case so by the time I find a bus and get down there, Tracey's already waiting and checking her watch she don't cut you no slack whatever does that one, we say Hi! and go straight to the ladies to tidy ourselves up.

Well, I'm just coming out of my cubicle and there's Tracey stood at one of the sinks with her hands all covered in soap pulling her wedding ring off her finger. I'm completely shocked.

"What on earth are you doing?" I says.

"What does it look as though I'm doing?" she says. "I'm not going out on the town with this on."

"Why ever not?" I says.

"Why do you think?" she says, looking at me as if I'm stupid.

"I'll tell you what I think," I says. "You're a married woman and you're denying the vows you made in the name of our Lord, that's what you're doing and it's blasphemy." I know this for a fact, my Martin being a regular churchgoer an' all.

"Ooh," she says, twisting a reddened lip. "We've gotten very self-righteous all of a sudden, haven't we? I suppose you've forgotten the time Jamie Jones had his hand up your skirt in the graveyard at the back of St Wilfred's. How blasphemous was that?"

"Ah," I says, blushing to the roots. "That was before I saw the light."

"And that ain't all you saw that night either," says Tracey. "Well, not according to Jamie Jones it ain't, so don't you go giving me no lectures."

There's no comeback on that one so I decide to leave it alone.

We have a couple at Barnaby's to start with then trawl off up the High Street on our usual run. I can tell Tracey's wanting to hit it pretty hard so I'm trying to slow things down and take it easy. I'm well out of practice and I've no intention of making a spectacle of myself and going home in a taxi even remotely trolleyed, so I'm backing off and making every other round a soft one but Tracey's not interested in that. I'll give her credit though, she always could hold her drink could that one, she's seen me well under the table on more than one occasion in the past I don't mind telling you.

So by the time we get to The Lizard Lounge Tracey's fairly steaming and I'm dragging along behind, we're just inside the door and my mobile goes off, it's Martin, he's got a problem and can I come home and help. Well it's that loud in there I can hardly hear a word he's saying, Tracey's shot straight off to the bar and I'm shouting *Well just see if you can get her to go down for the moment, leave the mess and we'll clear that up later* and when I turn round, she's hooked up with that Terry Bennett from the garage.

Now that's a surprise. Like I said before I always had her figured for something romantic, a pop star or a footballer would have been fine even the boxer was okay but a used-car salesman just ain't the type you'd expect to find on Tracey's menu. I thought she had grander plans than that, maybe he's got a nice motor or maybe she knows something the rest of us don't. Anyways, before you can so much as blink an eyelid they're sailing off into the sunset on a sea of champagne and I'm on my way home to contemplate the scene of domestic bliss that now awaits.

I can't blame Martin. I did rather land it on him unexpected but he's got himself into a right pickle and by the time we get cleaned up and into bed it's gone twelve. I'm just dozing off when he fancies rolling over under my side of the blanket.

"Hold on," I says. "Hasn't there been enough excitement for one night already? It may be alright now but weren't you going to get yourself sorted out and have the snip before we started that game again, let's make sure you get your tap turned off before you cause any more damage."

Men? They're all the same.

Barry

Next thing you know Ronnie does the dirty on me and takes the car away. Yes, *THAT CAR*, the Mini Cooper S, the one I sweated blood over, the one that wasn't worth a light when I got it, the one I drove from here to God knows where, the one that's still got my name on the side, the one he said was mine. I can't believe it.

"You must be joking," I says.

We're stood in his office with the door wide open. We should really keep this private but I can't bring myself to shut it or there won't be room enough for him, me and the way I feel. Plus I don't much care who knows it.

"Nah," he says. "I ain't joking. You don't need that no more."

"What do you mean?" I says. "*You don't need that no more.*"

"Well," he says. "Now that the boxing finished an' all."

Kick a bloke when he's down why don't you.

"I still need to get from A to B," I says. "And in case you hadn't noticed, A to B is pretty much the same as it was before. How d'you expect me to get to work for Christ's sake?"

"You'll have to catch a bus," he says. "Anyways, that's your problem, not mine." Then he goes quiet for a minute and gives me that "I'm sucking a lemon" face. "To tell you the truth, it's getting to be a bit of an embarrassment. I mean, *BARRY MULLINS – SPONSORED BY BIG RONNIE'S*? Trouble is, Barry Mullins don't cut it no more. So you have to admit that don't exactly work too well."

"Worked well enough when it suited you," I says. Though I suppose he does have a point. "Besides," I says, "it's mine – you gave it me."

"Ah," he says. "That's where you're wrong. If you look close, I think you'll find I only lent it. Have you got the logbook?"

"You know bloody well I haven't," I says. "Seeing as it's still sat in your drawer."

"Well there you are then," he says. "Fact is, I'm having it back and that's the end of it. I've got a business to run. Or had you forgotten about that while you was busy swanning round the East of England? Somebody's got to keep things going." Then he looks at his watch like he's got some big meeting to go to and I'm holding him up. "I expect you've got work to do," he says. "Don't let me stand in your way."

So this is what I get after all I've done for him. I ain't worth nothing to him anymore, he's had all he can get out of me. Except for my labour that is, the sweat of my brow, and that comes cheap. *Broken hand, broken nails*, that's what I say. And there's not much to show for them now either.

I head back to where I belong, in the workshop and with something I can understand – oil, dirt and three ton of motorised metal.

The upshot of it is I'm having to walk home. It's three mile all told and no lift so I'm back late and Tracey's already gone out. Though it wouldn't make no difference if I came home early, she'd still go out just the same.

There's no lights on this time and the house is cold and empty. I pick up a takeaway at the Chinese on the corner and I sit in the kitchen to eat it. Chicken chow mein, king prawn curry and boiled rice. I could do with a beer to go with it but there's none in the fridge and I can't be bothered to go out again and fetch one. When I was boxing, I had steak twice a week. Now I can't afford it. To tell the truth, I ain't a fan of junk food neither – but then I never was much of a cook.

I finish eating and go upstairs. I'm wrong about the lights and there's one on over her dressing table but you can't see it from the road outside. She must have left in a hurry – the table top's a mess, there's odds and ends of makeup all over the shop and she's tipped her jewellery box out in a heap.

The wardrobe door's still open so I start looking through her dresses to see if I can tell which one she's gone out in. That's never an easy decision for a woman, especially one like Tracey, she must have more than twenty to choose from. There's every size, shape and colour, from that red one with the low cut back right through to the black piece I bought her to wear on ABA finals night. She always did like to dress well. I should know, I've paid for most of it, nearly every penny, it's money I've earnt with my own hands, one way or another.

Then it gets to me, looking at her clothes and remembering how we used to be, and suddenly I'm all boiling up inside. I struggle to keep a lid on it and I dig whatever nails I've got left into my palms until my knuckles are white – though it ain't no good and I've got to let it out. But the only thing I can smack right now is the wardrobe door and I've still got that pot on my big right hand. I give it three of my best and listen to the sound of splintering wood – *bitch, bitch, bitch.*

Terry

So Tracey Williams and me, we start getting it together so to speak – Friday nights, Saturday nights and in particular, Wednesday afternoons. I say goodbye to Bernie and on Friday nights I don't go down The Bell and The Lion no more. Friday's pay day so we do the bars and the clubs, while on Saturdays we might go somewhere quiet to avoid the crowds. And Wednesday afternoons? Well put it this way, seeing as it's her day off, Wednesday afternoons we're round at hers for a bit of relaxation and domestic entertainment. And why ever not? I hear you ask. After all, Tracey's a girl with a healthy set of needs, wants and desires, and in that respect we're well suited, I've a few of them myself. So when you look at it that way, it's only natural ain't it?

Now you might think different, but I ain't as daft as Ronnie makes me out. A one-nighter – fine. A few days on the trot, okay – but week in, week out, no matter what and I'm thinking *So what's the attraction?* Well it ain't the way I look, that's for sure. I'd be the first to admit I'm no Robert Redford though a friend told me once I bore a passing resemblance to Bruce Willis – but we'd both had a few and it was dark at the time. And I ain't exactly Albert Einstein either so there has to be something else as keeps me in the frame. But let's not beat about the bush, it's obvious, ain't it? It's got to be the money, the moulah, the cash, the green folding stuff. Because like they say in the song, it's money makes the world go around and it certainly makes Tracey's spin, she just can't get enough of it. Talk about spend, spend, spend, I reckon she could make Viv Nicholson blush – some nights I'm hard pushed keeping up. It's a good job I work Saturdays and we don't go shopping together else my tank would be drained dry. No wonder Barry works the hours he does, the bills in his house must be a challenge.

Talk of the devil but I'm looking to keep things quiet for the time being. Broken hand or not, Barry could still be a problem, so

I ain't taking no risks and Tracey and me, we don't go nowhere that's going to cause trouble. I ain't looking to rub his nose in it – well, not in public anyway, in private on a Wednesday afternoon'll do fine for me, I ain't fussy. He can't do nothing now anyway – like I say, he's finished – but all the same it's just as well he don't catch on. And there's times I get to thinking...

"You've gone quiet," says Tracey.

Which I have, it's true. But then I'm a bloke and it goes with the territory. Especially at her place after you know what and I'm lying there with my head on his pillow and the guilt thing going through my head.

"I was just wondering," I says.

"You was just wondering what?" she says.

"About Barry," I says. "Whether he suspects. It's been on my mind a bit of late."

"Don't be silly," she says. "Of course he don't, I make sure of that. Anyways, he wouldn't see it if it was right under his nose. To tell the truth, I don't see much of him these days – he keeps himself to himself. And he certainly don't come in here without my say so."

"So where does he sleep then?" I says. Because I can't help being curious.

"In the spare room. Has done for weeks."

"Really?" I says. "So you two don't..."

"You must be joking," she says. Then she looks at me, all playful. "Can't you tell?"

But I ain't ready for that again yet so I don't make no move.

"Besides," she says, "I know Barry and the last thing he'll do is go back to his parents – he's far too bloody proud. Frankly, it's just as well because I couldn't afford to keep this place up on my own and there's no way I'm going back to Campion Street in a million years. So we're stuck with it I'm afraid. Unless you..."

"Out of the question," I says. "You know my position. There's not a hope in hell of that happening. Not with my commitments."

"No," she says. "I didn't think there was."

"So we're safe then," I says.

"Absolutely," she says.

I put my head back down on the pillow and relax. So if that's how she wants to play it, I reckon I'll keep her dangling for as long as. As long as what? you might ask.

As long as Barry don't find out.

Barry

I knew there was something wrong the minute Terry started coming into the workshop. That's my patch, always has been, and he knows it. He don't set foot unless he's invited – which up until now he hasn't been.

It's a Wednesday morning and he wanders in from the car lot like he's got all the time in the world. His shoulders are all hunched up, he's cupped his hands together and he's blowing into them like as if it was cold. Only it ain't, the sharp snap finished a week or so back and I ain't had the heater on in the workshop for the best part of ten days. He sidles in, looks at me out the corner of one eye, then shoves his hands in his pockets and starts fiddling with a set of keys.

"So what you up to, Baz?" he says.

Now that's a bloody silly question if ever I heard one.

"Fixing cars," I says. "That's what I do – in case you hadn't noticed."

"Yeah, yeah, I realise that," he says. "But, um… Busy, are you? Got plenty of work on?"

It just so happens that I have. I'm still playing catch up with the backlog, a big estate's come in with faulty transmission and there's three MOTs booked between now and the end of the week.

"Enough," I says. "It'll keep me out of trouble for a couple of days. How's things with you?"

"Pretty dire," he says. "Often is this time of year. To tell the truth, it's dead out there, mate. It's as dead as a doornail." He may be right about the motor trade though when we got to be mates is open to question. "Had a woman in yesterday," he goes on, "wanted a people carrier. But we've nothing on the lot under five grand so I'd no chance."

Which ain't of any interest to me. And I'm beginning to wonder if he's simply come in for a chat or whether he's going to ask for a favour when he finally gets round to the point.

"Anyways," he says, "Ronnie's given me the afternoon off."

"That's nice," I says. "Trouble is, you won't know what to do with yourself."

"Ah, well that's where you're wrong," he says. "Fact is, my mother ain't too well. I've got her booked into a home in Tiptree so I'm off up there for a visit. All come on a bit sudden, it has."

It must have done because it's the first I know about it.

"I'm real sorry to hear that," I says. "You should look after your mother. You won't get another one."

"I intend to," he says. "So that's where I'll be. This afternoon. In case you was wondering."

Which I wasn't, but still.

"Alright then," I says. "Have a nice day. And give her my regards."

But suddenly he's gone. And I'm left thinking *What the hell was all that about?*

Then Terry takes another afternoon off. Then another and another and pretty soon it's regular, once a week, always a Wednesday, and I start thinking either his mother must be in a really bad way or Terry's just acquired a brand-new sense of responsibility. Because he ain't never had one before, not Terry. He don't exactly strike me as the most responsible person in the world to start with and even then, I don't recall looking after his mother being very high up on his list of priorities.

The weird thing is, he comes and tells me about it every time. It's always the same routine. I'll be in the workshop underneath some vehicle or another, up to my elbows in muck and bullets, when the side door creaks open and there's the sound of his big size nines pattering across my floor.

"Baz?" he says.

"Yes, Tel," I reply, and I haul myself out to talk.

"I thought I'd best let you know. I'm off. To Tiptree. To see my mother."

"Yes, Tel," I says. "Give her my best wishes. I hope she makes a swift recovery."

"Cheers, mate, I will do." Then, "Baz?"

"Yes, Tel."

"You busy?"

"Yes Tel, I'm always busy."

That's true if nothing else – right now I can hardly get out of the place.

"So that's alright then," he says. And he buggers off again.

Only he ain't going to see his mother, I know that for a fact. Not unless they've moved her nursing home fifteen mile up the road he ain't. Because the one time I don't crawl back under, I stand at the workshop window and watch him drive out the front gate and turn left. And you can't get to Tiptree turning left. I should know. I turn left every day. It's the way you get to my house.

Then it starts niggling me and I have to find out what's going on. There's a part of me says I don't want to know, because whatever it is, it's going to hurt. Then there's the other part of me, the part that tells me to be a man and face up to it because whatever else happens you're going to find out sooner or later so you might as well do it now. It's like the feeling I got walking down the corridor to a fight, all gloved up and ready to go. My stomach's churning and it keeps telling me *You'll get hit, you'll get hit.* But my head's saying *Go on son, you can do it, you're better than he is, it's what you were born to.* And my heart? Well that's pounding so fast I can't even tell what it's saying. Then the red mist comes down and wipes everything else away.

I pick a Wednesday when Dad's off work and I get to borrow his car. I let Terry go through his routine just as normal and half an hour after he's gone, I stick my head round the office door. Ronnie's sat there with his feet up on the desk reading the paper. My guess is he's on the racing pages because he don't even bother looking up.

"Ronnie," I says. "I've got a tooth giving me gyp. I'm going to the dentist and get it fixed."

"Yeah, yeah," he says. "Whatever. A man's got to do what a man's got to do."

He certainly has, but I don't need the likes of Ronnie Bent to tell me that. I lock up the workshop, drive out the front gate and turn left towards mine.

I come in at the top end of the street so I'm on the other side of the road from my house. My palms start sweating and I have to get a grip on the wheel. I slow to a crawl and park fifty yards off, then force myself to look up.

Yup, his motor's there alright, slap-bang outside my front door. And my first thought is *How stupid is that? What kind of a dickhead would leave it there?* Then I remember who I'm talking about – Terence Bennett, Terry, Tel, a bloke who hasn't even got the gumption to park the evidence round the corner somewhere and walk. So that just tells me where his brain's located right at the moment i.e. somewhere down the front of his trousers.

I look at the house. The upstairs curtains are drawn and there's a dull light on behind them. It's half past two in the afternoon, it's broad daylight and they need a light on. What the hell are they looking at that they need a light on, for Christ's sake?

I don't want to think about it.

I try and turn my mind off.

But my arms are shaking and I've got hold of the wheel that tight that my knuckles are going white. And I'm thinking *Don't let go of the wheel, don't let go or you'll do something you'll regret. Please God don't let him come out now, please don't let him come out, if he comes out now, I'll kill the bastard I swear to God I'll kill him.*

Part Six

Counterpunch

Ronnie

So here's the thing. Remember me telling you how lucky I was? And how my mother kept reminding me of it when I was a kid? Well right now (as they say in the song), if it wasn't for bad luck, I wouldn't have no luck at all.

Goldstrap's got my ten large (God knows if I'll ever see that again), Barry's out of commission and I've got Smithson breathing down my neck all the time about my bloody accounts. Well not so much breathing down my neck as more bleating in my ear as there's hardly a day goes by but what he ain't on the phone wittering on at me about one damn thing or another. *How are sales looking this month, Mr Bent?* Answer? Crap. *When you've got a moment, do you think you could bring me up to date with your latest cashflow position?* Not if I can help it. And best of all, *Could you let me know the moment your accountant gets back from Bermuda?* Now that's a good 'un, that is, what with me never thinking he'd take it serious and my accountant (if he is one, which I have every reason to doubt) residing closer to Clacton than he does to the Caribbean. Plus there's the small matter of that embezzlement case that comes to court next week. Maybe I'll have to tell Smithson he's decided to emigrate – permanent.

Most of which I can handle. It's all part of a normal day's work in the motor trade, along with *You promised me a rebate on my Road Fund Licence* and *That pair of tyres you said would last for years wore down to the canvas inside six weeks.* You know the sort of thing I mean? Standard stuff. It's mention of Her Britannic Majesty's Revenue and Customs as makes my nerves jangle. The last thing I need is for them to come poking round, they're bound to find skeletons in cupboards where I didn't even know I had cupboards. So please spare me that or we'll all be down the drain quicker than you can say VAT.

Though you can't tell me I haven't made an effort. I've tightened up in just about every place you can tighten up –

there's no fancy soap in my bathroom anymore and if we had any pips they'd be squeaking. Barry squawked, that's for sure, when I took that car back off him. But it had to go, no question about it. I phoned around a few of my professional acquaintances and sold it as a collector's piece – got £5k for it in the end and that's what's kept us going these last few weeks. And seeing as I sold it myself, I didn't have to pay Terry no commission – that's how hard I'm trying.

Talk of the devil and it's times like these I could use a good salesman. And I know what you're going to say, Terry's all of that, I don't have to be told, but just at the moment he seems to have switched off again. Maybe that burst of effort earlier on took it out of him as it looks to me like his head's somewhere else. And come Wednesday afternoons, so's the rest of him because he's forever telling me he needs to take them off on account of some regular appointment he has to keep.

"So what's this all about?" I says.

"Ah," he says, "it's my mother." And he starts hopping about from one foot to the other like he does when he's telling porkies.

"I thought your mother was dead," I says.

"She is," he says. "Or was... As good as... Got that demented thing... I've got her parked up in a nursing home near Tiptree. Need to visit her once a week."

"Really?" I says. "I seem to recall you had an afternoon off a couple of years back to go to her funeral."

"Um... No," he says. "That was the hospital. Fell down the stairs and broke her hip. Never properly recovered."

"Well okay," I says. "It's up to you." The last thing I want to do is come between a bloke and his mother when she needs him. That's the thing about mothers – I've got one myself somewhere.

So on Wednesday afternoons it just leaves me and Barry. And right now, he's a bit of a puzzle. One minute he's off work and the next he's here doing all the hours God made. Then on this particular Wednesday, he's gone to the dentist and comes back looking all hot and bothered. Now I hate dentists almost as much as I hate bankers though I can usually cope with them if I put my mind to it. But that tooth of his must have been a real bugger as he storms in and goes straight past me and into the workshop without so much as a howdy-do. The door bangs shut behind him and I get the message it don't want opening, so I get back to reading the paper.

Half an hour later he's upped sticks and left so when I come to close up, I have a good look round the workshop just to make sure it's okay. And there it is, thrown in the skip, his pot, sliced through from top to bottom and a pair of bolt-cutters from his toolbox left lying out on the bench. Which is real strange seeing as he's normally such a tidy bloke. Next thing you know, I get word he's been seen at the gym. So there's something going on, I can feel it my water. But just exactly what, as yet I haven't a clue.

Barry

It's dark and I can hardly read the sign in the dim glow of the lamplight. But there it is – *CHELMSFORD CITY BOYS CLUB* – just as it was all those years ago. The paint's peeling off the windowsill and that crack's still there in the same pane of glass. Don't look to me like anything's changed much at all.

I push the door open from the street and it's like going back to another life. Grey lino, green walls, it all comes flooding back. I don't have to look too far for Albert neither. He's stood in the corridor with his back to me, talking to some young hopeful who's just got gloved up and at first he don't see me. Then the street door bangs shut and he turns round and I think his jaw's going to fall off. It takes him a second or two but there's no way he's forgotten.

"Well bugger me," he says. "Look what the wind's blown in. If it isn't Mr Barry bloody Mullins. Didn't think we'd be seeing you again so soon. How the hell are you?"

"I'm alright," I says, and I give him a respectful nod. "And how the hell are *you*? And a bit less of the 'bloody' if you don't mind, you make it sound like I'm some kind of butcher."

"You was, mate, you was." He pauses, like he's taking it all in. "You're a sight for sore eyes, you are, Barry, and no mistake. Let's have a look at you." He puts his hands on my shoulders, then runs them down my arms, gauging the condition I'm in. "Hmm... You could do with beefing up. You've let yourself go a bit over the last few weeks. What about these?" He takes me by the wrists and turns them over to look at the state of my hands. The one's dirty black, oiled and bloodied while the other's blanched white where it's just come out of the pot. He winces.

"Jesus Christ. What the hell have you been doing?"

"Beating up the underside of a motor vehicle," I says. "Only work I can get."

"And this?" He taps gently on my right hand, the white one,

the one that got mashed. I've cleaned it up as best I can but you can still see the marks where the plaster's been.

I shrug my shoulders.

"Aches a bit from time to time. Other than that, it's fine," I says. I flex my fingers to show him they're still working. My hand ain't perfect but what the hell do you expect when two hundredweight of car jack drops on it and it gets all busted up? There's a minute's silence while we both mourn the passing of my boxing career. Then Albert tries a change of tack.

"So how's Tracey?"

Maybe he thinks he's being polite – he ain't to know. But I can't lie, even if I try.

"Don't go there," I says. "Things ain't turned out too well to tell the truth. Maybe it was my fault, maybe it was an accident waiting to happen."

"And has it happened?" he asks, sounding concerned.

"Pretty much," I says.

"I'm sorry," he says.

I shrug my shoulders again and there's another minute's silence. Albert breaks it for the second time.

"Well I'm sure you didn't come down here just to say hello," he says. "What can I do you for?" It's like he's got a gym to run, there's no time to chew the fat.

"I was thinking about getting into shape," I says. "I could do with working out."

"You're right there," he says. "You certainly could. That's something I can help you with at least." He's more confident now he's on home ground. "Besides, Micky's getting on a bit – it'd be good to have someone like you around. You could teach some of these young kids a thing or two. Bloody tearaways most of 'em, they do my head in. Come on, we'll go and get you set up."

We walk down toward the changing rooms. He opens the door and shows me in.

"Feel free," he says.

I step through and it's as though I've gone back seven years – it's the same as the day I arrived. I breathe deep and there's that old familiar smell of stale sweat and sawdust. Someone's singing in the shower and round the corner there's the sound of a locker clanging shut.

It feels like I've come home.

Terry

There's a few weeks gone by since I hooked up with Tracey Williams and she starts asking me awkward questions, like *How much money have you really got and where does it all come from?* Because she ain't stupid, not Tracey, her head's screwed on facing forward and I suppose you can understand her wondering, what with me being a second-hand car salesman an' all with no other means of support. So I guess I should have been prepared. But to tell the truth I ain't really blessed in the thinking department anyway and when she drops it on me, it's a bit of a bombshell.

So what the hell am I supposed to say? *Oh, I forgot to tell you. But now you're asking, I got paid off by an East End mob for making sure your husband got crippled. Which in case you didn't know it, is what got us into this position in the first place.* Somehow, I don't think so. And even if I did, she ain't going to believe me. You'd think a woman in her position would be grateful for the attention and happy to get on with it. What with vodka and orange at five pound a double, she's an expensive habit – not to mention the smokes, the perfume and the nights out. But oh no, she's got to start prying and poking her big Mary Rose in right where it ain't wanted.

It's a Wednesday afternoon at her place and we've just finished our usual piece of business, so Tracey's already lit up a smoke and she's lying back taking a big draw. Me, I'm fumbling for my watch on the bedside table trying to see what time it is and wondering how long I've got before you know who returns. Forget the idea he's out of it these days, I still reckon it's best not to be around at the same time he is. He could still do some damage with that pot, never mind anything else – I've seen the mess he made of that wardrobe.

Anyways, my trusty timepiece says it's early and there's no need to rush, so I slide out of bed and off to the bathroom to get tidied up. And I guess that's when things go wayward on me and one of Joe Black's little brown envelopes slips off the table or out of the back pocket of my trousers and winds up on the deck. Because when I get back from the bathroom, there she is leaning over my side of the bed and picking it up. And here I am wearing nothing but a towel to cover my embarrassment.

"So what's this then?" she says.

"What's what?" I says.

"This," she says, waving it at me like it's the winning ticket in the lottery.

"It's an envelope," I says, trying to play for time.

"I can see that," she says. "But what was in it?"

Now my mind's been elsewhere the last half-hour as you can imagine, and I ain't quite with it yet. So, good plan or not, I say the first thing that comes into my head.

"It looks like a wage packet," I says.

"Oh it does, does it?" she says. "I thought you told me you was monthly paid and your money went straight into the bank."

Which I did, mostly as a matter of convenience so's she can't always get her hands on it. But she's sharper than a stropped razor is Tracey, especially when it's anything to do with finance.

"Ah," I says, having to think on my feet. Which ain't altogether easy considering I've no socks on and I'm stood on some other bloke's bedroom carpet. I've not much else on either and that towel's beginning to slide. "It does," I says. "But that's a bit extra. On the side, you might say."

"Oh," she says, sniggering. "And I thought I was your bit on the side, ha, ha, ha!" She has a good laugh and then gets back to the serious stuff. "So is that where you get your money then? Doing odd jobs for Ronnie Bent? It's a funny way of going about things if you ask me."

"Not exactly," I says.

Although on reflection, it might have been easier to admit to. "What then?"

And because I ain't thinking straight and I need to make up

something quick, I tell her much the same thing as I told Ronnie.

"It's me Mum," I says. "She's worth a few bob, is Mother. But she ain't too well to be honest. Losing her marbles, if you know what I mean. I've got her tucked away in a home near Tiptree. There'll be a bit to come when she goes. But in the meanwhile, she lets me have something on account. Carer's allowance, you could call it."

Now you know as well as I do that's a fib. But if you're going to tell one, you may as well make it a whopper, that's what I say. And now it's out there and I'm listening to it, I'm happy with it. *Yes,* I'm thinking, *I can live with that. Give me long enough and I could even believe it myself.*

"Oh," she says. "That's a shame, what with her being your mother an' all." And then she pauses, just long enough to make it sound respectful. But you can tell what's on her mind. *So how long do we have to wait?* "Serious, is it?"

"'Fraid so," I says. "It's very serious, could even be terminal. But how long she's got, it's difficult to say. Could be next week, could be next month, could be next year – you just can't tell. There could even be a message when I get home."

Which, incidentally, is precisely where I should be heading.

"I see…" she says, her grey cells working overtime. Then she cuts straight to the chase. "So how much will she be worth, your mother, when she goes?"

I suck in air like it's a tough one – but I've had time to see it coming.

"Ooh, it's hard to say," I says. "Two hundred thou'? Might even be a quarter of a mill." I shrug my shoulders. "Nobody really knows."

Which is all bollocks seeing as my mother died three year ago and left me with a bill for Social Services that I'm still paying off. But every now and then a dead mother has her uses. And you can tell Tracey's impressed by the way her eyes light up.

"And you're the only one?" she says.

"Yup," I says. "I'm the only one."

"Well, you're clearly a man of resources," she says, only this time she ain't talking about what's underneath the towel. "So why don't you take me away somewhere?"

Now if there's one thing I ain't ready for, it's commitment, so this sends a shiver down the back of my neck. "What?" I says. "Permanent?"

"No, don't be silly," she says. "Not yet anyway." *Not until your mother dies.* "There's a few formalities to go through first. Like I'm still married to Barry, remember?"

As if I could forget.

"No, I was thinking about a holiday. A few days away. Somewhere nice. In the sun. That sort of thing."

"Oh," I says, sounding relieved – for a minute she'd had me worried. And now the pressure's off so I agree. "Alright then," I says. "Why not?"

"Good," she says. "I'll get something organised. Now why don't you take that ridiculous towel off and get back into bed?"

Which sounds like a good idea – if it wasn't for the fact I'm on the clock.

"But what about Barry?" I says.

"He won't even notice I've gone," says Tracey.

That wasn't what I meant. But I look at my watch and see there's still time so I get back into bed anyway.

Barry

My first Tuesday back at the gym and I'm down there for six-fifteen. It's early so there's really no one about yet. Except Fat Micky that is, and he's busy readying up, laying the towels out and organising the kit. He sees me and nods in that funny way of his, bobbing to and fro. I nod back then head toward the changing room. It's cold in there, waiting while the heating comes on. Maybe that's what gives me a shiver or maybe it's the memories. I put my sports bag down, looking for my locker. The key's still in my pocket where I kept it. That's one thing they ain't had off me yet.

They're hanging there, just like I left them, my gloves, the red ones Dad bought me when I started out. Ain't nobody touched those since I've been gone. Maybe Albert's looked after them, or Micky even, I know they'd do that for me. Red outers, white palms, white laces, the maker's name in black on the wrist, 8oz lightweights. I feel like I'm staring at a previous life, the one I had before that truck came crashing down. But to look at them now you'd think they'd never been used. It's like they're floating there, suspended, just like they was brand new, stiff and empty. But I can remember the places they've been and the fights they've been in, the long nights in a cold sports hall with only the boxing to keep you warm.

Albert's calling from the corner.

Watch him, Barry, watch him!

I peer out over my guard and shift to one side as a big hook comes slanting in.

Now jab him, son, jab him! Get that left going!

There's an opening so I flick my hand out and catch a point. Always remember the points, says Albert, it's the points, the points. In the corner I clock Micky with his thumbs up. Ah yes, the boxing, I hear you say, all gone now.

You can't go back, says Albert.

Why not? I says.

Board of Control won't let you.

Bastards.

Then Albert's shouting again, his voice rising above the crowd.

Hit him, Barry, hit him for Christ's sake! Hit him with the right!

And suddenly someone's lying there, sprawled on the canvas, and they're lifting my arm up and saying I'm a winner. Or maybe it's Ivan with his face stoved in and all the blood dripping. Sometimes it's hard to tell.

The noise of the fight fades away and it's all quiet in the locker room except for the hum of the heating and the crack of the pipes warming up. Then I hear the gloves talking, crying out to me and saying, *Put me on Barry, it can't do no harm. Why don't you put me on?* My fingers start to itch and I know I shouldn't and I know it won't do me no good but I reach out and take them down, cradling them like I'm weighing them up and feeling the power inside. My hands start to ache but it ain't with broken bones, it's with wanting and it's wanting I can't resist.

I get taped up good and proper – I don't want that hand to hurt no more than I can help it – then I pull the gloves on tight. One quick smack and they're there. It's like my fists are where they should be now, hard against the leather. I head toward the gym.

Albert's arrived and he's standing with his clipboard in the corridor. He takes one look at the gloves and then one look at me.

"Where d'you think you're going?" he says.

"Where does it look as though I'm going?" I says. "I'm going for a workout on the bag."

"You know you can't do that," says Albert. "You'll damage yourself."

"Oh I will, will I?" I says. "I think I'll be the judge of that."

"What about your hand?" he says.

"It's my hand," I says. "And I'll do what the hell I like with it.

It don't matter a damn now anyway."

Albert wrinkles his forehead.

"I thought you were coming back here to get fit and help out with the boys," he says. "I've got a programme all worked out for you."

"Maybe you have," I says. "But there's other things got to come first."

We've come a long way Albert, you and me. Don't cross me now. You can't stand between a man and what he's born to.

He sees my look and backs off. He knows I'll knock him down if I have to – but it won't come to that and he steps aside and lets me pass. I walk on by, only now I decide to leave the bag and climb straight into the ring. I might respect him but this ain't on Albert's say-so, it's because I want the real thing and the feel of canvas beneath my feet. I climb through the ropes then hold on and paw my feet like I'm readying for a big fight. I hear the bell ringing in my head and I turn and face. I know there's no one there but I can always beat the shit out of my own shadow.

If that's what it takes.

Tap, skip, tap, tap, skip. I'm dancing again and back to the rhythm of the ring.

Terry

"So are we going on this holiday or what?" says Tracey.

"What holiday?" I says.

"The one I mentioned the other day," she says. "And the one I spent my lunchbreak yesterday getting brochures for."

And now she comes to mention it, something stirs in the memory and I do recall her saying. Only my mind was elsewhere at the time, what with that towel slipping off and me being more concerned with what was going on underneath it than I was with what I was hearing. So maybe I didn't pay attention.

"Well, you don't seem very interested," she says, looking peeved.

"I am," I says. "Trust me. I was just thinking about something else, that's all."

"Yes," she says. "And I can guess what that was, an' all."

It's Sunday afternoon and we're sitting in a coffee bar in Colchester. In other words, well up the road and out of it – although gossip does travel down the A12 if you're not too careful. We don't always get together Sundays (a bloke's got to have a rest sometimes) but this meeting's been convened special. Now I know why.

She's brought a pile of them glossy magazines you get from the travel agents. "I fancy Spain," she says, flicking through the pages. "I've been to Tenerife already – on honeymoon."

As if I need reminding. I spoon the froth off my cappuccino while I wait to be told what we're going to do next.

"I've found a nice place with a pool," she says, pointing at one of the pictures. "And it's only a few hundred yards from the beach."

"Sounds lovely," I says. Then the penny drops. "Wait a minute though. Spain? Ain't that somewhere foreign? I mean like *abroad*?"

"'Course it is," she says. "What did you expect? You didn't

think I was going to spend two weeks sat in a deckchair outside some B&B in Brighton, did you?"

"Well maybe not," I says. "But..."

"But what?" she says.

"Well," I says. "That means *flying*, don't it? Like – in an *aeroplane*. I can't say I'm overly keen about that. Not with my dicky tummy an' all."

"Now he tells me," she says, getting all steamed up. "I've come here to book a nice overseas holiday and the man I've picked to go with gets airsick. Typical. Well you'll just have to take some pills – or get one of them wristbands. Because like it or not you'll have to get used to it if you're going to stick around with me."

I suppose it was worth a try but she's got her claws well into me and no mistake. I can see there's no putting her off so I decide to play along – until I find out the price.

"So how much is this little adventure going to cost?" I says. "All told?"

"Ooh," she says, pursing her pretty lips. "Given we could go all in, we might get away with a couple of grand – if we're lucky."

The shock of it catches me and I splutter the froth off my cappuccino.

"A couple of grand?" I says. "*If we're lucky?* That's a bit steep, ain't it? Where the hell are we staying for that kind of money? Hotel Majestic? Or are we renting out some A-lister's villa?"

"Don't be silly," she says. "A-listers don't have villas in Spain – they're all in Florida. And if *I* had one, I certainly wouldn't be renting it out to all and sundry. Besides, that price is all inclusive, flights, meals and everything. Face the facts, Terry – if you want the best, you have to pay for it."

Which is all very well – but it ain't her that'll be shelling out.

"Anyways," she says. "I thought you was a man of resources?"

"Oh I am," I says. "Definitely – you can rely on that." Trouble is, I can't afford to disappoint her, especially now I've got a reputation to maintain. "It's just that I don't happen to have that much spare lying around at the moment."

"Well then," she says, tapping her fancy brochure on the table and getting a touch impatient. "You'll just have to go and pay a visit to your mother and ask for some more on account."

What? Another trip to Tiptree? Ronnie says I spend half my life there already. It just goes to show how one bloody fib leads to another. Sometimes a dead mother just won't lie down.

I'll have to do a damn sight more than go to Tiptree to come up with two grand. Because what she don't know is, I'm down to my last knockings and it'd take a shedload more of those little brown envelopes to make up the rest. To tell the truth, I'm running short of funds and there's no prospect of building them up for a while. Which is all a bit of a bugger, seeing as how I'm supposed to be Mr Moneybags an' all.

So one way or another, someone's going to have to cough up. Or else.

Barry

I'm working late at Ronnie's again and I don't see the point of going home first. The bird's as good as flown and the house is like an empty nest so I'm straight off down the Boys Club. At least Albert's there when I walk in, so that don't change much.

I get gloved up and then go on out into the gym. It's as cold in there as it is in the locker room so this time maybe the heating ain't on at all. A few of the lads are working out to get warmed up, lifting weights and skipping. But the bag's left free and it's hanging there, waiting. It's still carrying that scar, the one I gave it when I spilt its guts out all over the floor. Remember that? I sure do. And maybe the bag remembers too because it's like it's got a voice and I can hear it taunting me.

Still think you've got it, do you? You hurt me once but you can't do that again.

But it ain't just the bag that's got ideas and as soon as my tapes are tied and tucked, I'm off after it. Only I give it some respect to begin with and I dance around it once or twice to show it how good my footwork is. I ain't going to stand off it for long though, and I let it have a couple of solid left jabs to loosen up with. Then a couple more and a couple more after that. Now I try a right cross but I mistime it a touch and catch it a glancing blow rather than full on. But my hand don't hurt me none and I start feeling good. I duck inside and land a couple of lefts and rights to the body before breaking off. Then it's back to the jabs – four, five, six, seven, eight in a row. This time the right cross comes off and lands smack on the button. I think the bag should go down, like they always go down – only it don't. So I come inside again and start pounding it to the body, left right, left right, left right. They're big shots, but still the bag don't crumble.

Then the red mist comes down and I'm lost in the fight. And when I'm in the fight, there ain't nothing but the fight. It's like the fight is all of me and I am all of it. But this time it's me or the bag so I'm hitting it again and again with everything I've got like I'm a steam engine on speed – woof, woof, woof, woof, woof – like I'm Sugar Ray Leonard, like I'm Marvin Hagler, like I'm Nigel Benn, like I'm the Dark Destroyer all rolled into one. But whatever I do the bag don't drop, it's still hanging there giving me lip. So I keep at it, punching, punching, punching, hitting the bag 'til I've got nothing left. And all time the red mist keeps swarming.

Next thing I know Albert's grabbed me from behind, he's got his arms around me and he's calling out.

Steady on, son.

It takes four of them to pull me off the bag and when the red mist clears, I'm lying on my back, panting, and there's two of them sitting on top of me. Albert's wafting a towel while Micky's stood by with another.

Laurel and bloody Hardy.

"So..." says Albert. "When's the big fight?"

"What big fight?" I says, pretending not to know what he's talking about.

"This fight you're fixing to have," he says.

"You know bloody well when it is," I says. "It's been in your diary for weeks. Last I heard it was about a fortnight off."

"Ah," says Albert. "That fight. You know as well as I do that can't happen."

"Can't it?" I says. "You just watch me."

"The Board of Control won't allow it," he says. "I've already told you that."

"Bugger the Board of Control," I says.

"That's a lot easier said than done," says Albert.

"You should know," I says. "You're the one that could fix it."

That shuts him up. He thinks I'm just a pair of fists but I know a lot more than Albert gives me credit for – only I don't always let on. All it wants is a word from him, or even the lack of one, and we could be back in the game.

"Hmm..." he says. "Maybe. But there's a lot more to it than

that. You've no idea who you'd be fighting for a start – and from what I can see I don't think you much care."

No, I don't – I'll take them all on if I have to. Ronnie, Terry, Spike, Ivan, the bloody lot, even the guy with the shoes – they all deserve it.

And I can see Albert saying to himself, I can't hold him. Don't matter what I say, I can't stand in his way. Don't matter what I do, somebody's in for a bloody good hiding.

And he's probably right – maybe somebody *is* in for a good hiding, although who that is, I haven't a clue. But that's the luck of the draw, ain't it? That's what it's all about, somebody picking the short straw. All I'm trying to do is make sure it ain't Barry Mullins that gets it, that's all.

Albert

What on earth made me think I'd seen the last of Barry Mullins? Experience, I suppose. I'd spent nigh on twenty years watching people come and go at The City Boys Club – and I knew that once they'd gone, they tended not to come back. No wonder I never questioned it too much when he left.

And yet with Barry I should have known different. I remember how I kept telling myself that he wasn't like the rest and that the urge to box ran through him just as blood ran through his veins. If it hadn't been for that hand of his (or so I kept saying) – well, who knows what might have happened. It was enough to stop the strongest of men.

Please don't get me wrong – I was delighted to have him back. Things had gone rather flat since his departure and quite frankly, the Club was in the doldrums without him. As soon as news of his injury had broken and the story had run its course, the press lost interest and moved on to the next set of headlines. The queue of people eager to watch him train had once stretched into the street but it virtually dried up overnight. Applications to join the Club dwindled from a flood to a trickle. As for Micky and I, I'm loath to admit it but we'd rather enjoyed being the centre of Chelmsford's attention and that was now denied us. Whatever fame we'd managed to garner was dramatically short-lived and we discovered how fickle celebrity life could be. Had I subconsciously hoped he would return? Is that really why I'd failed to send in that vital report on his condition? Or was it simply because I wasn't ready to let go? Whatever the reason, my letter to the Board of Control was still in the drawer, Barry was back in the camp and Micky and I couldn't deny we felt lifted.

We all deserve a chance in life, that's common knowledge. Everyone deserves to have an opportunity to make something out of themselves, no matter who they are or where they've come from. In this day and age, we've almost come to see it as one of our human rights. And for all I know, it is. It's probably written down in some obscure charter at the United Nations and enshrined in international law as though it were one of the ten commandments of existence – *Thou shalt have a chance.* It stands to sense.

And in my experience, most people get one. A point occurs in most people's lives when something comes along – a chance, an opportunity, call it what you will – and all they have to do is reach out and take it. So it's not the chance itself that's important – that's going to happen anyway – it's what they do with it when it arrives. It's all to do with that set of crossroads I was telling you about earlier. Do they turn left, do they turn right, or do they go straight on? It's a decision that will doubtless change everything. But the thing is, people don't always recognise that chance for what it is. And as a result, they don't always make the most of it.

Take me, for instance. I had a chance at the age of eleven. I sat at a desk in a big classroom, my socks falling down round my ankles and a pen in my hand but with barely a thought in my head except what was I going to have for tea when I got home. And so I blew it and my big chance went sailing by. I'd spent my childhood climbing trees and getting mud on my trousers instead of reading books and I didn't have a clue. Although at least I can say I had a childhood. That's more than most kids can lay claim to today – half of them don't get any further than the door to their own bedroom. But because of it all I failed an exam.

Prior to that there'd been a war. "Chance" had meant something else then – not so much the potential for gain, but more the possibility of loss. "Chance" was the odds of being hit by a bomb as you lay in your bed or crossed the road so you learnt to avoid risk and took the safe option. I was lucky and escaped with two years' National Service long after the conflict had ended – but it still meant my career prospects were compromised and I was forced to become a draughtsman instead of the architect I so desired to be. I consoled myself with the idea that if I couldn't learn a profession I could at least learn how to draw, both the buildings I yearned to design and the wages I needed to survive. I should be thankful for that if nothing else.

Do I have any regrets? Of course I do. No one can say that they don't and I'd be a liar if I didn't admit it myself. But what if I'd done things differently? Chances are I'd never have finished up as Head Coach at Chelmsford City Boys Club, a place where I get to work with and develop the young lads of today. So if I never did get to build museums, cathedrals – or even tower blocks – now I'm building character. And there's a lot of satisfaction in that, believe me.

We've never had a trophy cabinet in my office. There isn't enough room for a start and up until the time Barry arrived, there'd have been nothing to put in it anyway. Oh, we came close once. We had a flyweight, Freddy Jackson, cocky little bugger, but he lost a semi-final and never did anything after that. The Club has its own awards of course. There's a plaque we get engraved every year for Best Boxer and we have a little statuette for Most Promising Youngster. I keep those on a shelf over my desk. Above that there's another shelf for Barry's things – cups, medals, all the prizes he won over the years. As you can imagine, it's pretty crowded but there was a space I'd kept open in the middle, waiting for the big one, the cup for the National Title. Sometimes I'd look at that space and there'd be a hole in my guts as big as the hole on that shelf.

The morning after Barry went ballistic, I fetched his file out of the drawer. I took the letter I'd written to the Board of Control and tore it up and threw it in the bin. If I didn't tell them, they wouldn't know. And if they didn't know, they couldn't stop him. If they *did* find out, I'd probably lose my licence. *So what?* I thought. *Sometimes you just have to take a risk.*

So now it was Barry's turn. Now it was time for him to have

his chance, his opportunity to make something out of himself and to stamp his mark on the world. There was a big prize at stake. If he won, he'd be National Champion, he'd like as not become famous and his phone would be ringing the morning after. He'd worked hard and he deserved the right to have a go. Who was I to take that right away?

BARRY MULLINS DECLARED FIT

It would be in all the papers.

Terry

Now if anyone calls me an elephant, I might just take exception, but it's like I told you before – I don't forget things easy. Ronnie still owes me, big time, so I'm wondering why I don't just come out with it and ask him for it. It can't do no harm and there's a chance he might even say yes. Now seems as good a time as any. Especially as he's chuffed to bits on account of Mr Mullins being back in action – he's had a smile on his face as wide as a Cheshire Cat's ever since that piece of news popped out. So why don't I just do it, straight off the bat, and say, *Ronnie, I need a couple of grand.* Just like that. Simple enough, ain't it?

Trouble is, I know what'll happen next. He'll take me over to the window, put one of those great big arms of his around my shoulder and give me that *Have a look out there Terry, it's all tied up in the business* crap. *Blah, blah, blah.* Well, bugger that, I've let myself be fobbed off with that line more times than I care to mention. Why? Because I've never had the guts to push it, that's why. Only this time it'll be different. This time I'll put my foot down.

Ronnie, I need a couple of grand.

Jesus, Terry, that's a bit of a swipe. What on earth d'you want that for?

Never mind what I want it for. Let's just say I've got some bills to pay and we need to get started with some of the divvying up.

Divvying up? What divvying up?

You know, the partnership, what we've both been working for, that pot of gold at the end of the rainbow you keep talking about.

Look Terry, we've been through this a dozen times before. I'd love to help you out mate, you know I would, but it's all tied up. That pot of gold as you call it is all out there in the yard, the stock, everything you see around you, it's all invested in the business. And that's your future, my future. I'll see you right one way or another in the end, honest I will, you know that. But right now, we're just going to have to be patient.

Patient? You're talking to me about being patient? So how many years is it now since we started working together? Ten? Fifteen? I've lost count. But it's long enough that's for sure. And you remember how we started, the van, the markets, you and me, how we was going to build it up, the two of us? And in all that time I've worked my butt off and I've had nothing, not a penny. So don't you talk to me about being patient. I have been patient, I've been patient for the best part of fifteen years. Barry Mullins thought he could come between us and take it off me, but he couldn't last, not like I have. That's patient for you. But there comes a point when a man can't wait no longer, when a man's got to have what's due. And that point is now Ronnie, right now. I can't be held off no longer. All I'm asking for is two grand, two measly grand for Christ's sake, you can't deny me that. It ain't a lot to ask for after all these years.

Now hold on a second Tel, hold on old son. Keep your shirt on. So what's this all about? What's the big rush all of a sudden?

Then what?

So I can take Barry's wife away on holiday?

Somehow I don't think so. I'll have to do better than that – and it had better be something convincing. So how about this instead.

So I can pay Mother's nursing home fees.

That's better, I like that, that's a good 'un. It always gets to Ronnie, stuff like that. He may look hard on the outside, but underneath he's as soft as a piece of wet soap. Plus it's consistent, seeing as it's much the same story as I told Tracey. And what's sauce for the goose is sauce for the gander, or so they say. Yeah, Mother's nursing home fees. That should fix it.

But I will ask him. I've got to.

Ronnie

So now we start getting to the bottom of it. Barry's hand is all fixed up (or so we're told), the fight's still on and we're back in business betwise. In out, in out, shake it all about, this thing's got more twists and turns than the hokey-cokey. Which is fine just as long as there's no more surprises. And there was me thinking of another trip to Walthamstow to put it all to rights – but that's saved me the bother.

Conversely, the jury's still out on Terry. As for the Wednesday afternoons, I've given him the benefit of the doubt. But then he ups and asks for money – big money –and that gives me a problem.

"How much?" I says.

Like I'm well shocked.

"Two grand," he says.

"Two grand!" I says. "What the hell kind of nursing home is this?" That big trap of his opens up like a goldfish and I sense something gormless is about to come out of it so I put a stop on it first. "No, don't tell me, let me guess. It's one of them ones where the taps are all gold-plated and there's a herd of waiters wandering round with white gloves on serving tea and cake all day. Two bloody grand? Jesus Christ, Terry, there ain't a nursing home in the world worth that much. And from what I know of the one in Tiptree, you could probably buy it for that kind of money."

"I ain't looking to buy it," he says. "I just want to get some fees paid."

"Fees?" I says. "What fees?"

"Mother's."

"Ah yes," I says. "Your mother. I might have known. Got her booked into a nice suite, have you?"

"Don't be ridiculous," he says. "It ain't a hotel. These are care home fees. Been building up, they have – over the period."

"What period?"

"You know bloody well what period," he says. "Jesus, Ronnie, don't you ever listen to a word I say? Ever since she came out of hospital, that's what."

"With that demented thing?"

"Exactly."

Which proves I do listen – some of the time.

"Well," I says. "A mother's a fine thing, Terry, I'd do the same for mine." (If she ever got to find me.) "But sometimes you have to draw a line."

"That's right," he says. "And I'm drawing one now." And the next thing you know he's stood up straight like he's giving some kind of speech and he goes all serious on me. "This is it, Ronnie," he says. "This is what it's come down to – it's shit or bust. It's a poor job when a man can't get his own mother looked after. So it's two grand or I'm off. This ain't the only garage in the world and you know it. It wouldn't take me ten minutes to find a job somewheres else – then you'd be stuffed. And don't go thinking I don't mean it because I do – every word. So what d'you say? Are we doing this or what?"

Now I've known Terry a good few years and that's the first time he's ever pulled that one on me. You're probably going to tell me I should've seen it coming but in all the discussions we've had on the subject (and there's been a few) he's always taken a different tack. In the past it's been easy to defend but this time it ain't so simple. Fact is, he's right and if he ever goes, I'm buggered. God knows, it's been hard enough running a garage with a one-handed mechanic never mind what we'd be like with no salesman. So I'm well aware which side my bread's buttered, believe me, and I figure a bit of compromising's in order.

"Now steady on Tel," I says. "Calm down, old son, calm down. We ain't going to have a bust-up after all these years over a piddly little thing like two grand." Which in the grand scheme of things, it is, considering the amount of debt that's hanging over my head. "I'm sure we can work something out."

I do a quick mental calculation. Goldstrap's got my £10k, Barry wins (bless him) so we can double that to twenty. Now as far as I recall, Terry's on ten per cent and it just so happens as that works out at two. And if that's what I've got to do, so be it. Strange, ain't it, the way things turn out sometimes. I breathe a sigh of relief.

"So here's the thing," I says. "Don't shout at me," (which he will, given half a chance), "but I've made a small investment."

"An investment?" he says. "What kind of investment?"

"You needn't worry yourself about that," I says. "Let's just say it's a business arrangement – you know, the kind of opportunity that presents itself to business people such as myself and that we'd be daft not to take advantage of. Anyways, when it pays out, which I have every confidence it will do very soon, I can cut you in."

"Soon?" he says. "How soon?"

"Ooh," I says. "Let me see... A couple of weeks, three at the most." Personally, I'm banking on just a few days but I'd like to leave some wriggle room.

"But that's no good to me," says Tel. "I need it now. Things is piling up."

"What, right now?" I says. "Got the bailiffs at the door have you?"

"Yeah," he says. "Pretty much."

"Jesus, Terry," I says. "You sure know how to push a bloke."

I drum my fingers on the desk, wondering what to do. This is beginning to look like a tough call and I get the feeling it's the one time he ain't going to be fobbed off so easy. And then there's the thought of his poor old mother, sat there in that nursing home, suffering... Well, you can call me a sucker if you like, but in the end that's what decides me.

"You'll have to wait a while for the rest," I says. "But d'you know what? On this occasion I can help you out with a bit in advance. I wouldn't do it for everyone mind, but seeing as it's you..." And I pull open the bottom draw of my desk.

Now don't tell me you haven't got a bit of spare tucked away safe somewhere, we all have. You might keep yours in a cocoa tin on top of the kitchen cupboard, or put it behind the clock on the mantelpiece – but we all do it one way or another. I used to keep mine under the mattress but that went west some while ago – now I'm down to whatever's left in the petty cash. I bring the box out onto the desk and flip open the lid.

It don't look good to start with. There's plenty of paper clips, some sweet wrappers and a few odd bits of shrapnel – but I know where the treasure's buried. I lift out the cash tray and there it is lying underneath, a brand-spanking-new fifty-pound note. There ain't so much as a finger mark on it and it ain't even been folded yet.

"Well look at that," I says. "Seems like it's your lucky day." I take it out and wave it under his nose. "Here," I says. "Take it. That's the best I can do for now, it's all I've got 'til I get paid off."

He looks at it, sniffs, looks at me and then looks back at the fifty – and takes it. I guessed he'd go for it. That's the thing about Terry and hard cash, he finds it real tempting – the feel of it, the smell of it, the way it crinkles up when you shove it into your pocket. I should know, I'm sat on my wallet and I can feel the bulge of it warming the seat of my trousers. But I won't be telling Terry that – I might need it myself to buy some more time later on.

Smithson rang earlier – for the umpteenth day in a row.

Your ninety days are up, Mr Bent, your payment's due next week. I hope you've made the necessary arrangements. We won't be granting any extensions.

Bastard. So where's your bank manager when you need him? On your back, that's where. Ain't much changed in that department. Though with a bit of luck I won't be needing him much longer. With a bit of luck, come next week and I'll be in clover.

Terry

So that's it, is it? That's what I'm worth to him after all this time.

Fifty quid.

Fifty measly, miserable, effing quid.

What the hell does he think I'm going to do with that? You couldn't buy a decent day out in Clacton for fifty quid never mind two weeks in some swanky hotel in Spain. Fifteen years I've sweated blood for Ronnie Bent and that's how he treats me. He must think I'm an idiot. I know what goes on. You only have to look at the calendar on the wall behind his desk to understand that. It's a freebie from The Racing Post, it's hung open at October and there's a big red circle pencilled in round some date at the end of it. Investment? Investment my arse. That black briefcase of his has gone walkabout and I'll take a pound to a penny he's booked himself a day out at Ascot and the rest of it's gone on some three-legged donkey in the Champion Stakes. I haven't spent the best years of my life working with that pillock without knowing more about Ronnie Bent than he knows about himself. Fifty quid? I'll tell you what I'm going to do with his fifty bleeding quid. I'm going down The Bell, then maybe The Lion, and I'm going to get slaughtered – that's what I'm going to do with it. And don't be surprised if I happen to find a brick and put it through his window on the way back home. Fifty quid. I'll give him fifty bleeding quid. And it may not be all I'll give him neither. Like I said before – there comes a time when a man's got to have what's due. And right now, time's up.

Now don't get the idea I'm unduly nostalgic but The Bell and The Lion ain't nowhere near what they used to be. Maybe it's because I've gone up in the world what with doing the rounds with Tracey an' all, but these days I feel a lot more comfortable in The Lizard Lounge than I do in The Dog and

Duck. But this here's a drinking night, I'm on my own and you can't get a decent pint in the Lounge for love nor money. So I figure on going back to my old haunts and slumming it. Come half seven I'm nicely settled in at The Bell and I start thinking *Can I really be bothered to go next door? Bernie'll be in there and I can't be doing with the stick he'll give me.* And it ain't as if I'm going to miss the company. Besides which, the fruit machine's behaving itself and I'm on a bit of a roll. So *Bugger it,* I says. *I'm staying put. I'm happy where I am, thank you very much.*

Anyways, it gets to half eight and I'm still in there. By this time, I'm well into my fourth pint (Adnam's, best bitter, on draught), looking at the froth coating the bottom of the glass in fact and thinking about getting another one. But I'm held up by two fat cherries waiting for a third, then low and behold, the red fruit arrives and I catch a big payout. The coins come tumbling out faster than I can pick them up and that's my night's beer paid for and never mind Ronnie's measly fifty.

"Nice one." There's a voice pipes up behind me.

"Yes," I says. "You don't get too many like that." And I shape to move off, thinking *I'll leave that to you – you're welcome to it. Ain't nothing left in there now I've cleaned that lot out.*

Then the penny drops and I know who's talking. I turn around and sure enough, it's my old mate Joe Black.

"What, you again?" I says. "Can't you leave a bloke in peace?"

"Not when there's work to do," says Joe.

"Oh there is, is there?" I says. "And what makes you think I'm the right person to do it? Let me guess. You've been talking to Bernie in The Lion again."

"If that's what you call him," he says. "But I'm always going to find you, one way or the other, whoever I talk to."

"I see," I says. "You don't give up easy, do yer?"

"It ain't a question of giving up," says Joe. "It's a question of getting the job done."

"So what is it now?" I says. "Barry Mullins got more bones want breaking, has he? You've left that a bit late."

"Maybe," says Joe. "We could always try a bribe."

"Forget that," I says. "I know the little bastard inside out and he's as straight as they come. He wouldn't touch it with a bargepole."

"Well we need to come up with something," he says.

"Like what?" I says.

"Like what if the unthinkable happens..."

"...and the little shite wins."

"Exactly."

"Well my guess is, Mr Goldstrap ain't going to be too happy."

"No," says Joe. "He ain't. Fact is he'll be quite upset."

"Well don't look at me," I says. "I did what I was told. You're the ones that screwed up on it."

"Hmm..." Joe ruminates on past failures and the thought of what might happen if things go wrong again. His forehead knots up as the vision of a pair of thumbscrews goes floating by. "There is an alternative..."

"Such as?"

"Such as, let's say we agree to hand over the money to Mr Bent's personal representative – namely, you. After an appropriately short period of time i.e. on the way home, you might become involved in an accident, a mugging say, and the briefcase might go missing in the process."

"Whoa, whoa, whoa," I says. "The dish is running away with the spoon here. You'll have to slow down a bit while I do some catching up. Let's start at the beginning, shall we. First off, what money?"

"The £20k."

I take a deep breath.

"£20k?"

"Yes – the proceeds owing to Mr Bent should Barry Mullins

win."

Ah... So it wasn't a horse after all. Crafty bastard. No wonder... Well, no wonder a lot of things, but let's not worry about all that now.

"That wouldn't happen to be a black briefcase by any chance, would it?"

"You sound surprised. We'd assumed you'd know all about it by now."

"Naturally..." I stall for a minute while my brain goes into overdrive. "You mentioned something about a mugging..."

"I did. Nothing serious. Just a few cuts and bruises to make it look realistic. We don't want you ending up in hospital."

"Well thanks for that," I says. "I appreciate your concern." Don't matter how he puts it though, the thought of violence on my person gives me the creeps. Not to mention what Ronnie might say about me losing his briefcase. All the same, a plan's a plan... "You'll be paying my usual fee, I take it?"

"You don't miss a trick, do yer," says Joe, his thin lip curling into a sneer.

"Not if I can help it," I says.

"So that's agreed then?"

"Sounds okay to me," I says.

"After the fight?"

"After the fight. If he wins."

"Yes," he says. "If he wins."

We shake on it, his pure white hand sliding out from the sleeve of his black coat like some nocturnal beast emerging from its cave, his nails all buffed and polished.

Well, I don't hold no candle for Barry Mullins, as you well know. Tried to fix it once and it didn't quite come off. But a deal's a deal and sometimes a bloke has to make compromises.

I wait 'til Joe's gone, then fetch that pint I was looking forward to. I take a sip and contemplate the evidence in front of me – another brown envelope, Ronnie's fifty, and my jackpot winnings from the fruit machine. Not bad for a night's work, even though I say so myself. I've enough to make the deposit for the holiday – I'll bung the rest on my credit card and sort the balance when Ronnie's money comes through. I won't tell Tracey just yet though, I'll keep that as a surprise.

Plus there's a chance to get my hands on that briefcase...

Albert

It's hard to recall exactly what went on during those last few days before the big fight. With so much to do and so little time available, everything seemed to coalesce into one hectic blur.

The main problem was the fact that Barry wasn't fully fit. The weeks he'd had off nursing his broken hand had left him sadly out of condition and it was a race against time to bring him back to anything like his best. A race that had to be carefully run by the way, as to set off too quickly at the start might lead to him becoming exhausted before the end. He needed to be at his peak on the day – and that meant timing was everything.

As you can imagine, Barry was impervious to these considerations and wanted to go at it like a bull at a gate. The boy was so pumped up you'd have thought he was a balloon about to explode and there was a danger he'd go off pop before he got as far as the dressing room, never mind climbing into the ring. One thing I do remember is standing outside my cabin and watching him doing his press-ups. We'd got as far as thirty and he didn't look as if he was anywhere near ready to stop. I called across to try and catch Micky's attention.

"Come and have a look at this."

I asked him how many press-ups he could do at that age. It was a rather silly question. With Micky being the way he was, it was hard to imagine him doing any press-ups at all and as soon as I'd said it I wanted to bite my tongue off for being so stupid. But I could always rely on him to get me off the hook.

"You mean before I put on a bit of weight?" he said.

"Yes," I said, grateful for the get out. "Before that."

He pondered for a minute. "Oh, twenty, maybe twenty-five if I was to push it. Why? How many has Barry got up to?"

"I don't know, I've lost count while we've been talking. But he'll wear his arms out if he's not too careful." I decided to call him off. "Barry!" I shouted. "Pack that in and come over here. I want a word in your shell-like."

Barry gave in and came across but all the while he kept jogging up and down. It was as if his mind wouldn't let his body rest. I tried telling him he should cool it a bit, you know, slow down and take it steady, but I felt as though I was wasting my breath. If you could see words, I'm sure you'd have seen mine go in one of his ears and come straight out of the other. They didn't seem to make a scrap of difference and my attempts at restraint were hard to enforce.

Then there was the question of what to do about his hand. In theory the bones had repaired but the underlying structure might still be weak. Did it hurt when he used it? Barry said not – but was he hiding something from us? And sparring with it was one thing but standing up to the rigors of a full-on fight was quite another. We thought of administering pain-killers, or even an injection, but in the end rejected both. There was always the risk they might dull his reactions and that could prove suicidal. Not only that but we never really knew what these medications contained and the threat of an adverse doping test was something to be avoided. Eventually we settled for bandaging, as much as we were allowed, and hoped it would suffice.

All this would have been far more problematic had we not taken the decision to shut the gym to outsiders. The pressure their presence would have brought would have been unbearable. As much as Micky and I may have enjoyed the limelight, we had no immediate desire to return to a situation where there were queues of people hammering at the door to get in. Nor did we want to attract undue attention from the press – the thought of some ruthlessly probing reporter uncovering our weaknesses filled us with dread. And so Barry trained behind closed doors where, for the moment at least, we could cope with our difficulties in private.

It gave me the chance to study the opposition. We were going to be up against "Desperate" Dan Hampton, aka "Soldier Boy" as he was a corporal in the Parachute Regiment. Well, all I can say is he must have had one hell of a parachute because he was built like a brick outhouse, short and stocky, almost seventy kilos of toned muscle packed together with shoulders like a bull. He'd held the title for the last two years so he wasn't going to give it up that easily. Not only that but he was a nasty piece of work, a bruiser, a battler, and in my eyes not worthy of being called a boxer at all. He'd no interest in the noble art, that was for sure, and all the boxing that would get done would be coming from Barry's side of the argument. It put me in mind of Beauty and the Beast.

"You'll have to stand off this man," I told Barry. "Don't let him pull you in close because once he gets you on the inside, he'll hammer you to pieces. You've got a longer reach than he has so keep your distance. Stay back out of trouble, use the jab and pick him off when you can."

"In other words," said Barry, "box him. And pile up the points."

"You've got it." It had taken a while but I'd taught the boy well. "And keep an eye out for his left hook. I'm told it's vicious and it'll take the side of your face off if you're not careful."

Barry nodded and this time I was sure he was listening as he responded to what I'd been saying.

"Okay, Albert. But what about my right hand?"

It worried me when he started talking about that.

"You keep that in reserve. Remember, you're only going to be able to use it the once – maybe twice if you're lucky. It's always there to fall back on but if everything goes according to plan, you won't need it."

Barry gave me another nod, then went back to working on the bag. I admired his technique for a while and tried to convince myself things were going to be alright. They should have been as he was much the better boxer. But then, I was only Albert Hyde, his trainer, and what did I know? And when did anything ever go according to plan?

Barry

So the big day arrives, the day of the fight, the day I take on Dan Hampton for the National Title at the Albert Hall. I've waited a long time for this. *Bring it on*, I'm thinking, *bring it on*.

This last week and Ronnie's been fussing round me like an old mother hen.

"You look after yourself," he says. "We don't want any more accidents."

You're damn right we don't. Not after Black Monday.

All very well him looking out for me now but what he forgets is how he took that car away when I needed it. Anyways, he decides to give me a couple of days off after the fight like he's trying to make up for it.

"You'll need them to recover," he says. "Come back when you're ready."

"I don't want them given," I says. "I'll take them as holiday."

That way and it'll stop Terry bleating. Which he will be. Plus I've a few days owing. I haven't had a break since the accident and that was a while since. It's been hard going, I can tell you.

I cop for some free tickets. I ask Ronnie if he wants one, seeing as I've got a couple spare. Dad won't be coming. His emphysema's gotten real bad and he can't walk a hundred yards without he starts wheezing. Besides, we haven't exactly spoken a great deal since that thing between us down at the hospital. And as for Mum – well, she won't go without him and to tell the truth, she was never that keen on me boxing in the first place.

"Cheers," says Ronnie. "Tell you what, make it two while you're at it."

But that's Ronnie for you – give him an inch and he takes a mile. He slopes off back to the office mumbling something about bringing a friend – seems he can't stand the tension on his own. Well if he can't, I don't know how the hell he thinks I can.

"Just make sure you win," he says. "That's all."

"I'll do my best," I says.

I don't count on giving Terry no tickets, that's for certain. But Ronnie's friend's already sorted so it ends up with the both of them coming and I can't do nothing about it. I give the rest to Albert. If he can't use them, he can pass them on to someone down at the Club. Or Micky, I don't really mind, they're welcome.

We travel separate. They've a load of kit to carry so Albert and Micky plan on driving up. They offer me a lift but I prefer to take the train. I've got some thinking to do and I reckon that's best done on my own. But I can't settle and I'm jittery the whole journey, shadow-boxing anything that moves. Someone only has to slide back a door or rustle a paper and I'm ducking and diving like the fight's already begun. I just want to be on with it, it's the hanging about that gets me.

It's half five by the time I land at Liverpool Street so everyone else is going the other way. The tube is packed and I wonder whether to take Circle or Central. I opt for Central so's I can get out at Lancaster Gate and walk across Kensington Gardens. I reckon a breath of fresh air will do me good.

On the way I pass Albert's Memorial. I have a good laugh as he ain't actually dead at all but he's waiting inside. It ain't no laughing matter, really, whether he's dead or not – it's just the nerves jangling. But it kinda breaks the ice.

I look across at the Hall and it blows me away. It's massive, like nothing I've ever seen before. I try to focus down and tell myself that somewhere in the middle of it all there's a ring, and that ring ain't no bigger than any other ring I've been in, and once I get into that ring I'll be fine.

There's a door marked for contestants and such so I show my pass and they let me in. The corridors are busy, bustling with security and trainers and people with sports bags and God knows what, so you can tell something big is going on. Then a steward comes to help me and takes me to my dressing room. Laurel and Hardy are already in there, setting up their act.

"Here he is," says Albert, trying to look cheery as I walk in. "How are you doing?"

Micky's sat in the corner, chewing gum. I give him a nod.

"A bit nervous," I says. "I just want to get started."

"That's alright," says Albert. "I'd be worried if you wasn't. Don't worry about it, we'll soon sort you out."

I tell them about Kensington Gardens and the statue. Now we're all laughing.

Micky's got hold of a programme with a running order in it. The show kicks off at seven-thirty and I'm third bout on, so we reckon it'll be about half past eight, all depending. Over two hours to fill and I'm as jumpy as a cat on a hot tin roof. I start to get changed but I make it as slow and deliberate as I can.

Albert goes to fetch a bucket of ice. He tells me to stick my hand in it, my right hand, the one that got busted up.

"It'll help keep any swelling down," he says.

And kill the pain, I reckon.

My right's a bit numb after an hour in the ice but I guess it's got to be that way. Eventually we try the bandaging, as much as I can take – both sides to balance things up. It's all I can do to get my hands into the gloves. I'm using the red ones, the ones Dad bought me and we try a couple of minutes' work with Albert against the mitts and the body jacket to get things moving.

Then it's on with a robe to keep warm, and I'm sat there with my leg jiggling. And all the time my heart's pumping faster and faster and I'm thinking *What happens if I get hit? I haven't come all this way just for that, stay out of his reach like Albert says and it'll be alright.*

The boys can see I'm jumpy so Micky tells me to chill out while he works my shoulders. I sit there and close my eyes as he plumps up the skin.

It's real quiet in the dressing room – except for the clock, that is, ticking. *Tick, tick, tick.* I try counting the ticks to pass the time. I get to three hundred then lose count and have to start again.

Tick, tick, tick.

There's a hell of a lot of ticks between now and half past eight.

God knows how long I sit there, it feels like the length of a lifetime. I daren't look at the clock and what with Micky's massage I might even doze off for a second.

Then suddenly it's all hands to the pump as I catch a break and they call us early. In the bout before mine it seems some poor bastard got taken out in round one so they're running ahead of schedule. I try to think about doing the taking out and not being the one that got hit. It don't help knowing though.

Albert stands me up and we do a couple more minutes with the mitts and the jacket, then before you know it my robe's back on and I'm out into the corridor and down toward the ring.

It's a real shock coming out into the auditorium – the size of it, the noise, the people. I try not to gawp around but just keep focused on the carpet in front of me. I can sense the crowd, mumbling low on either side, and down toward the front I catch the whiff of good cigars. Because this is it, the peak, the pinnacle of amateur boxing, the embodiment of the noble art, ABA finals night at the Royal Albert Hall. No fanfares, no music and no flashing lights. Just a collection of toffs relaxing after a good dinner and engaged in the quiet contemplation of honest pugilistic endeavour. Or so Albert says. I'll bet they're glad they'll not be sitting in my seat in a few minutes time though.

Tick, tick, tick.

I climb through the ropes and into the ring. There's a ragged cheer from the back of the hall but I can tell it's not for me. I turn around and across in the other corner I get my first glimpse of Desperate Dan Hampton, the Soldier Boy from Catterick. Front on and it's like looking at a bulldog. He's short and squat and it's hard to tell where his shoulders end and his arms begin, it's all one big muscle. And the thing about him is, he ain't got no neck, it's like his head's been stuck straight on top of his torso – and that looks as though it's fit to bust straight out of his singlet.

He's black, so his body's as brown as a berry and on each bicep there's a tattoo – a coiled snake and dagger on the left and a pin up with a heart on the right. He is one scary looking bugger. He ain't exactly pretty either – and that's before he puts his gumshield in and he starts snarling. Which he does, most of the time.

Tick, tick, tick.

I turn my back and face the crowd.

Laurel and Hardy are busy setting up our corner. Micky's got his bucket and sponge and Albert's folding up a towel.

"Look at me," says Albert. "And listen." He stares deep into my eyes so we're together. "This man is dangerous," he says. "Remember what I said, stay well out of his reach and box him. Keep that left jab going just like I showed you. Understand?"

"Yes Albert," I says.

"And whatever you do, don't think you can stand toe to toe with him and slug it out because he'll destroy you. Just stay clear where you know he can't get you and you'll be fine."

"Yes Albert. But what about the right?"

"If you're lucky, you won't need it."

"And if I ain't?"

Albert shrugs. "I'll let you know. And by the way, watch out for that left hook – it's a killer."

"Yes Albert, I will."

"Good luck."

Tick, tick, tick.

The MC taps the top of his mic and starts making his announcement.

"This contest is for the ABA National Title 69kg class, three rounds, three minutes each round…"

While he's talking, the ref calls us together in the middle of the ring. So at last we're nose to nose, me and Dan, staring each other out. And I can tell you now, he ain't no better looking close up than he was from a distance.

"Now then boys," says the ref. "I want a clean fight, break when I say break, no punching on the break…"

But we ain't listening, Dan and me, and all I can hear is him snarling. It starts to get on my nerves so I decide to piss him off. I point at his tattoos.

"You're in the Army, ain't you, Dan?" I says.

"So what?" he says, growling.

"They'll be military tattoos then," I says. "Ha, ha, ha."

But Dan don't seem to find that funny and he keeps looking straight ahead like he's pretending he ain't heard.

"I'm going to knock your bleeding block off," he says.

"Hmm…" I says. "Nice. Only trouble is, you ain't going to get close enough to try."

The ref sends us back to our corners. I wait a couple of seconds, the bell rings, then I turn and face. Dan and me touch gloves and the clock stops ticking. Now it's game on and we're off and running.

Most fights you're in start off nice and slow. For the first minute nobody tries anything daft and you take some time to feel each other out a bit, you know, see what the other guy's got, so to speak. Well it ain't like that with Dan. Dan knows what he's got already and he couldn't care less what you've got. So he's coming at you right from the word go. Did I say running just now? Well, straight from the off I'm the one that's doing it and it's mostly backwards. But Dan don't run, he plods and it's only in one direction and that's forwards. He's like a slow-moving tank with no reverse gear and fitted with this homing device so whichever way you move he's going to turn toward you and hunt you down. And when he's close enough, like if he's backed you into a corner or onto the ropes, he's going to pummel you to pieces – then all of a sudden he'll throw that left hook at you in the hopes of catching you out. Which at some stage during the course of the next nine minutes, chances are he will do. And if he does, you're as good as dead – if you ain't dead already after all that pummelling.

So me, I've got my dancing shoes on. And I'm dancing to my own tune, the tune I've danced to for years. *Tap, skip, tap, tap, skip,* I chassé round the ring. But it's Dan who's the lead and I'm following his every step but in the opposite direction and gliding away. As he plods toward me, I sometimes let him get close enough to try a swipe – but I can always see it coming and I dive out of reach. Then I feint, bob and weave my way off the ropes or out of the corner where he's trying to trap me. And as I do, he leaves a gap, a space where I can get to him, so it's *tap, tap, tap* and I'm collecting points.

But every tap I give him it's like a pebble bouncing off a piece of granite, it don't make no impression. I tap him, hard as I can, and he just blinks or brushes it off like I'm an annoying fly. Then the homing device cuts in and he turns toward me once more. *Plod two three swipe, plod two three swipe,* his is a different beat but it's so predictable I begin to know what to expect. And there's me, *tap skip, tap tap skip,* so pretty soon I'm tapping and skipping for all I'm worth. Come the end of round one and Dan's nose is flatter than a pancake where I've boxed him silly. But I ain't hurt him none, I ain't hurt him at all.

The bell rings out and I go and sit in my chair. The crowd stays quiet, just a few low murmers of appreciation. So far so good and there's been nothing to get excited about. Micky wafts a towel.

"Well done," says Albert. "You got through that alright."

"Yes," I says. "That was okay. It's hard – but he ain't got no surprises."

"Don't you be too sure," says Albert. "He won't have got this far without having a few tricks up his sleeve. Just you watch out."

"No worries," I says. "It's all under control. Leave it to me."

"Don't go getting cocky," he says. "And make sure you concentrate. Two more rounds like that and you're home and dry."

But maybe I do get cocky. Or maybe it's bad luck, but one way or the other I'm about to pay for it. I take a couple of breaths, the bells rings again and we're out for round two.

Plod, plod, plod. The tank comes lumbering out of its corner and blunders towards me. Only now it's got its motor growling that bit louder and it looks as if it's found another gear. Maybe his corner's said something to him at the break. *It's no good Dan, he's too quick for you. You haven't hit him yet and you're going to have to up the pace.* But one thing's for sure, he ain't changed his tactics. I'm not even sure he can, he's just speeded up. So Dan and me, we don't dance the waltz no more – now it's the quickstep and my feet are moving faster all the time. I'm thinking quicker too and I can tell I'm having to react. Each skip I make is under pressure and there ain't always time to get a shot off. And even if I do, it don't always connect. *Tap tap skip* goes out the window, and it's *skip skip skip* with maybe a tap if I'm lucky. I'm getting pushed and here comes Dan, *plod swipe swipe, plod swipe swipe,* faster and faster 'til you just know it's only a matter of time before he catches me and lands one on.

BANG! And there it is, a left to the body just as I'm coming off the ropes. Jesus Christ, it's like being hit with a steam hammer. *Get in there Dan!* A cry of hope goes up from his corner. Dan takes encouragement and resumes his forward march. Now he's hit me once, he knows he can do it again. And he does, *BANG!* This time it's a right and I catch most of it on the forearm but it smarts just the same. I slide away and get in a tap. But taps don't bother Dan and he just flicks them off. Now his dander's up, the tank's turned into a shark and it's smelling blood in the water. *Plod swipe swipe, plod swipe swipe,* it's relentless and I can't always fend him off. So every now and then he catches me around the body, and every now and then I give him a tap. It's even-steven as we head toward the end of round two. And that's when it happens, the setback, the bit that don't go according to plan, the bit where I fall foul of Dan's left hook.

The lights are off in the hall so it's dark beyond the ropes. Dan's still coming at me when suddenly there's a "pop" and a flashbulb goes off, blinding white. I blink out of instinct and in that split second my eyes are closed, he throws the punch. I see it late, a round black shape moving fast against the flash, and I flinch away. It catches me a glancing blow – but it's enough.

Then I'm swimming in the black ink. I'm tired and I want to lie down but I know I mustn't go to sleep. Albert said not to go to sleep in the black ink. I'm lying on my side looking out at the crowd – though maybe I'm still under the truck because all I can see is a pair of black shoes with gold buckles. But now they're stood next to a briefcase. Then I hear a voice. It's Albert's voice, calling me out of the black ink. Baz! Get up, he's saying. Get up Baz, for Christ's sake. I shake my head and push up toward the voice. The ink gets lighter and there's another voice, counting... Seven, eight... Then I'm out of the ink and I hear the bell ringing.

The crowd's roaring its head off, Laurel and Hardy have got hold of me and they slap me down on my chair. Albert's shoved something up my nostril, there's a sharp whiff of smelling salts and suddenly I'm wide awake. Meantime, Micky's sloshing water.

"Jesus Christ," says Albert. "What happened there?"

"Lucky punch," I mumble. "Flashbulb... Blinded..."

"Lucky?" he says. "You're right there. You're lucky it didn't take your head off."

They go on patching me up. The ref walks over, bends down in front of me and looks me in the eyes.

"You alright son?" he says.

"Spot on," I says.

"Hmm..." he says, waving a hand. "How many fingers am I holding up?"

I'm looking at six – but I know that can't be right so I guess at three.

"Fair enough," he says. "You okay to continue?"

"You bet your life I am," I says.

I nod twice and give him the thumbs up. It'll take more than a slap from the likes of Dan Hampton to stop me coming out for the final round. I get another whiff of the salts, my head clears, then Albert pops my gumshield in and I stand up ready. The bell sounds again and I come out for the last time.

The crowd is all abuzz now and they're expecting something special. *Plod, plod, plod.* Desperate Dan's on the loose and he's coming my way. He's that keen to get at me he's almost broken into a trot. The shark can't wait to finish me off and I brace myself for the onslaught.

Dan comes charging in and my mind goes back to the school gates and how it all began and how Parky came tearing in too, arms flailing, just the same. And then I remember the rest – McGuire, Spike, Ivan – each with a different style but no technique yet all having the same object, namely, to cut me down and prove a point. Then it was all about a Game Boy, my life, my future and the dream I had with Tracey or maybe it was just pride but instead of Parky, Spike or Danny, now it's Desperate Dan Hampton who's blocking my way, a soldier boy from Catterick, a brute, a bruiser, a man for whom the words "noble art" have no meaning and whose only intent is to destroy what stands in his path.

So maybe this ain't boxing any more. And never mind what Albert says, maybe it never was. Maybe that was just a cloak, a means of disguising the brutal nature of it all, like a mask to hide the shame. Because when you get to that crucial moment, the moment when you gain or lose what you've been striving for, that cloak falls away, the mask slips off and you see it for what it really is, a mean and dirty game. So then it's just a fight, a fight like all the others – but it's a fight you've got to win.

So then I'm in the fight. And when I'm in the fight, there ain't nothing but the fight. It's like the fight is all of me and I am all of it.

And everything that happens in the fight I see it coming a mile off like well before it starts. They only have to twitch a muscle or blink an eye and I can tell what's coming next – a jab, a cross, a hook, right or left, I know just what they're going to do. So next thing, I ain't there, I'm gone, moved that fraction of an inch that makes the difference between hit and miss. Or I cover up and take it on the arm and ride with it so it don't do no damage. But either way they can't hurt me. And every shot they throw, somewhere there's a gap. So I just pick them off, where I like and when I like. That's all I have to do. It's easy. And that's the fight.

Well that's the theory but things don't seem to work like that no more. The crowd's on its feet, Dan Hampton's all over me like a rash and he's throwing leather from every angle. I duck, I bob, I weave – but I can't seem to move away, it's like my feet are encased in concrete. My spirit's willing but my flesh is weak. I cover up and take the hits but they all hurt and it seems I can't avoid them. And with every one that lands, I can feel the strength sapping.

Dan swings big, trying to take me out. He's traded in his snarl and he's gone for grunts of effort. I lean back and let his shots slip by. Then he loses balance so I step out from under and off the ropes. I try to get a jab in as I pass by but it falls short. Then I hear Albert calling again, high above the crowd.

"Hit him, Barry, hit him!"

Yes, Albert, I'll hit him, just give me a chance.

I take a look in the punch cupboard to see what's available. It's empty and there's a sign hung up outside saying "Sold Out". My arms feel like they're made of lead.

"Hit him, Barry, hit him!"

You hit him, Albert, I'm too tired. I need a rest.

I'd like to lie down in the black ink but I know I mustn't. Meanwhile, the shark's turned back into a tank and comes homing relentlessly in. I retreat in the face of the onslaught but I feel like I'm wading through treacle.

"Hit him, Barry, hit him for Christ's sake!" Albert's screaming now. "HIT HIM WITH THE RIGHT!"

The right? What right? I ain't got no right.

The one he told you not to use, the one he said to put away. The one that got all busted up. Yes, that right.

But it's been so long since it last got used. I don't remember where I left it. I take another look in the punch cupboard but it still ain't there. Maybe I dropped it on the floor. I reach down to pick it up and there's something on the end of my arm that feels like a ton weight and it's starting to ache. But the tank's closing in fast and I need to hurry.

I pull the weight up and try shifting it forward. Dan arrives, snarling through the fetid air. Sweat glistens on his rocky chin, giving me a target. His left arm draws back for the final hook and while the crowd holds breath, I throw the weight, hurling it into the gap, the gleaming point where neckless head joins chest. There's a thud as I let go – and then the blinding pain shoots up my arm like that truck's collapsed on me again.

Now Dan's got the weight – only he can't hold it. It's landed on top of him, forcing him down, and he's struggling to push it off. The weight gets heavier, stifling his breath and robbing him of light. He stumbles backwards, staggering beneath it. He wants rid of it but it's too big and it's dragging him into the black ink. Desperate Dan crumples and there's a crash as he hits the floor like a felled tree.

Someone counts to ten but he don't get up.

Next thing you know the place erupts and everything goes wild. The crowd gives a roar, there's flashbulbs popping everywhere and suddenly the ring's full of people. Moments ago, it was just me and Dan, slugging it out, but now the world and his wife are in there and they all want a piece of the action.

Across the way, Dan's corner are crouched over the body and trying to bring him round. He won't be saying anything sensible for a while – though it ain't as if he did that before.

Albert's halfway across the canvas looking like the cat that got the cream, and some way behind, Fat Micky's having trouble getting through the ropes. It's Laurel and Hardy all over – pure slapstick. And wouldn't you just know it, here's Ronnie getting in on the act and planting that big hand of his around my shoulders. There's a smile on his face the size of the Dartford Tunnel.

"Barry, my son!" he shouts above the din. "I always knew you was a good 'un."

Somewhere along the line he's blagged a cigar and there's a waft of stale smoke and aftershave. I shake him off to give Albert a hug.

"I knew you could do it," he says, slapping me on the back. "I just knew."

Yeah, didn't we all pal, didn't we all.

A minute or two and things quieten down while they persuade Dan he needs to be vertical. They manage to clear the ring and we get together again with the ref because now it's time for the announcement.

"Ladies and Gentlemen... Your attention please..." The MC clambers in with a mic. "And the winner is... In the blue corner..."

The ref raises my hand. It's my right hand but the ice has worn off and it ain't numbed up no more so now I can feel the pain. It's sharp and there's something trickling too – though it ain't sweat and I watch as a thin red line starts dribbling down my arm.

Soon they'll give me a medal and call me a champion – but the truth is I'll still just be Barry Mullins, a car mechanic who wanted to be a boxer. I stare out beyond the flashbulbs and into the crowd, wondering if I might see those shoes again. But they're gone. Then I think about Dad and how I wish he could be here instead.

Ronnie

Jesus, that was close. So close there were times I could hardly bear to watch it – if I'd been at home I'd have been hiding behind the sofa. And d'you know what? For a minute or two I thought Barry'd taken a dive, thrown the fight and chucked his hand in, blown it if you know what I mean. That bloody flashbulb's gone off ping and Hampton's whipped over a wild one – though from where I'm watching it don't seem that bad, a glancing blow to the side of the head and it never looks enough to put a strong man down. But all of a sudden, Barry's flat on his back and looking up at the ceiling. Now I know what you're going to say – that it's all very well for me to talk, sat at the side of the ring with my palms sweating, biting my nails, while he's in there doing the work. Though this is Desperate Dan we're talking about and if you read what they say in the papers, he can really dish it out.

All the same, it's hard to believe it when you've never seen him go down before. Barry Mullins knocked over? That just ain't possible. So I start thinking *Somebody must have got to him, somebody must have marked his card* because that don't come about purely by chance. I always did wonder about that hand of his for starters, that was never right. Because that's what they'll do to you, the bastards, given half a chance. A horse goes sick, a dog don't run – how many times have I seen that happen? Too damn many, especially when there's been a bit riding on it, like there is with me. And maybe I ain't the only one, maybe there's others in on it too. Makes you wonder, don't it?

Anyways, he takes a massive tumble but the bell comes to his rescue. Don't ask me how but his corner get him to his feet, drag him to his chair and start waving the revival kit under his nose. I'm not expecting much to happen after that as it looks like they think it's all over. And sure enough, for a few seconds it seems like the lights are off and there's nobody in. There's no blood and I think he must get lucky with the ref because he gets the go-ahead to continue. Then, glory be, another whiff of the salts and there he is, ready and raring to go. The fat one wipes the sweat off and he's back out there again. So now we're in for a big finish.

Only to begin with it don't look like Barry's going to make it and that blow from Hampton must have done more damage than I thought. His head seems clear enough, it's just that his legs have gone to jelly – or maybe he's gone into shock. Meantime, Hampton wants at him straight away. He's got him pinned to the ropes and he's pounding him from all directions. Barry's covering up but it's that ferocious I'm wincing. And every blow he takes, you can see him sinking lower.

Then his corner start screaming, wanting that big right hand. At first, I don't think he hears them – or if he does, he makes no sign. They shout again but still no response. Hampton's bearing down so I start screaming too and this time the message must get through because Barry starts to move.

Then, *WALLOP!* He gives him one, straight out of the blue. And either Dan don't see it coming or he just don't care because he walks straight into it. What a punch! It's a peach. It catches Hampton slap in the kisser and he goes down like a sack of spuds falling off the back of a lorry. The next thing you know we're all jumping up and down, me included, and I can't wait to get into the ring.

So that's me sorted. It's like I kept on telling you – Barry Mullins is a nugget, a solid gold nugget. He's done the business just like I asked him and I'm out of the mire. The bank can phone me as much as they like, I'll be taking all their calls from now on. *Ah, Mr Smithson. How nice to hear from you again.* I'd like to be a fly on the wall in his office when he finds out I'll be making that payment – and then some. Ninety days and a cup of tea? He'll get a damn sight more than that from me. I'll be tap-dancing on his bloody desk before the week's out.

Barry

So that's it, that's the end of it, my boxing career's all done and dusted for the second time. And if it wasn't over before, now it's over good and proper – there won't be no comeback on this occasion. I've fooled Albert once, I won't be doing that again, not now he's seen things for real.

We leave the ring and get back to the dressing room. My gumshield's out but I've kept my gloves on (for obvious reasons). We get in, Micky pulls them off and there's a nasty red blotch seeping through the tapes on my right. I try pulling my hand back – but Albert's got eyes like a hawk.

"What's this?" he says, taking a closer look.

"Nothing that should concern you," I says. "I probably broke a few of my stitches, that's all. I wouldn't worry about it." Though what I don't tell him is it feels like someone's chopped my fingers off with an axe.

"Don't be daft," he says. "Your stitches fell out weeks ago – probably while you had that pot on."

"Maybe they did," I says. "I don't rightly recall."

"All the same," he says. "You should get that looked at." And he offers to call one of the medics.

"Nah," I says. "I can't be bothered with that. We'll just get it bandaged up for now. I'll go see the doc in the morning. Anyways, nobody's looking under there without my say-so." Fact is, I don't want to be looking under there, never mind anyone else.

Albert's got other ideas. "I not sure I can let you walk out of here like that."

"Yes you can," I says. "You looked the other way once before, you can do it again now."

"That was different."

"How so?" I says. "A busted hand's a busted hand – don't matter which way round you look at it."

"Hmm…" He wrinkles his forehead. "Maybe I shouldn't have…"

"Maybe you shouldn't have what?" I says.

"Let you get back in the ring."

"It wasn't a case of that," I says. "I was going to get back into it anyway."

"Even so," he says. "Maybe I should have sent off that letter."

"What letter?"

"I was supposed to send a letter to the Board of Control, telling them you weren't fit to box anymore. Somehow it got overlooked."

"I see," I says. "And now you're overwhelmed with this sudden feeling of guilt – is that it? A bit late for that now, ain't it? Besides, what do you care? You got what you wanted out of it, didn't you? You've finally got a trophy to put on your mantelpiece."

"That's unfair, Baz – and you know it." He's trying to defend but he's got this sheepish look. "Although I can't deny there's an element of truth in it."

"Yes," I says, "there is. And you'd better make the best of it. Because you can't tell me I'm going to get this fixed up a second time." I wave my bloody hand under his nose. "We ain't going to be doing this again next year, are we?"

"No," says Albert. "Cards on the table, Baz, we're not." He pulls a conciliatory face. "But look, we've had a good run, haven't we? It's been worth it."

"Good for you, maybe," I says. "You've still got something to fight for. Some of us just lost that."

"Don't say that," he says. "Look what we've achieved together. You've just won the ABA National Title for goodness sake – there aren't many people as can say that."

"Ain't no good to me," I says. "Not now. What am I supposed to do with it?"

Albert goes quiet on me and turns away like he's trying to

work it out – but then he turns back. "There's not much I can say really, is there?"

"Nope," I says. "There ain't."

"Anyway," he says. "Let's not part on bad terms – none of us want that. Like I say – we've had a good run. Let's shake on it and be friends." He holds out toward me.

He's right of course – I've just had one hard fight and the last thing I want is another. Not with Albert, anyway. But I can't take it, my fingers are all buggered up, so I have to shake with my left. He laughs, seeing his mistake. And that sets Micky off and then they're both laughing.

I get cleaned up as best I can and collect my kit. Micky finds me some painkillers. I take a couple and keep the box for later – it might hold things off 'til the morning. It reminds me I've not eaten for a while. Something hot would be good. Another night and we might have had a beer together. But it's too late for that now and besides, I've got a train to catch. I set off for Liverpool Street with my right bandaged up, a sports bag in my left and a medal round my neck.

Terry

It's a hard job, having to sit and watch Barry Mullins win. Well, you know how I feel about the little bastard. There's a big part of me hoping he'll get flattened, that Desperate Dan will whup his sorry arse and shut him up for good. I thought he had for a minute, too. Wouldn't that have been the perfect ending.

But there's another part of me says £20k is £20k and it ain't to be sniffed at. It's worth a bloody sight more than Barry Mullins is. Or was. Or ever will be. It'll see me right, that's for sure. Because here's the thing – I've done this deal with Joe Black, but if he thinks I'm going to hang around while he and his mates forcibly remove that briefcase, he's got another think coming. Like I said, I don't take kindly to violence on my person, stage-managed or not, and I wouldn't put it past him to put the boot in. So I've booked the flights and I'm off on holiday with Tracey. But what she don't know (and nor does any other bugger for that matter) is I ain't fixing to come back. In plain and simple terms, I'm going to do a runner.

But maybe you've worked that out already, maybe you've already guessed. Maybe you've told yourself that if Terry Bennett had an ounce of common, he'd take the briefcase, leave the country and lie low for a while 'til the heat dies down. Because they'll come looking – Goldstrap, Joe Black or another of his monkeys, they won't let me get away with it that easy. But I'll be gone, out of it, somewhere they can't find me, somewhere in the sun.

But that ain't the all of it, there's more. Fact is, I've had enough. I've had enough of bad boy Ronnie Bent and his broken promises. I've had enough of listening to him tell me about the stock and the garage, and how the money's tied up in everything I see around me and how he can't get his hands on it and how it'll be there for us come the finish and all that smarmy bullshit. I've had enough of standing on his forecourt in the whistling wind and the driving rain, not to mention the snow and God knows what else, waiting for some stupid bloody punter to stop umming and ahing and make their bloody mind up about whatever piece of scrap metal Ronnie's got dragged out of the back and had welded up especially for the occasion. Plus I couldn't stand being around when Mullins starts crowing. So I'm off. To the sunshine. Life of Riley and be done with it, I've got it all planned.

Course, Tracey ain't in on it yet, she thinks it's just a holiday but you wait 'til I show her the money, she won't be able to resist. Anyways, it's what she wants, a place in the sun, just the two of us. Any questions and I'll tell her Mother's come up trumps. As for the rest, I'll deal with that when the time comes.

I know what you're thinking. You're thinking Terry's gone ga-ga, he's delusional, because if he thinks he's going to get very far on £20k he's very much mistaken – especially when Tracey's around. Well, Biggsy went to Brazil and got away with it – this year Terry's going to Torremolinos. And okay, so Biggsy had a lot more than £20k I daresay, but Biggsy never worked. Me, I'm a grafter, I'll find something to keep me afloat. I'll work in a bar if I have to. I'll *buy* a bar if I have to. Let's just hope I don't have to. Our flight's first thing in the morning. Tonight, we're in a hotel next to the airport and I've got a train to catch so I'm in a bit of a hurry. But first I have to collect.

Now as you might imagine, collecting £20k off Joe Black and his crew ain't going to be entirely without its complications. He wants to beat about the bush awhile so I don't get my hands on the case straight off. There's this handover ceremony to go through first and he's brought some stooge along as witness. We meet in the boys' room.

"This here's Mr Weinbaum," says Joe, introducing his acquaintance.

Mr Weinbaum is on the short side, elderly and rather podgy in the kind of places you go podgy when you're elderly. He looks the type of bloke who's made a living from taking the gold out of dead people's teeth. We smile politely and bow.

"Mr Weinbaum has already inspected the briefcase and verified the contents. Haven't you Harry?" Joe Black gives Weinbaum a nudge.

Mr Weinbaum turns up his hearing aid and his head starts bobbing up and down like the nodding dog in a car back window.

"So, do you want to take a look?" says Joe. "Or are you happy to take Mr Wienbaum's word for it?"

Now I'm sure Mr Weinbaum is a gentleman, a scholar and a fine upstanding member of the community an' all, but the idea of taking a quick peak at £20k strikes me as rather appealing.

"No offence," I says. "But I'll just have a shufti if you don't mind." Because if there's one thing I've learnt off Ronnie, nobody buys a car and he don't count their money first.

Joe lifts the lid and there it is, all laid out neat and tidy in its shiny purple glory. I flick through a pile of twenties just to make sure there's no blanks.

"Looks okay to me," I says.

Joe snaps the lid shut and clips the catches.

"Good," he says. "You are Mr Bent's personal representative, I take it?"

"Oh, absolutely," I says. "Me and Ronnie, we're just like brothers. Family, you could say." There's a lot more I could say but I decide to keep shut.

Joe looks at Weinbaum to make sure he's listening. The nodding dog sets off again.

"Well, I think we're just about done," says Joe, and he slides that manicured hand of his toward me. It's like watching Ronnie closing a deal. We shake once more and I feel as though I've just bought something I didn't want.

"Cheers," I says, and I pick up the case.

"Cheers," says JB. "Let's hope we meet again soon."

"I'm looking forward to it," I says. "When did you have in

mind?"

"In about ten minutes," he says. "Out at the front."

"You mean somewhere round the Albert Memorial?" I says.

"That'll do nicely," he says.

"What, like I was about to walk across Kensington Gardens?" *In the dark. Carrying a briefcase stuffed with cash. I should cocoa.*

"Exactly," he says.

We both look at Weinbaum wondering whether he's turned his hearing aid back off. He smiles politely but you can tell he hasn't a clue.

We go back into the foyer and JB heads off toward the front. Which is fine by me because I'm nipping through the auditorium and out the back in completely the opposite direction. I look at my watch. Tracey will be waiting at the hotel. I leave a message on her mobile. *I'm on my way. And I'm bringing a surprise.*

Ronnie

So Barry's gone back to his dressing room, they clear the ring and for the time being the party's over. Things settle down and I get to thinking about my £20k and what I'm going to do with it. A new three-piece suit comes to mind – not to mention a night on the town. But first things first and I guess I'll have to get myself over to Walthamstow and have a word with Mac about picking up the money.

Meanwhile, I reckon it's time to leave. I have a scout round for Terry, having lost the run of him when I went off to the ring to celebrate. He ain't in his seat and he ain't in the aisle. In fact, he ain't anywhere I can see. I figure he must have gone to the gents so I catch another bout while I'm waiting. But then I clock him, walking smartly along the back row – and bugger me if he ain't carrying my briefcase. *What the hell is that doing here?* I wonder. *Well that'll save me a trip. Good on you.*

But hold up – something ain't right. Because he ain't headed back here, he's headed for the exit. And he ain't exactly hanging about.

"Oi!" I shout. "Tel!"

But he's either not heard me or he just ain't listening. So I set off in hot pursuit.

I catch up with him at the station, but I'm a few minutes behind as I'm struggling to keep pace. Terry's built like a whippet and he's quicker out of the blocks than most things I've seen at Walthamstow whereas I've probably had one more meat pie than is good for me and I'm well out of puff. Enough said.

So I arrive, panting my lungs out, but Liverpool Street's deserted with hardly a soul to be seen. I have a good look round but there's neither sight nor sound of Terry and I'm just beginning to think *The little bastard – he's done a runner* when he staggers out of the gents looking as white as a sheet. Problem is, there's no briefcase.

He clocks me standing there and it's like he's seen a ghost.

"Ronnie?" he says. "What you doing here?"

It's a fair question, seeing as we weren't fixing to go home together.

"Chasing after you," I says between puffs. "That's what."

"Whatever for?" he says.

"You know bloody well what for," I says. "So where is it?"

"Where's what?"

"My briefcase, you numpty. That black thing with the handle you was carrying it by when you raced off from the Albert Hall."

"Oh, that was yours was it?" he says, trying to play the innocent. "I had no idea."

First, I'm not liking "was". And second, I've worked with Terry for years and I know when he's telling porkies – like now for instance.

"Don't give me that, you lying little toe rag," I says. "Who else did you think it belonged to?"

"I don't know," he says. "They didn't say."

"*They?*" I says. "Who's *they* when they're at home?"

"Joe Black," he says. "Goldstrap's mate."

"Goldstrap?" I says. "What the mother of God are you doing getting mixed up with Goldstrap?"

"They asked me to look after it for a while."

That's the trouble when Terry starts lying – every ten seconds he changes his story.

"Oh they did, did they?" I says, nodding like I believe every word.

"Yeah," he says. "And I was going to give it to you, honest, but…"

"But what?" I says. "Let me guess. Curiosity got the better of you, you thought you'd have a look inside and then you changed your mind."

"No! It wasn't like that Ronnie, honest to God, I swear."

"So what was it like then?" I says. "Do tell me, I'm all ears."

"They said they wanted it back. So I thought I'd take it somewhere safe, somewhere they couldn't find me – I mean it. But then…"

"Yes," I says. "But then?"

Terry looks at me with that hangdog expression he has, the corners of his mouth all turned down and his bottom lip quivering like he's about to burst into tears.

"Then," he says, "I lost it."

There's a long silence whilst I digest this unwanted piece of information. Then the station announcer starts telling me the 22:50 to all stations east is about to depart and it jerks me back to life.

"You lost it," I says. "And how the hell did you manage that?"

"I went to the gents for a tidy up. I put the case down by the sink while I washed my hands. Then I needed a number two so I had a sit down for a couple of minutes – and when I came out it had gone."

"Hold on," I says, holding my hands up. "Slow down a minute – my brain's hurting me here. So let me get this straight. Out of the goodness of your heart, you kindly agree to look after a case full of money on my behalf. 'They' want it back so you decide to take it somewhere safe i.e. the toilet at Liverpool Street station. At which point you're overcome with a pressing desire to empty your bowels. And while you're sat there taking a shit, leaving the bag outside where the world and his bleeding wife can see it, somebody comes along and nicks it. Is that really what you're telling me?"

"Er, yeah," says Terry. "Pretty much."

By now I've got my head in my hands.

"I don't believe it," I says. "I don't bloody well believe it. What on earth did I ever do wrong to get landed with someone as thick as you. You stupid, stupid tosser. Jesus Christ. Have you any idea what you've done?"

Terry shakes his head like the pathetic little weasel he is.

"You've ruined me," I says. "That's what you've done. That was the ace up my sleeve and now you've gone and blown it."

"Oh," he says. "You mean that was it? The business, the garage, the stock – all those things we've been working for together all these years, all that stuff you kept telling me about?"

"We?" I says. "Hang on a sec, where does this 'we' come from all of a sudden? The garage – or rather, what's left of it now that you've inconveniently succeeded in losing most of it – is mine. Always has been and always will be. I'm the one as took all the risks and built it up. I'm the one who had all the sleepless nights worrying over how I was going to pay the bills and keep the bank off my back. What makes you think you had anything to do with it?"

"I thought we was partners," he says. "I thought we had an agreement. I thought we…"

"Well you thought wrong," I says. "All you ever had was the job I gave you in the first place – and you should be grateful for that. Because no bugger else would. Christ knows, I'm regretting it now."

Then all of a sudden, he stops being pathetic and he turns on me like the weasel's been cornered and it's baring its teeth.

"Hang on," he says. "So you're telling me I was doing it all for nothing. All those years I've stood out on that bloody forecourt, working my fingers to the bone, and it don't count for sod all? I've laid myself out for you, Ronnie Bent, and don't you forget it. Remember those markets we used to go to back in the old days? How we used to kip in the back of the van and all that? If it wasn't for me, you'd never have got started. The fact is…" (and he starts prodding his scrawny little finger in my chest) "…the fact is, you couldn't sell a pint of blood to Dracula, never mind a motor to an honest punter. You'd be nowhere without me and you know it. That money was mine just as much as it was yours. But now you're trying to tell me different. D'you know what?"

"No," I says. "What?"

"I don't know why I trusted you. I always knew you was a wrong 'un. I always knew you was going to run out on me sooner or later. All that crap you kept feeding me. *I'll see you right, Terry, don't you worry. I'll make sure you get yours.* That was just bullshit, you never had any intention. Well let me tell you something, Ronald Bent…"

But I never did get to hear what it was he was going to tell me. Because that's when I brayed him *SMACK!* right between the eyes. I'm no Barry Mullins but I reckon even he'd have been proud of that one. And Terry Bennett's no Dan Hampton either but his lights go out just the same. You have no idea how good it felt.

Then this white-haired guy in a black coat turns up and we're all three of us at it.

Barry

I've never really understood British Rail – their trains, their timetable, their rolling stock. Dad had the same problem. What was it he used to say? *They couldn't run a bath, never mind a bloody railway.* Here I am on the 22:50 to Chelmsford and it's hardly the most popular place in the world. Counting me, there's just the four of us and two of them are asleep – maybe they live here permanent. Okay, so some people need to get home late at night, but we're going to stop at every damn place you can think of on the way – like Harold Wood for instance. *Who'd want to get out there?* Dad used to ask. *Well, Harold would*, he'd say. Ghost towns, the lot of them, they'll all slip by grey and empty and no bugger seems to get on or off. Maybe that explains our clapped-out carriage – more than 40mph and it don't feel safe, starts to wobble like the wheels are coming off. When I sit down the springs creak in the seat. I'll be lucky if I'm in the house before midnight.

I've found a hot-food stall and treated myself to a baguette (bacon, brie and cranberry – I deserve something posh). I tuck in and brush the crumbs off. A couple more minutes, the train pulls out and we're into it, the concrete, the wires and just a few lights twinkling in the dark. It's started to rain and I try wiping the window to get a better look as backstreet London slides past through the grime.

There's something on my mind I haven't figured out yet. I'm starting to think how to fix it when Terry's mobile goes off and saves me the trouble. I take it out and check who's calling. The screen says it's Tracey. I press accept and she comes on the line but before I can say *Hello*, she's gabbing away all excited and I can't get a word in edgeways.

"I got your message," she says. "I'm at the hotel. You said you was bringing a surprise. What is it? I want to know, tell me now, I can't wait."

"Surprise is," I says, "this ain't Terry. It's Baz."

"Oh," she says and it goes all quiet like she don't know what to do next. I let her stew for a minute while she tries to work it out. Pretty soon the penny drops. "So what you doing answering Terry's phone?" she says.

"More's to the point," I says. "What you doing ringing it?"

Now she gets her wagons in a circle and goes defensive.

"Terry's a friend of mine," she says. "I can ring him if I like."

"Sure you can," I says. "Just don't expect to get the answer you were looking for."

"So where is he?" she says.

"Where's who?" I says. I ain't in the mood to be helpful.

"Terry," she says.

"Last I saw of Mr Bennett," I says, "he was playing catch-as-catch-can at Liverpool Street station with Ronald Bent and some bloke in a long black overcoat."

"You haven't hurt him, have you?" she says.

"No," I says, "not yet. Just give me time. Besides, it looks like someone's sorted that out already."

"What d'you mean?"

"Well let's just say Ronnie wasn't too pleased to see him."

"Oh... So how long d'you think he's going to be?"

"If either of the other two get hold of him," I says, "longer than you could possibly imagine."

"You're making me very worried," she says.

"And so you should be," I says. "For more than one reason."

"And what's that supposed to mean?"

"We're done," I says. "It's over. Our dream, your dream – whatever – it's finished. But then, so's mine so I reckon we'll call it quits. And maybe it never got started, maybe it was all wrong in the first place."

"No it wasn't," she says. "Not in the beginning, not when you had the boxing."

"Ah yes," I says, "the boxing. Well, now that's finished too," and I look down at my hand and the bandage and the blood seeping red. "I won't be doing that no more."

"Oh..." she says. "So what am I supposed to do?"

"You've still got Terry," I says. "Or what's left of him. But I wouldn't count on no surprises coming from that direction. Leastways, they won't be good ones. Face it, Trace, you've hitched your wagon to the wrong horse – twice. But you'll survive. My guess is, you always will. There'll always be some other sucker out there ready to take you on. Thing is, it won't be me. I'm out."

"But Barry..."

"But Barry nothing," I says. "This is it. This is the end of it. This is goodbye." And I cut the call and put the phone back where I found it.

With the plane tickets.

In the briefcase.

Well you didn't think I was going to leave it there, did you? I walk into the gents and there it is all black and shiny, stood beneath the sinks. And the last time I saw it The Shoes had it at the Hall so I'm thinking *He must be in here somewhere* and I start looking at the gaps below the doors of the cubicles. But I can't find him – which is all a bit of a bugger because hand or no hand, I'd like to have his back up against the bloody wall, wouldn't I just. All I can see is Terry and I'd recognize his size nines anywhere, I've seen them often enough in the garage. So what the rocking donkey is he doing with it? I ask. And it ain't as if it belongs to either of them, it's Ronnie's because now I get up close I remember how he used to keep it in the office. Besides which, it's got his initials, *RAB*, stitched on the side.

Now, I ain't in the habit of pinching other blokes' stuff, I left off being light-fingered when I was a kid. But I reckon I've a right, a vested interest so to speak, seeing as how it was The Shoes that busted my hand an' all. So before Terry can haul his trousers back up, I'm out of there, case and all and I'm sitting on the train eating my dinner.

This must be Terry's surprise. A surprise for Tracey, and my guess is it'll be a surprise for The Shoes and a surprise for Ronnie an' all I shouldn't wonder. And it ain't a bad one at that. I've never seen so much money. There's so much of it in fact, I don't even start to count it. I could do a lot with money like that. I look at my hand and feel the hurt. I won't be going back to the garage, that's for certain. So maybe I should open a gym with it or maybe I should do this with it or maybe I should do that with it. Only somehow, I don't feel that way.

It's a funny thing, money, when you look at it. I mean, it's just a piece of paper really, special paper mind – a picture of the Queen on one side, some bloke with a big moustache on the other. The green folding stuff, the moulah, the dosh, the wonga, call it what you like, it causes so much trouble but it's what they all want, it's what they all chase after.

But then I'm touching it and I remember where it's come from and I feel the sweat of their palms on it – their grime, their muck, their filth, the soiled dirt of their grubby lives, infecting my hands, my fingers, and staining the honest dirt of mine. And I feel the weight of it pressing down on me and on my shoulders like it's some kind of burden I have to carry. But I can't carry it, that weight, not now, not ever, not for the rest of my life and that's when I know I don't want it, it don't belong to me, it's theirs and I can't keep it. So I have to get rid.

I get up and walk to the lobby at the end of the carriage. I pull down the window sash and the air comes flooding in, the clean fresh air of the County of Essex. I put my head out of the window and let the air wash over me, wiping all the dirt away. Then I take a note from the wad and I hold that out there too, watching the air tearing at it like it wants it, like it wants to tear it away. I let the air wash over the note, wiping it clean, then I open my fingers and it's gone, flying up and swirling above the train and it's like the weight's easing off my shoulders. Then I take another, and another, sending them out of the window and out of my life, the weight easing all the time as I cleanse myself and I cleanse the notes, swirling upwards into the clean fresh air. Then they're all gone, the notes, and I don't feel so bad no more.

Because it was never about the money – well, not for me it wasn't anyway. It was always about Tracey and the boxing, there was never much of anything else. It was about fixing cars too, I suppose, but never in the same way. I might keep to that – it's something to hang on to – but the rest has gone, just like the money, and it ain't never coming back.

And what I reckon is, if I can't have it, then they can't have it neither – the Terry Bennetts, the Ronnie Bents, The Shoes, the Ivans, the shady people of this world, the people I don't want to know, the Parkinson and McGuires even, they're all the same. Tracey Williams too, come to that. Mustn't forget Tracey, why leave her out? She deserves it.

So fuck 'em, I say. Yeah, fuck 'em. Fuck 'em all.

Epilogue

Ken Cartwright

So there you have it. Our wondrous firework rocket, which once rose meteorically upwards and shone briefly in the heavens, has finally crashed and burned. Well at least it went off with a bang. But that's not quite the end of my story as there's a few loose ends I need to tidy up.

Barry returned home to what would have been a hero's welcome. At first the public clamoured for some form of recognition and there was talk of a civic reception in his honour. But when he announced his retirement from the sport, the authorities realised there was nothing to be gained by lauding a man whose glories lay in the past rather than the future and they quietly dropped the idea. And so, at last, he became an ordinary person again and nothing more of note took place in his life.

It's true that he retained a passing interest in motor mechanics, although with no formal qualifications and a broken hand that was always going to be a difficult path to pursue. He couldn't go back to the garage, not least because shortly after his return the premises were raided by the Essex Constabulary. Such files and papers that existed were taken away and the place was closed down. And so for the moment at least, there was nowhere for him to go. But when his hand had repaired for the second time and after a few short months on the dole, he managed to find himself a job as a tyre fitter at Kwik Fit. As a result, his nails remained cracked and broken for the rest of his life and his hands became dirtier than ever.

But he didn't abandon boxing altogether. For two nights a week (Tuesdays and Thursdays) he worked out at the gym in an effort to maintain whatever skills he'd retained and under Albert's guidance, he acted as a role model for the young. Later on, once Fat Micky had retired, he assumed his duties, setting out the equipment and folding towels. In the meanwhile, for a little extra cash and to satisfy some inner competitive need, on Friday and Saturday nights he took a post as a licensed door supervisor at The Lizard Lounge. Inspired by the thought of taking on a former holder of the ABA National Title, it was here that the latest aspirants to the crown of Chelmsford's hardest man would come to challenge. A brief but bloody encounter would ensue, after which the challenger would limp home, beaten, and Barry remained undefeated for the remainder of his door-minding career. And in the course of time and with the help of the local hospital, his hand healed – but not his heart, and he never loved again.

Of the others, there are some matters to report. The bank foreclosed on Ronnie's business, the bunting was taken down, the forecourt fenced in and the stock sold off to pay the debts – a process that Smithson meticulously took care of. Ronnie himself was declared bankrupt and subsequently convicted of tax evasion and fraud. He spent a number of years in prison. Some said he deserved it – they were mostly those he had crossed or to whom he'd owed money. A few said he didn't – they were mostly his friends and other random acquaintances. A significant number had no opinion on the subject, read an article about it in The Chelmsford Gazette, then turned the page and started on the crossword.

Eighteen months after it was shut, the site of Big Ronnie's garage was sold to a property developer. The buildings were demolished and nothing of it remains. More recently, Sainsburys have acquired the plot and a new supermarket is under construction to challenge the might of Tesco.

As for Terry, he simply disappeared and no trace of him could ever be found.

Except that Tracey was carrying his child – a fact which helped accelerate her separation from Barry and led to their eventual divorce. She had a girl, Scarlett, named after a favourite film star. Tracey was forced to leave her job and fell back to a life on benefits. The house in Walton Terrace could no longer be afforded and mother and daughter took up residence in a small one-bedroom council flat in Bell Meadows, a few blocks down from Sharon – a far cry from the six-bed mansion she'd once dreamt of.

Scarlett grew up to be utterly adorable. Barry, bless him, kept in touch and although he knew the child wasn't his, accepted her as if she were his own. He doted on her and whatever joy he found in life came almost exclusively from her.

As far as we know, Goldstrap escaped punishment. And if that strikes you as unsatisfactory, you should remember that life is an arbitrary affair – unresolved, unjust and full of imperfections. As for the rest of the characters in this story, they are of no real consequence and you must imagine what you will.

But, I hear you ask, what ever happened to Chelmsford? Well, it's still a county town. There's still a county hall. They still play cricket on the county cricket ground. And on hot, lazy, August afternoons, life resumes its crawling pace although the traffic at the Army and Navy roundabout is as bad as ever despite the introduction of bus lanes and a one-way system. But nothing else excites.

In short, Chelmsford simply went back to sleep.

Author's Note

The characters in this book are entirely fictional and are not intended to be a representation of any real person, alive or dead.

Biography

N.E. David is the pen name of York author Nick David. Nick began writing at the age of twenty-one but like so many things in life, it did not work out first time round. After a rewarding career in industry and then personal finance, he took it up again and had initial success with a series of short novellas. His debut novel, *Birds of the Nile,* was published by Roundfire in 2013 and quickly became their top-selling title in adult fiction. *The Burden* and *Malaren* soon followed, the latter being entered for The Man Booker Prize of 2017.

Nick writes character-based contemporary fiction where he focuses on stories of human interest and drama. He maintains he has no personal or political message to convey but his initial objective is to entertain the reader and he hopes this is reflected in his writing.

Besides being a regular contributor to literary events in the North East Region, Nick is a founder member of York Authors and formerly co-presented "Book Talk" on BBC Radio York. He has recently been appointed Chairman of York Literature Festival and enjoys contributing to the literary life of the city.

Other Works
Carol's Christmas
Feria
A Day at the Races
Birds of the Nile
The Burden
Malaren

For more information visit the author's website at www. nedavid.com.
You can also follow N.E. David on Twitter @NEDavidAuthor.

**ROUNDFIRE
BOOKS**

FICTION

Put simply, we publish great stories. Whether it's literary or popular, a gentle tale or a pulsating thriller, the connecting theme in all Roundfire fiction titles is that once you pick them up you won't want to put them down.
If you have enjoyed this book, why not tell other readers by posting a review on your preferred book site.

Recent bestsellers from Roundfire are:

The Bookseller's Sonnets
Andi Rosenthal
The Bookseller's Sonnets intertwines three love stories with a tale
of religious identity and mystery spanning five hundred years
and three countries.
Paperback: 978-1-84694-342-3 ebook: 978-184694-626-4

Birds of the Nile
An Egyptian Adventure
N.E. David
Ex-diplomat Michael Blake wanted a quiet birding trip up the
Nile – he wasn't expecting a revolution.
Paperback: 978-1-78279-158-4 ebook: 978-1-78279-157-7

Blood Profit$
The Lithium Conspiracy
J. Victor Tomaszek, James N. Patrick, Sr.
The blood of the many for the profits of the few... *Blood Profit$*
will take you into the cigar-smoke-filled room where American
policy and laws are really made.
Paperback: 978-1-78279-483-7 ebook: 978-1-78279-277-2

The Burden
A Family Saga
N.E. David
Frank will do anything to keep his mother and father apart. But
he's carrying baggage – and it might just weigh him down ...
Paperback: 978-1-78279-936-8 ebook: 978-1-78279-937-5

The Cause
Roderick Vincent
The second American Revolution will be a fire lit from an internal spark.
Paperback: 978-1-78279-763-0 ebook: 978-1-78279-762-3

Don't Drink and Fly
The Story of Bernice O'Hanlon: Part One
Cathie Devitt
Bernice is a witch living in Glasgow. She loses her way in her life and wanders off the beaten track looking for the garden of enlightenment.
Paperback: 978-1-78279-016-7 ebook: 978-1-78279-015-0

Gag
Melissa Unger
One rainy afternoon in a Brooklyn diner, Peter Howland punctures an egg with his fork. Repulsed, Peter pushes the plate away and never eats again.
Paperback: 978-1-78279-564-3 ebook: 978-1-78279-563-6

The Master Yeshua
The Undiscovered Gospel of Joseph
Joyce Luck
Jesus is not who you think he is. The year is 75 CE. Joseph ben Jude is frail and ailing, but he has a prophecy to fulfil …
Paperback: 978-1-78279-974-0 ebook: 978-1-78279-975-7

On the Far Side, There's a Boy
Paula Coston
Martine Haslett, a thirty-something 1980s woman, plays hard
on the fringes of the London drag club scene until one night
which prompts her to sign up to a charity. She writes to a
young Sri Lankan boy, with consequences far and long.
Paperback: 978-1-78279-574-2 ebook: 978-1-78279-573-5

Tuareg
Alberto Vazquez-Figueroa
With over 5 million copies sold worldwide, *Tuareg* is a classic
adventure story from best-selling author Alberto Vazquez-
Figueroa, about honour, revenge and a clash of cultures.
Paperback: 978-1-84694-192-4

Readers of ebooks can buy or view any of these bestsellers by clicking on the live link in the title. Most titles are published in paperback and as an ebook. Paperbacks are available in traditional bookshops. Both print and ebook formats are available online.

Find more titles and sign up to our readers' newsletter at http://www.johnhuntpublishing.com/fiction

Follow us on Facebook at https://www.facebook.com/JHPfiction
and Twitter at https://twitter.com/JHPFiction